WINIFRED HOLTBY

(1898–1935) was born in Rudston, Yorkshire. In the First World War she was a member of the Women's Auxiliary Army Corps, and then went to Somerville College, Oxford, where she met Vera Brittain. After graduating, these two friends shared a flat in London where both embarked upon their respective literary careers. Winifred Holtby was a prolific journalist, writing for the *Manchester Guardian*, the *News Chronicle* and *Time and Tide* of which she became director in 1926. She also travelled all over Europe as a lecturer for the League of Nations Union.

Her first novel, *Anderby Wold*, was published in 1923, followed, in 1924, by *The Crowded Street* (both published by Virago). She wrote four other novels: *The Land of Green Ginger* (1927), *Poor Caroline* (1931), *Mandoa, Mandoa!* (1933, also published by Virago), and *South Riding* (1936), published posthumously after her tragic death from kidney disease at the age of thirty-seven. She was awarded the James Tait Black prize for this, her most famous novel.

She also published two volumes of short stories, *Truth is Not Sober* (1934) and *Pavements at Anderby* (1937); a satirical work, *The Astonishing Island* (1933); two volumes of poetry, *My Garden* (1911) and *The Frozen Earth* (1935); a critical work, *Virginia Woolf* (1932); a study of the position of women, *Women and a Changing Civilisation* (1934), and numerous essays.

Winifred Holtby's remarkable and courageous life is movingly recorded in Vera Brittain's biography, *Testament of Friendship*, published by Virago.

Cruella Weir
August 29, 1984
Oxford, England

If you would like to know more about Virago books, write to us at 41 William IV Street, London WC2N 4DB for a full catalogue.

Please send a stamped addressed envelope

VIRAGO
Advisory Group

Andrea Adam   Zoë Fairbairns
Carol Adams   Carolyn Faulder
Sally Alexander   Germaine Greer
Rosalyn Baxandall (USA) Jane Gregory
Anita Bennett   Suzanne Lowry
Liz Calder   Jean McCrindle
Beatrix Campbell   Cathy Porter
Angela Carter   Alison Rimmer
Mary Chamberlain   Elaine Showalter (USA)
Anna Coote   Spare Rib Collective
Jane Cousins   Mary Stott
Jill Craigie   Rosalie Swedlin
Anna Davin   Margaret Walters
Rosalind Delmar   Elizabeth Wilson
Christine Downer (Australia) Barbara Wynn

Book Tokens

**Give them
the pleasure of choosing**
Book Tokens can be bought
and exchanged at most
bookshops

THE
LAND OF
GREEN GINGER

WINIFRED HOLTBY

WITH A NEW INTRODUCTION BY
MARGARET WALEY

Virago

Published by VIRAGO PRESS Limited 1983
41 William IV Street, London WC2N 4DB

First published in Great Britain by Jonathan Cape 1927

British Library Cataloguing in Publication Data

Holtby, Winifred
    The land of green ginger.—(Virago modern classics)
    I. Title
    823'.912[F]   PR6015.05

    ISBN 0-86068-250-1

        Printed in Great Britain by litho
        at the Anchor Press, Tiptree, Essex

CONTENTS

To

A PHILOSOPHER IN PESHAWAR

WHO SAID THAT HE WANTED

SOMETHING TO READ

INTRODUCTION

Winifred Holtby was proud to be the daughter of David Holtby, one of a farming family long established in the Wolds of the East Riding, where she was born at Rudston. Her mother, born Alice Winn, came from another farming clan of old standing in Wensleydale, the main scene of the novel *The Land of Green Ginger*. After being taught at home Winifred was sent, aged eleven, together with Grace her only and elder sister, to Queen Margaret's School at Scarborough, where she stayed until she passed her entrance examination for Somerville College, Oxford, in 1916.

At home in the holidays relatives and friends abounded. Among them was an orphaned Russian boy, George de Coundouroff, who introduced Winifred to the works of the great Russian novelists; apparently her only contact with European literature between the Latin classics and her own generation. More important still was Harry Pearson, elder of two local brothers who joined the Holtbys in Christmas theatricals for several years. In 1915 when Harry was already in uniform Winifred found she was in love with him, permanently it proved. But when a year later he became her suitor, shyly she repulsed him.

Before her third term at Somerville ended she went to London and enlisted in the Women's Army Auxiliary

Corps—the WAACS. Winifred felt too inexperienced to be an officer and after a short training was sent as hostel-forewoman to a camp in France, coping with English traffic on the local railways. Here her officer, Jean McWilliam, proved a godsend. A past Somerville student, aged about thirty-eight, she had taught English in schools and to teachers in training before joining the WAACS. In the mud of Huchenville she turned a place of misery and discomfort into an ordered happy community. The friendship between Winifred and Jean was immediate and permanent, but because Jean emigrated to South Africa at the beginning of 1920 it was later carried on largely by post.

Winifred returned to university after the war, her family having moved to Cottingham, a village outside Hull, following her father's retirement. Oxford in October 1919 was a very lively place and Winifred thoroughly enjoyed it. She knew she was going to be a writer and welcomed every new experience, though some were bitter. Harry Pearson, once destined for Cambridge and the church, was drifting, idle, dissolute, irresponsible and no longer her suitor. Slowly she realised she had lost her faith in the church, causing pain both to herself and her parents. There followed a turmoil of new ideas, difficult to define, which led towards a Christian mysticism which embraced pacifism. Throughout the 1920s she wrote regularly to Jean McWilliam. These letters were to be published in 1936 as *Letters to a Friend*, and proved valuable rehearsals for her later journalism.

At Somerville Winifred met Vera Brittain, another future writer, who had returned from war-time nursing extremely unhappy after the loss of her fiancé, her only brother, and their best friends. Intelligent, ambitious and with great integrity, she was physically attractive but acutely sensitive, jealous and prickly, unable to make friends with other women. Soon Winifred realised she could "manage" Vera and that Vera needed her. This friendship was of great importance to them both for the rest of Winifred's life. It was not of a passionate kind and stretched to include George Catlin, Vera's husband and her children in future years, but it made possible a shared London home after Oxford.

Thus by 1921 all the elements needed for Winifred's life as a novelist had come together. It was at a tutorial in 1921 with A. L. Smith, the Master of Balliol, when he spoke of the ruthlessness of economic processes and how the good of yesterday becomes the evil of today, that it flashed on Winifred that that was what she wanted to say in her first novel. From then on she was working toward *Anderby Wold*.

In the summer she learned she had got a second class in her history finals and at the beginning of 1922, with her family's blessing and financial help, she joined Vera Brittain in a London flat and took up part-time teaching and other work as it offered. The years 1922–24 were ones of apprenticeship, meeting people, notably Lady Rhondda, lecturing for her feminist 6-Point Group and for the League of Nations Union, working for a year in London's depressed area of Bethnal Green and teaching part-time. She sought for outlets for journalism and to publish *Anderby Wold*.

In April 1923 *Anderby Wold* was brought out by John Lane. This was brave of them for it did not sell at all well. It was however widely reviewed without any consensus of opinion. A short book with a simple plot ending tragically, it stays within the years 1912 and 1913 and covers familiar places in the Yorkshire Wolds and the lives of its farms and villages. In this way it can be read as a prologue to *South Riding*, set nearly a generation before. In John Dobson, the middle-aged farmer, one senses her feeling for her father and his perplexities.

While at Cottingham she had planned out her second novel, eventually called *The Crowded Street*, and published late in 1924. It was a book that was troublesome to write—indeed was once torn up and restarted—and is based on her homesickness for Rudston, her dislike for Cottingham and its society, her troubled denial of conformity inside the Church, and her difficulty in moving away from her family background. This book sold even less well than *Anderby Wold*.

In 1924 Winifred was still teaching, lecturing and trying to place journalism, some of it about Bethnal Green. This is what caught Lady Rhondda's eye. It started Winifred's connection with the weekly *Time and Tide*: from then on no article came back rejected, and so she could relax from teaching which she had found absorbed all her vitality. In 1925 she knew Vera was going to marry, though eventually her wedding to George Catlin was postponed till 1926. This led to a break in their London life which Winifred filled with a six months' visit to South Africa. Here she was to lecture for the League of Nations Union, and to stay a part of the time with Jean McWilliam, by then established as a headmistress in Pretoria, and to visit every large town and enterprising school in South Africa.

South Africa changed her future, for it brought her face to face with the problems of race—not only the one she had foreseen of continuing soreness between the English and the Boers, but behind that to the great majority of Black South Africans, mainly illiterate and used as unskilled and lowly paid workers in the cities, cut off for years from their homes and families. From then on she worked to improve their lot and found to her surprise that her chief allies were the English-speaking missionaries who had been working in South Africa for over a century.

At an isolated farm near Bloemfontein Winifred heard a tale "embracing passion, tuberculosis, suicidal mania, neurasthenia, lack of sanitary accommodation and stifled desire". The book this engendered, *The Land of Green Ginger*, was begun in Pretoria and is the first which shows her concern for South Africa. She never felt she had the knowledge to set a book in that country—this one is placed in Hull and Wensleydale—but its heroine is the daughter of a missionary in the Cape.

The idea which runs through the novel is that crucial help can come in times of trouble from vivid imagination. The Land of Green Ginger is the very old name of a street in Hull which thrills the young Joanna, heroine of the book, with its enigmatic suggestion of the poetry of far-off places. It is a characteristic Joanna shares with her creator, as she does her tall fair physique and her untidy habits. However, Joanna has splendid health and has neither religious doubts nor intellectual ambitions.

Joanna certainly needs all the solace she can find to face disaster after disaster with her temper unsoured. Married to Teddy Leigh, still lovable but disintegrating in character under the strain of his disease, they have had to abandon his planned career in the church for life in the country. This has placed them in a small isolated farm, with little skill for their task, losing money year by year till verging on bankruptcy, short of help and with two young children.

A plan by the local squire to have his woods harvested by foresters from abroad convincingly arouses xenophobia amongst the villagers, and the well-intentioned billeting of the Hungarian interpreter on the Leighs, meant to add to their miniscule earnings, leads to prejudice outside and emotional tensions inside their home with a final catastrophic outcome. After this the pace quickens and the end of the book balances the beginning in a striking and very successful manner. This is Winifred's first mature novel, by no means flawless—particularly in the central section which loses its way—but unforgettable because Joanna is a complete, vital human being; imperfections included she stays in one's memory.

A year and a half later Winifred wrote another novel, *Poor Caroline*. The novel is carefully compartmented—a new feature—to show us very disparate people. It has some well-directed satire against well-meaning societies, which did not please Lady Rhondda, and a caricature, unpleasing to him, of George Catlin as a high-church curate.

Before she had written another novel her tightly-filled life was suddenly checked by a kidney failure. Her collapse of health appeared absolute and the trouble was un-diagnosed for months. It was the long-delayed sequel to a girlhood attack of scarlet fever.

Eventually brought under control by careful regime it subsided into a chronic state by mid-1932. For the rest of her life she was subject to almost constant severe headaches and to prostrating attacks of vomiting. She remained constantly at work and few people realised how ill she was. During the months of most acute illness she wrote the novel *Mandoa, Mandoa!*—showing no weakness of approach though it took long to complete. It was conceived when she heard a first-hand account of the comic tribulations suffered by guests at Addis Ababa for the coronation of the Emperor Haile Selassie. Dealing with a part of Africa she knew only from research, this is a splendidly rich piece of writing. Set in an imaginary African state, it is nevertheless most impressive in the city and people described.

For a long time she had wanted to write again about Yorkshire. The agricultural depression there moved her deeply, but it was listening to her mother's talk about local government that lit the spark. By this time Mrs Holtby was an East Riding Councillor about to become its first woman Alderman, and a member of many committees whose minutes came Winifred's way. Winifred moved between London and Yorkshire helping nurse her father, and after his death in April 1933 stayed on with her mother to transact business. It was a sad time but helped by Harry Pearson who showed his ingratiating trait of generous understanding and co-operation.

With so much to do in London it was not till March 1934 that she was able to disencumber herself and spend eleven weeks alone in a workman's cottage in Withernsea on the Yorkshire Coast. There at last *South Riding* was begun. In these weeks the main plot was laid out, the chief characters took shape, the name was chosen, and a first draft of about half the book was written.

Then London life was resumed until early in 1935, when

she was able to take a further Yorkshire interlude, this time a ten weeks' stay in rooms in Hornsea, where the rest of *South Riding* was drafted.

Back in London her total exhaustion told her that time had run out. Those nearest her were not told this, only Jean McWilliam who would be far away. With the rough proofs of *South Riding* still uncorrected, a short final illness in London carried her off in September 1935. *South Riding* was published early in 1936. It is her greatest achievement and has been thoroughly acclaimed, translated into several languages, and constantly kept in print. It is her mature work, and by it she must be judged.

Margaret Waley, Wiltshire, 1981

CHAPTER ONE

THE ADVENTURERS' CHILD

§ 1

WHEN the Reverend Ambrose Entwhistle had been for six months in his grave, his widow besought an Eternal Father in Heaven to substitute His Providence for that of a mortal father upon earth, and to assist Nature and Society in the provision of husbands for her girls. She therefore felt appropriate gratitude when the Bishop of Kingsport developed jaundice, and the S.P.G. Bazaar was opened for him by the Reverend Robert Harringly Burton. Mr. Burton came from the Fort Carey Mission, Eastern Province, Cape Colony, and if his opportune arrival resulted from the intervention of Providence, to Mrs. Entwhistle alone belongs the credit for selecting her daughter Edith to superintend the African stall at the bazaar.

For Edith, tall, brown-haired and dreamy, had an incongruous taste for travel, and spent time more profitably devoted to the occupations of needlework and distributing Parish Magazines, in devouring unladylike literature from the Kingsport Free Library, such as *A Voyage up the Amazon*, *The Coast of Blood and Gold*, and Kelsey's *Islands of the Pacific*. Mrs. Entwhistle had read none of these works, but she had her own ideas about Amazons, and considered that the sooner this sad failing was transformed into advantage, the better for Edith, for herself, and for the household in Park Street, Kingsport.

The advantage revealed itself. The yellow beard and uncouth gestures of the middle-aged missionary, which aroused the derision of Emily, Kate and Helen, were glorified for Edith by the glamour of his adventures. She stood with soft parted lips and glowing cheeks while in abrupt and disconnected phrases he told the ladies at the S.P.G. Bazaar of the native Missionary College, built by his efforts, of the chapel in a rondavel, where he celebrated Holy Communion to brethren black, but in the Lord's sight, comely; of the round thatched huts among the prickly pear bushes where the baboons walked in grotesque procession, and of the lordly warriors who laid aside the ochre-stained blankets of their heathen life to don the sober raiment of Christianity.

And the Reverend Robert Harringly Burton, seeing her slender figure in white spotted muslin, her gentle rapture, and her wondering eyes, suddenly knew that he had been sore with loneliness, and that the Gospel light would burn far brighter if illuminated by such innocent and tender grace.

Their courtship was necessarily brief, because Mr. Burton had promised to attend three missionary congresses, to read a paper before the Geographical Society, and to return to South Africa after Christmas. But Mrs. Entwhistle was a practical woman, and Edith's trousseau grew under the flying fingers of herself and her four daughters, until on January 14th,

1896, Edith found herself leaning over the railing of the steamer, while the deep brownish-grey water of the Thames rushed past with silent dark intensity.

The boat seemed to be perfectly still. It was the low white coast between Tilbury and the sea; it was the smooth subtle river, which flew away from her. England was flying away. The red-brick rectory at Cattleholme on the wolds, where the snowdrops in February pierced the black earth below the briar bush; the bedroom with blue knots on the wall paper, which she shared with Kate in the house at Park Street, Kingsport; her workbox in the back sitting-room, the Mothers' Union meetings; the red plush hassocks in the Church of St. Michael and All Angels — all these were flying away. While she herself, since the day not three months ago when she had stood by the African Stall selling kettleholders, had done nothing at all. She had remained as quiet as the snow-wreathed ship. And yet she had done everything. She had left Kingsport for ever. She had been married. She was sailing out on a real ship across the sea. She was Saint Paul, setting forth towards Rome. She was Sir Walter Raleigh, seeking El Dorado.

With the low, flat coasts, ridged by their frozen roofs, the familiar things all fell away from her, and a small round unfamiliar sun, flat as a sovereign thrown on a grey silk tablecloth, hung in the snow-filled sky to watch them go.

She turned to her husband. " Oh, I'm happy, happy, happy. It's too lovely. Too romantic. It seems to me impossible."

He regarded her with hungry yet detached affection. "My dear," he said. "With God all things are possible."

His hand met hers in her little seal-skin muff.

§ 2

Edith Burton's child was born eighteen months after her marriage, fifteen months after her arrival in Fort Carey.

The journey had enchanted her. Its discomforts enhanced its magic and destroyed its tedium. Fort Carey itself with its oak trees, its village green, its wooden houses, and the gossiping, vivid, restricted social life of the officers' wives, both pleased and disappointed her. An Africa which tried to be as much as possible like England dissatisfied her craving for the remarkable, and the barely concealed distaste of the ladies for her husband's calling aroused her indignation. She learned that officers' wives thought the natives happier and better without missionary interference, which "put ideas into their heads," and augmented the danger of risings. "Ah, my dear," they told her, "when you have been in Africa as long as we have, you will think differently."

She climbed with relief into the ox-wagon which was to convey her, her brass bedstead from Port Elizabeth, and the cases of new books, out to the mission station forty-two miles away.

She saw the parched and twisted valleys where the baboons walked in colonies. She saw the bushes of prickly pear crouched in fantastic attitudes, thousand-

armed, pulpy-breasted, like the lascivious goddess of
the Ephesians pictured in her Bible Concordance. She
saw the cool, transparent cup of the evening sky
warmed at the rim by burning hills, and the goats, with
bearded, provocative faces, mocking her from their
grim banquet of thorns.

She saw the group of rondavels which formed the
mission station, the chapel hut with its smooth, earthen
floor, its circular walls and pointed roof of thatch, and
all the curiously assorted treasures collected for it by
her husband, the Crucifix fashioned from a Russian
Pax, its brass kissed smooth by pious lips, the hood of a
cope made from a Kaffir blanket, embroidered in gold
thread from Persia; the altar cloth, that had once
decorated the tea-table of a colonel's wife.

She saw the hut provided for her use, not thirty
yards from the main building of the college, where her
husband had slept on the veranda with his students, his
bed at one end only distinguished from theirs by a neat
white sheet between the rough brown blankets. He slept
with her now on the new brass bedstead bought in Port
Elizabeth, but his days were completely occupied by
the discovery of misfortunes which had occurred during his absence, by disagreement with his white as-
sistants, and by perturbation of spirit over the short-
comings of his black but comely brethren.

Edith was therefore left to learn many things for
herself.

She learned that a missionary's life was not, as she
had supposed it, a series of fervent journeys into
heathern lands, illuminated by moments of spiritual

radiance, when a few kneeling converts opened their eyes to the Gospel Light. It was rather a succession of skirmishes with official prejudice about the transport of mealies, the local status of native preachers, and the enclosure of commonage.

She learned to house-keep upon chickens, rice, goats' milk and yams, to endure mosquito bites, the ravages of white and brown ants upon her furniture, and the labour of dealing with a people whose tongue she did not understand, and whose alien colour, scent and presence she found unexpectedly disturbing.

She learned, moreover, that life cannot be lived quite objectively. Her eyes and ears were rich with wonderment; her heart was curiously bare. Her husband, a kind, affectionate and preoccupied priest, hardly showed more concern for her than had her father, who had also been a kind, affectionate and preoccupied priest. She was lonely beyond description, but not at all unhappy, diverted from hour to hour by the strange ecstasies of discovery, the perilous delights of an enchanted world. Always the doors of her heart stood a little ajar to receive some new wonder. When she found that she was going to have a child, she thought, " This is the wonder."

To have a child in Kingsport was, she knew, an ordinary and somewhat prosaic business. There were doctors; there was a nurse; there were presents from relatives, of woolly coats, and cot-covers. There was a whispering atmosphere of pleasurable fear.

To have a child in South Africa was a somewhat perilous but wholly desirable adventure. The ladies of

Fort Carey urged the expediency of bringing Mrs. Burton into the township. Mr. Burton, however, believed in the efficacy of Black Labour. Edith, prejudiced against the ladies by her recollection of unhappy tea-parties, and assured of her husband's infallibility, elected to remain.

On a fresh, exquisite June day, when the air challenged the shadows with a clear blue light, she walked down the path to the valley and stumbled on the shadow of a rock that swarmed suddenly about her face in a cloud of purple butterflies. Her surprise and consequent fall terminated in the birth of a girl child before the doctor could be summoned from Fort Carey. When he arrived, accompanied by Colonel Fanshawe's wife, who had most irritated Edith by her superiority, but who now rode the forty-two miles to her assistance, the child was wailing healthily, but Edith lay flushed and in pain, her wide eyes bright with dismay. She could not believe in this abrupt ending to her pilgrimage, while its supreme adventure still eluded her. She died three days later of puerperal fever, demanding from her distracted husband a bowl of aconites and snowdrops from the shrubbery at Cattleholme Rectory.

Mrs. Fanshawe's indignation at Mr. Burton's ineptitude was quenched by her pity for his despair. His militant spirit could fight all wills but that of the Lord, so clearly manifest in His injunction of celibacy. When Mrs. Fanshawe suggested that the Mission was an unsuitable place for the upbringing of a child, and that it should be conveyed as soon as possible to its aunts and grandmother in England, he acquiesced. The Lord had given and the Lord had taken away. Blessed be the name of the Lord.

So in the third week of her life, Edith's daughter was christened in the rondavel chapel. She was called Joanna, after the Spanish wife of Sir Harry Smith, who followed his camp in the Peninsular War, and later accompanied him to South Africa, to give her beautiful name to hills and towns in the Eastern Province. The small Joanna, attended by a subaltern's wife going home on leave, thus returned by the route along which her mother had adventured, to the house in Park Street, Kingsport.

§ 3

On the day before Christmas Eve, Joanna walked with her aunts Kate and Emily up Friarsgate, Kingsport. Friarsgate is a grey, narrow canyon between beetling cliffs. Usually the cliffs are blank grey and angry brown, but at night they blossom surprisingly with orange flowers that leap to light in a dramatic climax of surprises.

Joanna, who was eight years old, danced two or three yards ahead of her aunts, singing in a soft little happy voice, " Christmas is coming! Christmas is coming! " Because of the shop-windows full of holly and toys and groceries in scarlet frilled paper, and silver tinsel, and trumpets, and mistletoe, she was so happy that her little blue serge dress felt as though it must burst from the swelling of her breast.

" Joanna, Joanna," called Aunt Emily, and Joanna stopped.

"We turn up here," said Aunt Kate. "Helen said that she thought he lived in Commercial Lane."

"Helen thinks a great deal too much," replied Aunt Emily acidly. Aunt Helen was engaged to Mr. Braddon, of Braddon's, Elk and Braddon's, Coal Exporters, and did think a good deal of herself, which was hardly surprising, considered Joanna, seeing that she had such lovely underclothes all with little tucks and embroidery, lying out on the spare room bed.

"I don't think that this is Commercial Lane," said Aunt Kate, screwing up her short-sighted eyes behind her glasses. They were seeking an electrician who, Aunt Helen had thought, might come even at the eleventh hour to mend a bell, dumb at so inconvenient a season. Joanna, who rarely went out on late shopping expeditions, jigged up and down singing her private song.

"Joanna, my dear, your eyes are younger than mine," said Aunt Emily. Joanna was always hearing that her eyes or her legs were younger than other people's, an observation so apparent that she wondered why people troubled to make it. But being an obliging child, she never resented the requests to make use of her youth which invariably followed.

Joanna stood on tiptoe, feeling tremendously important, and peered up at the letters half hidden in the obscurity of the dirt and darkness.

"The — Land — of — Green — Ginger," she read incredulously. "The Land of Green Ginger."

It was unbelievable. It was inevitable. On such a night of course such things must happen. Only they never had happened before.

"Aunt Emily. Auntie. Auntie! It's called the Land of Green Ginger."

Why did her aunts not share the wonder of her delight?

"Of course," said Aunt Kate crossly. "Commercial Lane is the next turning. I told you that it was right at the end of the street. If I'd known it was so far I'd never have said I'd come."

"But the Land of Green Ginger, Auntie? The Land of Green Ginger?"

Was it really possible that having found it, they would not enter in? That like Moses — or was it Abraham? — Joanna was not very good at Scripture, except about the countries — That like Moses they would look at the Promised Land and never enter it?

But they were gathering up their skirts. They were settling the strings of parcels more comfortably across their gloves. They were moving on.

"But Auntie, Auntie, we can't just — just leave it, can we?"

To be offered such gifts of fortune, to seek Commercial Lane and to find — the day before Christmas Eve and by lamplight too — The Land of Green Ginger, dark, narrow, mysterious road to Heaven, to Fairy Land, to anywhere, anywhere, even to South Africa, which was the goal of all men's longing, the place where Father lived in a rondavel, the place. . .

Her aunts were moving away. Relentlessly, majestically, with skirts well lifted from the muddy road, and firm boots laced against the slithery grease of the pavement, they moved forward.

" But Auntie, we must stay, mustn't we? We shall come back, shan't we? We must just look, just a little look? " If she were very modest in her requests she might perhaps break this monstrous spell of indifference.

" Now come along, Joanna, and don't be a naughty girl," chanted Aunt Kate in the accepted formula.

" But Auntie . . . "

" Hurry up, dear, and walk nicely. Don't drag your feet like that. It spoils your new boots. Yes, of course we shall come back some time. Well, Emily, what about some chestnuts for the turkey stuffing? Mother said that if there were any nice ones . . ."

The three moved on.

§ 4

In the summer of 1914, misfortune came upon Joanna. Her father died while on an expedition through the Transkei, and she failed to matriculate in Mathematics and Latin.

Her aunts Kate and Emily — Aunt Helen, now safely married, had children of her own, and Grandmother was dead — became seriously perturbed about their niece's future. The Reverend Robert Harringly Burton had left a will but no money. All his earthly goods had been expended upon the Mission College. The house in Park Street had been maintained partly by remittances every year from Fort Carey, and Joanna was just eighteen. They wept a little over the combined misfortune.

Joanna did not weep, but with a stiff little smile and

a queer pain in the side of her chest, she sought her two great friends at the Kingsport High School, Agnes Darlington and Rachel Harris.

They took counsel together.

Joanna told them the facts as she had heard them, then added the real cause of her fears.

"Of course this means that I can't go to Fort Carey."

They nodded sympathetically. Both girls knew that Joanna regarded England as a place from which one sailed for South Africa, or possibly China or Bolivia or Thibet, or anywhere attractively remote. Yet all roads hitherto had led to Fort Carey at last.

"You can still travel," said Rachel firmly. "You can always do what you want to do, if you want hard enough."

"Darling, it's beastly for you. Come and stay with my family in Manchuria," murmured Agnes, biting a daisy stalk.

They lay together in a corner of the cricket ground, and as Rachel was a prefect, and Joanna the tennis captain, and all three in the sixth form, they were left undisturbed in Olympian detachment.

"All that you have to do is to want enough," said Rachel. She was a small ardent Jewess, with the rich beauty of her race and most decided opinions. "Look how I fought my parents to get them to let me try for Somerville. People will always give way to you if you really mean to do something, and all getting on in life is making people give way." Rachel always talked as though she knew all about life. As a matter of fact, her physical and mental maturity was remarkable, though not so remarkable as Agnes and Joanna thought. "It's your own fault, Joanna, if you're a lazy little hound. Look at the way you messed up your matric. It's the indolent people, pleasant and popular like yourself, who make things so hard for the fighters. We're never so nice as you are because we see beyond our noses and try to get there."

"Rachel, dearest, don't scold to-day. Our beloved Joanna is distressed," remarked Agnes, peacefully weaving a daisy-chain but glancing from Rachel's vehement little face to Joanna's flushed agitation.

"Joanna wouldn't like me half so much if I didn't scold her. She prefers to think of her friends as more clever and virtuous than herself, because this excuses her from making the efforts that she ought to make, and justifies her illusions about a very wicked world."

"My lamb," comforted Agnes. "Rachel went to a Suffragette meeting in the Town Hall last night, and it went to her head a little. The Hebrew mind takes its politics seriously, as Miss Phillips said in O.T. class yesterday." Rachel was, fortunately, one of those Jewesses with whom one could discuss anti-Semitism and jokes about Jews. "Don't let her bother you. My family's moving to Kirin Province next August. Come out with me when we leave school and we'll see lovely things. Korea is cold, and Japanese hotels lack privacy, but they are clean and there are lovely down quilts and paper screens and friendly little policemen. And we'll go South to Yunnanfu, where the streets are full of brigands and mandarins, and palanquins and swaying oxen dragging heavy carts."

Joanna's eyes grew dim with pleasure and consolation. She cupped her chin on her long hands and smiled across at Agnes.

"It must be wonderful to be the daughter of a Chinese customs official."

"Not nearly so wonderful as to go to China because of your own efforts. It's the curse of women to think of themselves just as 'somebody's daughter.' What do you think of men who think of themselves as 'somebody's son'?"

"But that's just how all the best sons in China do regard themselves. Joanna has a Chinese mind," said Agnes serenely. She and Joanna smiled at one another, lazily, secretly, sharing a deep extravagant love of the strange places where both had been born. Joanna's mind became full of palanquins and exquisitely caparisoned camels, and temples with roofs ingeniously curled, tinkling with bells and brilliantly coloured; and as she smiled across the daisies at her friends, she forgot that her heart was sore with disappointment and the shock of amputating from her personality an unknown but always anticipated father. She became intoxicated by her own vague, lovely vision of a world enriched with so many curious and coloured creatures.

"When I leave school I shall see all the world, and travel for ever and ever," she crooned dreamily.

The daisies opened their eyes wide in wonder that anyone, having seen them, should desire more abundant pleasures.

CHAPTER TWO

SIR WALTER RALEIGH

§ 1

SIX weeks later the declaration of War provided an unmatriculated Joanna with the remunerative position for which her aunts had prayed.

Sister Warren of the South Park Nursing Home, Kingsport, where Aunt Helen had stayed during the birth of her first baby, lost two valuable nurses, and had to attend to operations herself in consequence. Therefore she took Joanna into her office as assistant secretary at a salary of twenty-five shillings a week.

Joanna thus left school for ever, bought three grey overalls and a fountain pen, pinned up her thick fair hair, and set herself to learn the mysteries of petty cash, night-specials, and reduced terms. Because she was, beyond all her other loves, in love with life, she found it very interesting.

She was, moreover, an unexpected success, for though she sometimes forgot messages, or sorted linen into the wrong bundles, the nurses liked her. And even when she charged 4d twice for soda-water, the patients liked her too. Her capacity for endowing the commonplace with transcendental qualities enabled her to see South Park Nursing Home as the Best In England, her work there as Part of the Great Effort Made by Gallant

Women to Win the War, and Sister Warren as a splendid Leader and Chief — an attitude of mind commonly appreciated by employers.

§ 2

One Monday morning, when Joanna was closeted for two hours in a dark and stuffy cupboard sorting linen by the light of a hissing gas-jet, her long back ached with weariness, and her fingers with cold; but her mind was very happy.

. . . For Queen Elizabeth raised a petticoat quilted with silver threads from her small crimson shoe. She took three paces forward and spoke as she dropped to a low curtsy.

"Ah, Sir Walter, we doubted not your zeal but your discretion. Our cousin of Spain may break his teeth on this bone of contention; but we — we bide our time."

She rose slowly from her billowing skirts and moved like a ship in full sail across the gleaming floor. In the shadow behind her, tall, handsome, but damnably proud, strode the man in slashed doublet pricked with seed-pearls. Great drops of pearl and filagree swung from his ears. As she turned in the dance, swaying to a tune from unseen fiddlers, he stood and looked daringly into her eyes.

. . . Joanna dropped three more towels into the linen bag . . .

"If I had known other way to win, your majesty. If I had imagined how greater adventures might have been regained, if I could conceive what further means I yet might use but to appease so powerful a displeasure,

I would not doubt but for one more year to hold fast my soul in my teeth till it were performed."

. . . The hands picking up table-napkins were still . . .

" Aye, but when you fail then must a woman work. Hark ye, Sir Walter." She leaned a little nearer and he went down before her on one knee. In the candle-lit alcove the moving jewels on her breast shot ruby fire, deep royal amethyst, the clear water of diamonds. Glittering, perfumed and regal, she bent over him. " Think you," she said, and Joanna began with a mechanical rhythm to throw table-napkins from one pile to another. " Think you I let my gentlemen run from sea to sea, from cape to cape for the pillaging of ordinary prizes? Think you I hold my honour so light a thing that by rank piracy ye might enrich it? Think you I have not here," she tapped her forehead and the great pearl quivered, " devices which, were I to utter them, would freeze the seas and hold the pale moon spellbound? But ah, this woman's part, sister's part, queen's part, it is less easy than your wild adventures. For every ship that crosses the high seas draws after it a cord pulled from my heart. This way and that, warp and woof on the waters, they weave a web to draw my sons to me home. I cannot see your sudden-flowering isles, your El Dorados glittering with gold, save in the treasure brought by you to England. I face no rack of Spain, save that the inquisition of my heart tears nerve from nerve when I hear news that this lad died in the Azores, this is Guiana, this on the Spanish coast." She pressed her hands to her eyes and stood swaying a little. Joanna now stood with her hands against her eyes. " It is all here, here in my mind. I have seen without eyes, heard without ears. I have spread my nets and drawn them home to my mind. Nets — would ye break my nets by a rash word, a shot fired in the dark? "

He caught her hands and covered them with burning kisses. " Ah, your majesty, but I hope that there shall appear a way found to answer every man's longing, a better Indies for your majesty than the King of Spain hath any, which, if it shall please your highness to undertake, I will most willingly end the rest of my days in following the same."

. . . " Eighty-five, eighty-six. Damn. These should be the nineties." Joanna tucked Sir Walter Raleigh's *Discovery of Guiana* into her pocket and picked up a table-napkin ruefully, just as the office bell rang and she had to turn and fly downstairs, three steps at a time to hurl herself unexpectedly upon a tall young man who stood unseen in the shadow.

" Oh, I'm so frightfully sorry! " gasped Joanna.

" Not at all. Not at all. Why, it's Miss Burton." They moved forward into the office and the light shone on his fair, good-looking face, his slender, familiar figure. " I don't suppose that you remember me. I'm Teddy Leigh. My people know your aunts and we sit near you in church."

" Why of course I remember. I can always remember people's faces, although I never know their names." Joanna stood still, a little breathless, and talking too much as she always did when shy. " I know that I shall get up and look in the glass one morning and say,

28

'Dear me, I seem to know your face quite well, but I can't remember your name! ' "

" I, on the contrary," he said, " can always remember as many names as in a street directory, but I fit them on to the wrong faces."

Joanna, accustomed to young men who received her more absurd statements with frozen manners and an outraged sense of the decorous, began to laugh. The young man laughed too, with charming friendliness. He was, indeed a most charming young man altogether.

" But I thought that you were at Oxford or somewhere," said Joanna most incorrectly.

" Cambridge. I was. But there happens to be this little matter of a war on, and even incipient curates become lieutenant-colonels, and whatnot, and I've been passed as a perfectly good specimen of British manhood. No. Don't look so sceptically at my grey suit. I do not go into camp until next Friday week. Meanwhile my tailor. . . . "

" You look frightfully pleased about it."

" I've just been given the world to wear as a golden ball."

Did he really say that? Or had he just said, " I've got nothing to wear, it's an awful bore? "

He hadn't. He was adding excitedly, " The world is a wonderful thing to wear at the end of your sword-belt."

" O-oh," so nonsensical a young man was an uncovenanted mercy from Providence.

It took Joanna a moment before she could ask seriously, " Did you want anything special here? "

It appeared that the aunt who kept house for his

father had a son, a detestable little urchin, who had an
appendix. And, instead of removing the son, which
would, in Teddy's opinion, be preferable, they proposed
to remove the appendix, and sought a vacancy in South
Park Nursing Home. And since Teddy was idling in the
intervals of visiting his army tailor, his father and his
aunt thought that he would be better employed by
visiting Miss Warren. And so on.

Joanna moved to the desk to consult the book.
Teddy looked at her. She was tall and grandly propor-
tioned, like an immature young goddess. Soft golden
hairs curled graciously against her firm, milky neck.
Her full lips, parted eagerly, belied the severity of her
nose and brow; her blue eyes, deep-set below heavy
lids, laughed at a pleasant world. She appeared to be a
singularly happy and healthy creature.

Teddy Leigh drew towards her happiness and youth
as a chilled traveller draws towards a fire. She seemed
so young, so strong, so sure that life was good. He, who
snatched sudden joys from an uncertain world, looked
at her with envious longing. She seemed as strong and
stablished as a golden tower.

He nearly told her so, but decided instead to say,
" Have you an extra room in your nursing home? I am
suddenly afflicted by a malady of the heart."

She thought his facetiousness refreshing after the
solemnities of a middle-aged world. Besides, her acquaintance with Sir Walter Raleigh made her think
pretty speeches very becoming in a tall young man.

Detestable though the mother's sister's son's personality might be, Teddy Leigh came to visit him six

times at South Park Nursing Home, and at the sixth
time he told Joanna that he loved her.

§ 3

Joanna had frequently been in love before, with
Hiawatha, with the Scarlet Pimpernel, with Coriolanus,
Christabel Pankhurst and a colonel who came to lecture at Kingsport High School on Arabia, whose name
she had unluckily forgotten.

But what befell her when Teddy Leigh drew her into
Miss Warren's sitting-room and shut the door so
quietly, was something very different.

He said, " My dear, I love you. I adore you. I cannot live without you."

He kissed her as she had never imagined kisses. He
held her in fierce, impatient arms. He brought the struc-
ture of her tranquillity toppling about her. She was
possessed by an overwhelming desire for tears, to be
left alone to cry and cry, and then to sleep away the
exhaustion that his kisses brought. He left her tremu-
lous, but exultant in a world grown suddenly quite
strange, its values twisted.

When Rachel Harris came home from Oxford for the
Easter vacation, Joanna took her for a walk along the
embankment of the River Leame to tell her that she
was engaged to Teddy Leigh.

" Good Heavens. You're mad," cried Rachel. " Why,
you hardly know him."

" That's the lovely part," said Joanna. " Our marriage will be one long voyage of discovery."

" The only sort of voyage you'll ever make then,"

prophesied Rachel gloomily. "Why, he was going to be a clergyman, wasn't he? And his father's a retired bank manager and his mother died years ago. And they haven't any money. Good gracious, my dear child, what about your travels? What about your ideals?"

Joanna made a little comic gesture. "I've forgotten those trifles," she said. "My dear, he's adorable. You'll love him. He says the most ridiculous things in the world. I never knew that men could be so silly. And at the same time, so frightfully, so — so good. He wants to be good. He's, he's that sort of person, Rachel, I love him."

"You don't love a slum rectory in Birmingham. However, it's not my business. You're all the same. I hear you sound so frightfully keen on things, work and books and a career, then the first man comes who says he loves you and away you go . . . everything forgotten. Oh, what is the use of fighting and struggling to make it possible for women to work? You don't care. You don't care." Rachael had one of her unexpected lapses from the rôle of strong, silent — or sometimes most voluble — young woman, and began to cry.

It ended by Joanna, who rarely cried, lending the humiliated Rachel a pocket handkerchief, and the two friends walking with linked arms along the twilit river-path.

"Whatever happens, it won't make any difference to my loving you and Agnes. But oh, Rachel, this damned war. This damned war. Suppose he never comes back? Suppose . . . Oh, blind or crippled or anything, anything. If only I may have him to look after him. Rachel, if there's a God — "

" There isn't," said Rachel, gloomy but indomitable.

" If there's a God, He must let me have him back, just somehow, anyhow. In the world. Alive."

" You don't really feel like that. It's a madness. You really love islands and places more than you'll ever love people. Don't I know you? It's the hysteria of this damned war."

" It's not, it's not. You don't know what you're talking about. You don't know Teddy."

" I know you, my love. However, it's no use, I suppose, talking about it. This is a disease. Do look at that adorable little house wearing its chimney all on the side of its head like a best hat."

Rachel was, on the whole, unsympathetic.

§ 4

Old Mr. Crowle in Number 7 was still alive.

He had been operated upon three times for cancer of the tongue and now he could neither feed himself nor speak. His restless, despairing little eyes hunted the shadows of the darkened room until they rested on Joanna. She sat stiffly in her chair by the bed, trying not to look from the basins and forceps on the dressing-table that she had prepared to the bandaged horror which was old Mr. Crowle's face.

She told herself, " He was a hardware merchant and a Unitarian. He used to sing bass in the Philharmonic. He had a wife whom once he must have loved, as I

33

love Teddy. That mouth kissed her." She began to shudder violently.

Old Mr. Crowle saw the outline of her young figure against the shadow. Among the nightmare humiliations and unrealities of his illness, her youth and comeliness alone assured him that life had once held sweet and wholesome pleasures. Seeing her shiver, he thought that she must be cold, sitting so quietly there in the darkened room. His plump, feeble fingers moved on the counterpane and fumbled for her arm.

Joanna began to pray.

"Oh God, if you exist, why do you let such things be possible? Such horror, such pain? The world is lovely, lovely. But You won't let us see its loveliness because of this frightful cruelty of our bodies. Such terrible things happen to people's bodies. And then it doesn't matter how beautiful the world is." The seeking fingers found her wrist. "Oh don't . . . don't let him touch me. I can't bear it." The shadows jeered at her. "You've got to bear it. You can't hurt the poor old thing. You can't escape from pity. Pity will pursue you always. If you run away from here, it is out in the streets, it is on the battlefields. It is in your private room, everywhere. It has marked you down. You can't escape, ever."

The large gold watch beside Old Mr. Crowle's bed had a soft fluttering tick. The small second hand chased round and round as though racing the time till Old Mr. Crowle should die.

Joanna dared not look to see how long she would have to sit until Nurse Brooks should come on duty.

34

She dared not breathe deeply, because below the faint perfume of eau-de-Cologne the air was tainted with blood and corruption. She dared not think of Old Mr. Crowle, because it was not he alone who lay there. It was Teddy and all men whom women had loved. It was youth, and the recklessness of physical beauty. Everything fair and brave and strong could come to that helpless perversion of humanity. Not war alone menaced the loveliness and worth of life.

" If life is like this," she thought. " I don't want to go on living."

She made a violent effort of will to escape from her body in the darkened room. Her mind fought for its liberty.

" Teddy, Teddy," she called.

He came running towards her along the goat-path leading to the Dam. The tall reeds shook their spears beside them. Hand in hand they ran, till the golden willows tossed their fountains above the water, which was warm and dark, with a firm soft surface like brown agate. From far away on the thorny hillside, a Kaffir boy played three little soft notes on a pipe, limpid and clear as the water. They stepped into the boat and pushed out above the forest of feathery green weeds, waving below the water. If she put down her hand, she could feel them there, soft as a kitten's fur, between her fingers.

" Now we sail to Manoa," said Sir Walter Raleigh. " The willows are fountains of gold. The kopjes are silver mountains. Here will I kiss the bowl of bliss . . ."

There was a sudden movement from the bed. Joanna saw a dark stain spreading softly across the sheet.

Old Mr. Crowle died of hæmorrhage after his third operation.

" A mercy, poor old thing," said Nurse Brooks.

" We must send a nice wreath," said Sister Warren. " But really, I'm glad he's gone. These cancer patients are so trying."

CHAPTER THREE

THE FACE OF FACTS

§ 1

"BUT we must look facts in the face, mustn't we, Mrs. Leigh? " Mr. Boyse, the curate, shifted his tea-cup and took the last of Joanna's scones.

" No, no. There are some facts that you should never look in the face. Some facts are like Medusa. Their faces would turn you to stone."

Mr. Boyse looked at Joanna with round eyes and an expression that hovered between amusement and disapproval. He could not make up his mind if she were joking or being smart. Mrs. Leigh had a reputation in Letherwick for being a bit too smart. Poor thing, she had a lot of trouble, of course. But trouble should be meekly borne. It should be grateful for the pity of the fortunate. It should not aspire to wit, to ridiculous gaiety. It should not — the curate's eye travelled down from Joanna's bright, if shapeless green jumper to her shabby, smart shoes — it should not wear green stockings.

He reminded Joanna that she was a Poor Thing by asking, " How is your husband? "

" He's much better. The air here is splendid. Really, he's able most days to lead a perfectly normal life."

" That's splendid, splendid. Thanks, I will have another scone — er — er — bread and butter will do,

37

thanks. The climb up here does give you an appetite. Two miles is it? Two and a half, I should say, and three by the low road. Pretty awful roads, what? But they put beef into you. Beef, eh? that's what Captain Leigh wants. A little more beef. Does he use " beefers," dumb-bells, you know? I use 'em every morning. Eugene Sandow. Great chap. But he got fat, you know. Dreadful pity. I must get your husband to try dumb-bells."

" I'm afraid that he's hardly up to dumb-bells yet, he gets very tired still about the farm."

" Ah, but we'll soon have him on his feet again." If trouble will not be meek, then it must be ignored. We must have nothing tedious to sadden us. " I hear that he's writing a book. That's awfully interesting. I wanted to talk to him . . ."

Joanna was hardly listening. She was wondering about Teddy, and whether he had got over his mood, after tramping like that out to the cow-house. Going off without saying a word.

She felt miserably apologetic, with that sick ache at her throat which always attacked her when she was most conscious of Teddy's unhappiness. She had failed him again, of course. She was always failing him. If only she had remembered to post that letter about the linseed cake, it would have gone off three days ago, and the consignment might have reached the station before now. It was her fault, and yet she cursed the malignity of fate which made her pull the unposted letter from her jersey pocket just when Teddy was standing there. Facts, thought Joanna. Those were the facts of life: her forgetfulness, and the cake not arriving, and Teddy's temper, when he must on no account be upset, and Mr. Boyse eating the last scone, which meant that the children would have to go without, for she had no time to bake some more. Though she seemed always to be cooking at odd times of the day and evening, so often the most essential things somehow ran short.

It could not be helped. If only Mr. Boyse would go away. His jolly complacent optimism infuriated Joanna. It would outrage Teddy's jangled nerves. People had no business to find life so simple.

She wanted to say, "Oh, do go away. Do go away, and let me have a moment of peace to write to Agnes. I want to hear from Agnes more than anything in the world just now, and how should she write if I never answer her letters? How can she know that I am pursued through the days by little irritating duties, and whenever I find an hour to write, they capture me, they swarm all over me, and before I have swept them away, the time has gone?"

Mr. Boyse was saying, "But I said to her, 'My dear young lady, I know that you are one of these modern young women who think that they can get on all right without organized religion, yet don't you think that you are missing something, do you never feel an emptiness?'" Mr. Boyse leaned above his tea-cup, breathing heavily. Joanna wished that he would go, yet seeing his warm, earnest face, she could not refrain from looking sympathetic. Her distraction lay always in her loving heart, which warmed too easily to pity. She knew just how people felt when they knocked at your door for pity and it slammed in their face. Her door, she re-

flected, must be a trifle loose on its hinges from standing so long ajar.

She was feeling tired, so tired that the brown tea-pot
weighed at least a ton. She had been up since soon after
five, lighting the fire because she had no oil left for the
stove and Teddy wanted a cup of tea. And then it was
time for milking and for the children to be called, and
all the clamour of the day tumbled on top of her.

" Hullo, Boyse. By Jove, it's good to see you. So
you've managed to climb up to our mountain loosenesses? "

Teddy stood in the doorway, making a sensation.
Joanna knew that he had got over his mood. He was
elated again, blown to the airy heights of his own
ephemeral happiness. She could see him, seeing himself
as he stood there, fascinating the curate, handsome,
tragic, debonair Captain Leigh, in his college tie, and
his leather gaiters, his slender elegance encased as it
were in bucolic roughness, the gassed, tubercular ex-
officer, who had given everything, and yet remained
undefeated, gallant, radiant with perilous charm. Well,
he was happy again, anyway. Joanna's burden of
fatigue fell off her like the weight of Christian's sins.
She began to laugh almost hysterically.

" Loosenesses, fastnesses, you know," she explained
to the curate's puzzled face. " Scatterthwaite's roof is a
bit loose, you know; a tile off, Teddy says. So we can't
call it our mountain fastnesses."

She was watching Teddy pull out his beautiful purple
silk handkerchief and dust his slim white fingers. How
unlike a farmer he looked. The darling, the darling.

40

The anxious tenderness that he aroused in her pulled at her heart.

He came towards her and laid a careless hand on her shoulder. She felt stupid with relief that his mood had passed.

" Any tea, woman, tea, tea, tea, blast ye? " He removed the cover of the tarnished silver dish. " You've eaten all the scones, you skunks."

" Talking of skunks," observed Joanna, pouring out tepid tea, because in her pleasure at Teddy's returned tranquillity she had forgotten to fetch the kettle, " Colonel Badderley said that if you went to Nova Scotia and brought back a dozen skunks and built little houses for them on the moor, in three years' time you would have thirty-six dozen, and in six years . . ."

" We should all make our fortune. Boyse, will you come in with the deal? Blast this filthy tea. My wife is an angel, Boyse, but she makes tea like cabbage water, and is always forgetting to brush her nails."

He began teasing her, his gentle drawling voice aiming sharp little arrows of raillery at the tender places in her self-esteem, until she shivered with soreness. She told herself, " He is feeling better. He can't help it. It's the pains of convalescence. He's feeling that he was rather a pig, and he's taking it out of us both to pay himself back." But she was interrupted in her thoughts by the sound of wheels, and Thorley's booming voice, and then her children's laughter.

" Yes, yes. Come in, darlings. Here's Mr. Boyse. Pat, dear, say ' How do you do ' nicely. Oh, Pam, I told you to take your scarf."

41

The two little girls created a diversion in the firelit sitting-room. Pamela danced forward eagerly, her eyes bright with excitement, her little button of a nose red with cold. Patricia, pulling off her woollen gloves, sidled ostentatiously round the table away from Mr. Boyse. She was slender and fair, with a skin so delicate that colour blew up and down behind it like flames behind glass. A lovely child, fragile and stubborn and self-conscious, who turned on Mr. Boyse a look of sullen hostility, then drooped her long dark lashes, and stooped over the fire, warming her hands. She took off her felt hat, shaking her mass of fair, waving hair, and went forward to the table. With a movement extraordinarily like her father's, she lifted the cover of the dish.

"Aren't there any scones for us? Mother, haven't you left any scones for us? Oh, Mother, and I was so longing for a scone, a little round buttery scone, all hot with currents in it. All the way up the hill in that horrid rattly cart that makes my head ache so, I was thinking, 'Never mind, Mother said we'll have scones for tea.'"

"But darling," Joanna gave a conscience-stricken glance at Mr. Boyse's purple face.

"I think that you are a horrid, cruel mother. You always think of visitors before you think of us. If the house was burning down, you'd always run to rescue other little girls before Pam and me. We're always thinking of ways how to please you. I laid the table for breakfast this morning all myself, and you hardly said 'Thank you.' And you couldn't even keep one little scone . . ."

She fled sobbing from the room.

"My elder daughter," observed Teddy, "would have made an excellent militant suffragette. What a pity we gave women the vote. People like Patricia will miss their vocation. But perhaps she will become a Bolshevist."

"Oh my little daughter, my darling, my darling," cried Joanna to her stricken heart, shocked by compunction and by foreboding at such vehemence, such resentment, such bitter sense of wrong.

Mr. Boyse shifted his bulk uncomfortably in the arm-chair and turned to Pamela. "Are you the little girl who rides every day down to school in the milk-cart?" he asked.

Pamela helped herself placidly to another slice of bread and butter. "No. Pat goes to school. But I sometimes ride down in the milk-cart to meet her. And it's not a cart, but a float, although it goes on wheels." Pamela was a sociable child, accustomed to the filling in of some hiatus left by the devastating violence of her sister's temperament. She slid down now from her chair and laid her hand on the curate's fat knee. "I am very good, though not so clever as Pat. And I like you very much, though your hands are furry. Will you marry me when I grow up?"

"Er — er — certainly, my dear," said the curate, embarrassed but somehow gratified.

"That makes my fifth husband," remarked Pamela complacently. "I hope that you don't cough at night like Daddy, so that I shall have to sleep in the box-room too. It makes a cleavage between husband and

43

wife, I think, don't you? My doll Malcolm has eighteen wives. Mummy, may I have some of that cake? the one that's gone a bit sad in the middle? "

§ 2

The facts, as Joanna had admitted, wore no agreeable face.

She had married Teddy Leigh in the second year of the War, when she was just nineteen. Nine months after their brief honeymoon at Scarshaven, Patricia had been born, a most delicate but beautiful baby. In 1917, Teddy came home for a gunnery course, and went back to France leaving Joanna in the house at Park Street, to await the arrival of Pamela. In June, 1918, he returned to England for good, and wrote to his wife from the Yorkshire Military Sanatorium.

Joanna, leaving her babies with the aunts at Kingsport, went to Wellingham to see him. She hated the rows of huts with open sides, the scrubbed floors, the bleak cleanliness of the officers' quarters. The courage which had supported her during her journey became transformed to fury at the sight of Teddy on his hospital bed, his body — her gay slender boy's body — shaken and tortured by the racking cough. She could not face the hunted anguish of his eyes, the twisted jokes that he made to her.

Down in the waiting-room, she interviewed the military doctor, a kind colonel accustomed to such grievous work. But he was not accustomed to women who took it in Joanna's way.

" How dared they do that to him? " she stormed.

How dared they? How dared they? Blast them, damn them, blast them! "

She was shaken and blinded by rage. She stood beside the wooden table, locking and unlocking her hands and swearing with a hushed vehemence of profanity. " Swine. Huns. Bloody brutes. Damn them." She used expressions that she thought she had never heard, astonishing herself and the colonel who had thought her a lady.

Then she put her hands over her face and stood very still.

When she withdrew them, he saw that she was smiling steadily. " I'm so awfully sorry. I did not mean to treat you to that outburst. I don't know what came over me. Teddy says that you've been so kind. I do apologize."

" Please don't. I do understand. I am so sorry. But you know we must remember that it was amazing, considering his record, that he lasted as long as he did."

" His record? His record? What do you mean? "

" Well, I mean that his lungs can't have been in such a bad state. I mean that old patch . . . er . . . I . . . "

He stared at her, for she was staring at him with wide blue eyes. " You don't mean that you didn't . . . I mean . . . " Good God, didn't the woman know that she had married a consumptive?

" Please go on. I . . . I'm just a little stupid."

It was she who was quite composed now, shocked into stillness.

" Well, of course, I mean that that old trouble, when

45

he was a boy, sent to Davos, you know . . . I mean that it was remarkable they passed him in the first place. He confesses that he was surprised. Of course, it was madness. Considering how deeply rooted the trouble was, it is nothing short of miraculous that he kept going so long. His mother, of course, he tells me, picked up in a wonderful way before she died in Switzerland. It's no use blinking at the fact that he's got a wretched history. But that's no reason why we need give up hope. None at all. It's largely a matter of keeping up his spirits. He was going to be a clergyman, wasn't he? "

" He wanted to be. He was at Cambridge."

" Madness, of course. He never should have tried anything but an open-air life. However . . . there's no reason, absolutely none, why we should not get him on his feet again. Farming, poultry or something like that, I should say. We shall have to keep his spirits up. That will depend largely on you, Mrs. Leigh. Are you staying here? "

" I have to go back to Kingsport to-night. My children are there. But I can come again. Friday, perhaps. I'll arrange to stay."

" Ah. You have a family? "

She nodded, pulling on her gloves and avoiding the grave compassion of his glance. " Two little girls."

" Are they pretty well? "

She glanced up, startled at the significance of his casual question. The solid earth of her world cracked beneath her. She stared into a bewildering abyss. Such questions meant . . . meant . . .

"Oh, yes, yes," she whispered.

"Oh, I say, Mrs. Leigh." Suddenly he was appalled by the stricken terror of her face. He saw what the tall maturity of her figure and the anxious gravity of her voice had hitherto hidden, how young she was, and how defenceless. She was nothing but a child, and he had laid upon her the burden of an intolerable fear.

"Please, please don't look like that. It's all right. We'll get him all right. You know. You know. There's no reason why tuberculosis should be hereditary. It's by no means established yet that there's certain danger."

She flashed on him a smile of disquieting brilliance. She said, "It's quite all right. I'm not going to lose my head again. Be kind to him, please," and turned about and fled, leaving the poor man more troubled than he had been by anything for years.

Walking to the station, her tread was unusually light and gay. She inspected the groceries and woollen stockings in the little country shops. She bought a copy of *Home Chat* on the station bookstall, and looked at the fashions while eating her tea in the refreshment room. She ordered three eccles cakes, and ate them with enjoyment, wiping up from her plate the flaky crumbs of pastry, and nibbling luxuriously. For eccles cakes were luxuries in war time, and only in country station refreshment rooms could you eat three at a time.

But back in the train, alone in a third-class carriage, her fears swooped down upon her. Teddy, Teddy . . . Her young body writhed in torment at his pain. Patricia, Pamela. What had she done to them?

Why had he never told her? Switzerland? Of course he had told her that he had been to Switzerland. He did not like the mountains. They were too much on top of one another, he said, as though the Lord were trying to economize space. They looked like cakes with pink icing on at sunset time. The Swiss were great goths.

He thought that he was all right. He had been passed for the army. That was why he was so much delighted.

He had said, " They've given me the world to wear," didn't he, didn't he?

She sat up very straight, gripping her hands together on her lap.

" I know him so little. What after all, do I know of him? "

She realized that she had been in his company only four times: during the brief period of their courtship at the Park Street Nursing Home, during the ten days of their marriage and honeymoon, during the three weeks of his gunnery course, and now. Yet during those three years he had been her constant companion. She had built up a picture of him, solid and unquestioned.

" I am married to a stranger," she told herself.

" I am hateful, because in his misery, I have still pity for myself."

In her aunt's house at Kingsport, she knelt between the cot and the cradle where her two children lay.

" My darlings, I'm so sorry. I didn't mean to bring you into this horrid world, with this — this — hanging over you. I didn't know. I didn't know. Oh, and Teddy didn't know either. He thought that he was cured. He thought that as he was cured his mother didn't count.

It's not always hereditary. The doctor says it's not always hereditary. Oh, don't hate us. Don't hate us. Oh, God, God, God, don't let them be consumptive."

She bit her hand to check the choking sobs.

It was no use. Patricia woke up and began to whimper. Joanna gathered her up into her arms, and sat rocking her backwards and forwards on the floor, while the tears ran down her cheeks as though they would never stop.

§ 3

Scatterthwaite lay two and a half miles from Letherwick in Lindersdale. Like many other farms in the North Riding of Yorkshire it had a house built of grey stone, with a steep roof of dark slate. The house faced a narrow strip of garden with some gooseberry bushes, a mossy path and a weed-grown flower-bed. The back opened on to a yard entered by two gates: one from the high road over the hills, one from the low road round the Fell. Beyond the yard lay a potato patch, and surrounding that, and the house and the buildings, three fields. Beyond the fields, which dipped in a cup-like hollow, rolled mile after mile of the dark lowering moors.

Joanna used to think that the house was like a ship, and the rolling curve of the moors like great ocean waves. Its windows at night shone like the port-holes of a tramp steamer, ploughing its way up the North Sea in dirty weather. She had never seen ships except in the Kingsport Docks and from the esplanade at Hardrascliff, but she felt sure that they were like this.

49

They had come to Scatterthwaite after Teddy had received his discharge from the Yorkshire Military Sanatorium. With a gratuity from the Government and the legacy left by his father, now dead, they had bought the farm and hired an old foreman and his wife, Mr. and Mrs. Thorley, to come and live with them. The children slept in the big south room, with its square windows always open, and Teddy farmed with six cows, four pigs, a little colony of white leghorns, and fifty black-faced half-bred sheep scampering on the moors.

He had been here for five years, and he had lost money every year. He had assets, but no ready money, and small debts prospered as did nothing else on the land. Sometimes he felt pretty well, and sometimes he felt very ill, and always he felt a miserable discomfort of mind because he was not doing the thing that he had intended to do. He was trying to farm when he ought to have been a clergyman, and was cut off from all intellectual companionship, and felt so wretchedly useless and weak and ill.

Joanna, also, was not a first-rate manager. And Patricia was very delicate.

Teddy attributed all his troubles to the War, and the Peace assured him that he had been right in thinking that good could never come from evil. He was indignant about the Russian Revolution, the Anglo-Catholic movement, and the "Life of Christ" which he had intended to write and could not.

He became a guinea subscriber to the League of Nations Union, receiving small pamphlets decorated

with a map of the world surrounded by stars. He belonged to the British Legion which had an ex-soldiers'
club at Letherwick. He continued to call himself " Captain " Leigh.

Joanna used to welcome the pamphlets from the
League of Nations Union, and ran her finger lovingly
over the little maps. But she failed lamentably to take
an interest in the question of Disarmament, or the No
More War Movement, or the Letherwick branch of the
British Legion.

She used at first to write long letters to her friends,
Agnes Darlington and Rachel Harris. But as the chickens increased and the prosperity of the farm decreased,
she had less and less time somehow to answer letters.
Therefore the letters which she never answered dwindled and dwindled. She seemed utterly removed from
the world which she had known before her marriage.
Besides, Agnes was now in China and Rachel in the
Transvaal, lecturing in economics at the University
there. She said that South Africa was, on the whole,
kind to Jews.

So Joanna looked after the children and Teddy and
the farm, and received occasional calls from Mr. Boyse,
the curate, and Doctor Hutton, the doctor.

Teddy never mentioned to her that as a boy he had
been sent to Davos, nor that his mother had died of
tuberculosis.

CHAPTER FOUR

THE BLACK PIG

§ 1

SIR WENTWORTH and Lady Marshall asked the
Leighs to dine at Lindersdale Hall. When the in-
vitation at first came it was Teddy who was all eagerness
to accept, Joanna who doubted whether Mrs. Thorley
could manage the children or whether the farm would
collapse in their absence.

" Darling, we are modern parents. We must learn to
be dispensable," said Teddy; but when the day of the
dinner party arrived, he was seized at five o'clock with
such a fit of coughing that he sat on the hay in the
cow-shed, holding his head and trying not to faint. The
combination of nausea, dizziness and exhaustion, which
followed a coughing fit, seemed to Teddy unsuitable
companions at a party. He pulled himself together at
last, and went indoors to tell Joanna that he did not
want to go.

The sitting-room was dancing with firelight and
lamplight. On the floor, surrounded by strips of black
silk and gay embroidery knelt Joanna in a blue petticoat.
She had pulled off her old woollen jumper in order to
try on the dress that she was renovating, and her disordered hair fell in soft, bright waves over her bare
shoulders.

She loved dressmaking, especially when she could
make new garments out of old. She dyed and cut and

tacked with a rare audacity of speed that brought her either astonishing success or devastating failure. Because of her poverty she wore both successes and failures with equal ostentation, so that though she frequently looked shabby, she always looked remarkable.

She hardly glanced up now at Teddy, but mumbled with her mouth full of pins. " My dear, this is going to be perfectly brilliant. I make clothes by faith rather than by sight, and gamble on my touch of genius. This time I think I've won. It's perfectly dazzling."

Teddy swept out of his arm-chair a bundle of faded trimming, some artificial roses, and a fraying strip of gold brocade. "You can put away all that," he said. " The fierce he-man declines to endure the social inanities."

He sat down in the chair and rested his head on his hands, dreading lest he should cough again.

Joanna knelt upright, her petticoat strap slipping off her shoulder, a limp silver rose in her hand. She stared at him in dismay. Was it a mood, or did Teddy really not feel well enough to go? She knew his intense egotism and his perversity. She knew that he just might be making a bid for her sympathy. On the other hand, he might be really ill.

She wanted to go to the party. She had felt during the long autumn days that she must have some moment of gaiety, of bright colours and warmth and light, or she could never face the bleak monotony of the winter. She had sewn her dress in a frenzy of excitement. She must go.

" I don't like the looks of the black pig," said Teddy.

" Mochen Dee? Poor Mochen Dee? Isn't he all right again? I told Thorley to keep an eye on him. If he doesn't get better we shall have to get the Vet. in."

" And pay I don't know how much. We're not made of money."

He was fighting himself not to sound querulous, to be ironic perhaps and even a little acid, but not just cross with the irritation of the invalid.

Joanna knew all about their financial situation. It was she who wrestled with the ruthless logic of accounts, but to-night she had wanted to forget, just for once, all disagreeable things. Yet she cried, " Oh Teddy, darling, you're tired. Don't let's go."

He saw her flushed cheeks, the bright wilderness of her hair, her warm vitality. It was all wrong that she should glow with life and he be wasted with disease. His weakness became intolerable to him.

" It's all right. I'm perfectly well. I'm a bit worried about the pig. Of course I'm going. Why, what dinner party would be complete without me? Lady Marshall thinks that I'm a charming fellow and very handsome. She told young Brindley so."

Pamela and Patricia, playing on the floor with strips of brocade and cotton reels from Joanna's basket, had been whispering together since the first mention of the black pig. It was a famous pig, which had once distinguished itself by winning first prize at Clarington Agricultural Show, and thus imparting to Scatterthwaite an unwonted air of agricultural success.

Patricia, who considered that the grown-ups had ignored her existence for long enough, now began to sing in a high, shrill little voice:

> " Och, how sad indeed are we,
> Och, how sad indeed are we!
> There was grief and tribulation
> When we lost our Mochen Dee."

" Mochen Dee means black pig in Welsh, Daddy," she explained. " I know some more."

> " Mary Jones and Mrs. Thomas
> Came and laid our Mochen out,
> For our Mochen's gone to glory
> Oh, how sad indeed are we . . . "

" What's to lay out? " asked Pamela, well trained as commentator to her sister's performances.

" It's what you do when people die, like Thorley when we killed the pig last Christmas, and you cut it up and rub it with salt, and if your hands are chapped it hurts like anything."

" Poor pig," sighed Pamela.

" Lucky pig," said Patricia, who, having won no applause from her parents, turned gloomy eyes back to her work. " I think that it was a happy pig to die and go to heaven. People who go to heaven meet Gentle Jesus who is always kind, and never goes out to parties and leaves little girls at home."

" I don't like Gentle Jesus. His face in the pictures is always furry. I hate furry men. I'd rather go to the

Prince of Wales when I die. He's much better looking."
Pamela had inherited her mother's inconvenient capacity for hero-worship, and at present inclined to one
member of Royalty who had not a furry face.

"Well, any way, I'd like to die," continued Patricia,
winding herself up to a satisfactory grievance. "Then
people might be sorry that they went off to parties and
left me behind, and made themselves lovely new dresses
and only left me the bits to play with."

The big tears brimmed up to her beautiful resentful
eyes. Her small lips quivered.

"Oh, hell," muttered Teddy. "That kid's my conscience. Whenever I'm feeling particularly intense and
sorry for myself, she always comes on with a caricature
of my own emotions."

"Oh darling," said Joanna, who did not bring up
her children at all properly, and who measured her
iniquity in going to the party by the extent of her desire
to go. "You shall have parties one day. Lots of them.
And lovely silk dresses when, when . . ."

She did not say "when our ship comes in," because
for her the merit of ships lay in their sailing out, away
from Scatterthwaite and the North Riding and the grim
menace of poverty, the hostility of the land, and the
haunting fear of physical disease.

§ 2

Sir Wentworth Marshall was a small, frosted, pug-
nacious creature, having a fringe of white hair round
his shining skull and blue eyes twinkling with perverse
enthusiasm. His vagaries swept him from a plan for

driving electric power stations by the tides to a belief that the universal use of Latin would abolish wars. His ownership of a considerable portion of the surface of England enabled him to experiment with afforestation, small holdings, and sugar beet, but his lack of any suitable strip of sea-coast somewhat cramped his style with international frontiers and the tides.

He continually exploited his position as landowner to attempt the impossible, and passed his time very pleasantly accomplishing nothing but a reputation for eccentricity. His wife, on the other hand, passed her time in a succession of small sensible accomplishments. She was a round ball of a woman, with immense energy, and the unshakable complacency of a mother of seven, conscious of duties numerically fulfilled — after all, the least ambiguous way of fulfilling anything. This achievement had influenced her whole career in the direction of numerical successes. She sat upon ten committees; she was a justice of the peace, a voluntary worker for Lindersdale district under the Ministry of Pensions, the organizer of a Nursing Association, a Woman's Institute, a Girls' Friendly, and a Mothers' Union. She rejoiced in quotations like " Do the work that's nearest, though it's dull at whiles," or " God's in His heaven, all's right with the world," and used them with effect when opening bazaars and new Church Halls. She was continually engaged in helping Lame Dogs over Stiles, though mildly resenting the tendency of lame dogs to be independent rather than submissive. She had a fine sense of property, which affected her attitude towards servants, pensioners, villagers, and

" Friendly " girls, and she enjoyed the unquenchable optimism produced by an assured income, good health and small imagination.

She had first suggested that the Leighs might be asked to dinner because she had tried and failed to secure for Teddy a grant from the Ministry of Pensions to rebuild his pigsties; but when she remembered that for the same week-end, she had previously invited Sir Gordon Maclarran and Lorna Lavine, and nice Freda Langham and Howard Norton, she wanted to postpone the dinner party. Sir Gordon was an engineer with an imperial reputation, Lorna Lavine, a Scottish-American sculptor, who had wandered round the globe making rugged but surprisingly successful busts of American senators, Soviet ministers, Chinese War-lords and Thibetan monks. Eric Marshall was at the moment in love with her, an exercise which, being without possible result in matrimony, his mother thought quite profitable.

To these inappropriately distinguished guests, Lady Marshall explained what a nice couple the Leighs really were, poor things, and how one had to be kind to them, and what a nice fellow Captain Leigh really was, and how much she had been able to help him, and what a pity it was that he had not married a sensible country woman who could help him with the farm instead of a little secretary from a Kingsport Nursing Home, who knew nothing at all about poultry and dairy work.

She liked to create what she considered to be a proper atmosphere about her guests, lest any should judge each other according to standards differing from hers.

And since she had been unable to prevent an undesirable combination of lame dogs and great lions, she could at least assure her lions of her estimation of the dogs.

But right into the middle of her explanation, the lame dogs walked.

Lorna Lavine, turning to greet the little secretary of a Kingsport Nursing Home, saw instead a tall, magnificent young woman in a flamboyant dress of black and gold, cut far too low (the scissors had slipped at the last moment), about her splendid back and shoulders. Joanna's eager vitality dimmed that evening her husband's delicate charm. With lips slightly parted and bright, glowing cheeks, she seemed to be a little breathless, a little defiant, brazen in her determination to snatch from fortune one golden hour.

To Sir Gordon, she said, " Oh, but my father knew the Eastern Transvaal awfully well. Didn't you build the Wildebeestepoort Dam? He once wrote to me about it. How lovely to meet you."

To Lorna Lavine she smiled with a dazzling confidence.

She began to tell the story of their misadventures during the drive from Scatterthwaite. The pony had got a stone in its foot, and the road had been rutted and deep with mud, so she had taken off her shoes and stockings to tramp about in the puddles.

" It was cold, but delicious, and the mud squelched scrumptiously through my toes. I wanted to dance barefoot under the moon, but Teddy did not like it. Teddy is always reminding me that I am a wife and a mother."

She talked too much. Her happy excited voice filled all the pauses in conversation with absurd, exaggerated nonsense. She laughed at Sir Wentworth, she flirted ardently with Howard Norton, absorbing the vitality of the whole company and giving it out again with irrepressible animation.

They went in to dinner.

They ate oysters and clear soup and sole with mushroom sauce and grouse and ice pudding and cheese straws and wonderful heavy grapes. There were salted almonds in small silver dishes and tinted Venetian glass on the ivory lace. From the dim shadows behind Joanna footmen appeared like ghosts. When her table napkin slid from her knee, somebody picked it up again for her. Her glass was filled without consultation. In all her life she had never known anything quite so rich and wonderful. With dancing eyes and bubbling laughter, she said as much. Teddy, across the table, made one patient effort to repress her, then relapsed into the silence of outraged dignity.

Sir Wentworth, perfectly oblivious that any of his guests were behaving in an unusual manner, and believing Joanna to be a charming young woman, so far as he was aware of her at all, began to explain his intention of planting a great new forest along the slopes of the Five Fells. English labour, said he, was out of the question.

"As a nation, we know nothing about trees. The island was once covered by forest, and now look at it. What Englishman knows or cares for a bit of decent timber?"

"When we killed the trees we killed magic," said Lorna Lavine. "The Irish know that every tree has a personality, the permanent stable personality of form and colour, not the noisy, ephemeral personality of speech and action."

Lady Wentworth listened respectfully, because it was Lorna Lavine who said this, though she did not approve of nonsense at the dinner table.

"My husband wants to import foreign labour, Mr. North. Most unwise of him just now with all this unemployment. It might be done for a few months just to begin things, but I say that it would be far better to have a camp of ex-service men."

"If they have character"; Sir Gordon was reverting to Lorna Lavine's remark, his slow Scotch voice rolling his rrs deliciously. "Then the Scotch trees are the most friendly in the world. Canadian trees are a wee bit overpowering, and South African trees positively hostile."

"Yes, I know," Joanna said quickly. "They have thorns instead of leaves, and the wait-a-bit bushes lie ready to pounce on you and hold you prisoner till the sun shrivels you and travellers years afterwards find your withering skeleton. And the prickly pears are covered with tiny spears and the pepper trees give no shade."

"I thought you said that you'd left Africa when you were a few months old?"

"Yes, I did, but I'm going back there again. I know all about it. I know all about everywhere — Mexico, Labrador, Burma, Teheran. I'm going, you know." She challenged them, sweeping her excited glance round the table. "I'm going everywhere and going to see everything, all the queer places that nobody has ever seen, and I shall have to start soon, I shall soon be thirty and I haven't even seen London yet."

"Don't go, Mrs. Leigh," said Lorna Lavine. "Believe me, when you're at home you can always imagine that foreign countries will be lovely and surprising. It is harder to believe when you have been to them and got hung up in trains and bitten by insects and divided from your friends and infected with fever."

"Don't you think," interpolated Eric Marshall, who considered that Lorna had listened to other people for long enough, "that places are always just what you think they'll be? There's no surprise in travel, and that's its hideous secret. Places are just like their picture postcards. I remember when I went to Venice during my first Long Vac., I found Raphael Tuck scrawled all over it in my mind."

"But that's just why I must go," cried Joanna. "I know that my places are lovely, so I should see them lovely. I know I should be a happy traveller, because I should be so humble about it, quite ready to accept what fortune brought me and to be grateful. I must go because there are places which nobody has ever loved before waiting for me to find them lovely. It isn't fair to deprive them of my gratitude."

But Teddy decided that Joanna's bright manner was all very nice at home, but hardly improved by three glasses of champagne and a distinguished company. Teddy had a horror of exuberance, and lack of control and breaches of the exquisite ritual of social behaviour.

He himself could use oaths as a pretty licence in privacy; he could match absurdities with anyone. He knew that he owed Joanna's love largely to his capacity for nonsense. But he had his comprehension of time and place, and was shocked to the soul by his wife's indecorous abandonment of those conventions which alone make tolerable the contact of imperfect mortals in society. He was feeling quite horribly ill, and consciousness of his physical imperfections always rendered the decencies of intercourse more dear to him, by their contrast with the humiliating intimacies of sickness.

He made a heroic effort.

" Then you're really going to import Finns to show us how to plant larches, Sir Wentworth? "

" Why not? Why not? Finland's a great timber country, the best in Europe. Chief trade from Kingsport with the Baltic. During the War we had a camp of 'em here cutting down trees for pit-props and dugout props. Got a promise from the Government that I could build up again what they made me destroy."

" But won't foreign labour complicate things a bit? I'm all for international co-operation myself, and removing customs and labour barriers, but I do see that there may be feeling."

" I suppose," said Lorna Lavine's cool, deep voice, " that it really depends whether you think trees or people most important, and that really depends on whether you have the artistic or the reforming outlook. Mrs. Leigh and Sir Wentworth are both artists. They are interested in things as they are. They aren't always wanting to tackle the problems of human imperfection.

The seeing's enough for them, or the creating. I'm like
that too. I like Communists and Thibetans. I don't at
all want to convert them. I like insanitary Persian
towns. So does Mrs. Leigh. Sir Wentworth likes planting larches and making windmills. Lady Marshall and
Captain Leigh can't be content to look. They've got
the reforming instinct. It's very admirable. They're
always interrupted in looking by their preoccupation
of pity."

But only Eric and Joanna were listening to her, for
Teddy was saying with his ironic precision, " I shall be
much interested to see the attitude of the local League
of Nations Union to your imports. It's one thing to say
' Dear Little Finland, of course she ought to have a seat
on the Council,' and quite another to watch dear little
Finns snaffling your jobs."

The conversation about the Finns, however, unfor-
tunately waned. Joanna had become absorbed in this
idea of the reforming outlook and pity. Leaning across
the unlucky Eric she bombarded Lorna Lavine with
eager questioning. " What do you mean? Oughtn't we
ever to enjoy anything properly? Can't you see how
red the hibiscus flowers are in a country where there's
forced labour? Do sweated coolies really spoil the
beauty of blossoming islands? Aren't we ever free? "

" You may be, though I doubt it. I am. That's why
I go about the world so easily. Captain Leigh, I guess,
has the reformer's mind. Whenever he hears of something wrong he thinks, ' What can be done about it? '
whereas I think, ' How awfully interesting, I wonder
what it looks like? ' "

64

Teddy shrugged his shoulders. "You hold too high an opinion of my altruism, Miss Lavine."

"It's not altruism. It's self-defence for the really politically minded. They just can't endure the disorder of incompetence. It soothes them to do something even if it's all quite hopeless."

"She's talking for effect," thought Teddy. "There's an answer to her somewhere. Damn it, this is my kind of talk. This is the sort of society which I like, articulate, smooth, luxurious society. The woman's right. It's this disease of impotence which is killing me. I have the reformer's instinct. I am torn with a preoccupation of pity, only now I haven't got much pity to spare for anyone but myself. If I could do something, even if it were only pushing forward a municipal order, or a resolution at a Church Congress, it would be something. Any small activity in the direction of my desire would cure me. And here is Sir Wentworth, here is this fool Lady Marshall, able to do what they like with their property. If they feel compunction, it can be a fruitful pity. They can watch it materialize into reform. It does not remain inside them, corroding their thoughts, eating their heart away. Their will can set new policies, however small and futile, into action. They have power, power, power."

The sick exhaustion of the earlier afternoon was returning. Something had gone wrong with his digestion, it seemed. His senses swam with nausea. His hands and forehead grew damp. It might have been the champagne, but he had only taken half a glass. There was Joanna, with her unconscious strength, her splendid, radiant vitality, laughing, talking, enjoying herself. She did not care that he was suffering the torments of the damned. Damned, he was damned, damned to this hell of his imperfect body. These strong, competent people were too much for him. It was all too much for him.

He began to cough a little and felt the intolerable, tactfully hidden pity of all these people, mocking his ache for competence and power.

§ 3

The party was over. It was time to go, though the long drawing-room still glowed with soft warm light from alabaster bowls. In the tall mirrors before and behind Joanna, she could see an interminable series of rooms, with Adam fire-places, and slender pedestals on which a dragon of white jade upheld a perfect crystal ball. In each room Lorna Lavine sat on a deep gold sofa; her rich red dress grew smaller and smaller till in the distant chambers it flashed like a jewel of vivid crimson. In the nearer rooms her black hair swung aside from the ardent pallor of her face. Her voice, like the smoke rings blown from her cigarette, trailed away into oblivion.

Joanna knew by all the signs of her small experience that she was in love again. She did not want to part from Lorna Lavine.

" Are you going abroad again? " she asked, suddenly shy.

" I'm not sure. Probably." Lorna narrowed her dark eyes at young Eric Marshall. He was too young, too young, but so charming. And the view from Lindersdale

Hall was the most tranquil view in the world. And the green leisure of a Yorkshire dale soothed her after the turmoil of her adventures.

" All the nicest people sail so far away," sighed Joanna.

" Well, isn't that wise of them? They make a friendliness for you in the world's strange places. Half the world grows part of your property, if you have friends in it. Look at the two friends that you spoke to me about, in South Africa and in China. Why, I believe that I may be going to China and I'll look out for your Agnes, I think that I like Agnes. Though Rachel sounds to be a most admirable person."

" Rachel is far more beautiful than Agnes." It had been for Joanna the rarest fortune to find someone to whom she could speak of her friends. And she had never thought of talking about them until three glasses of champagne loosened her tongue.

Teddy was saying, " My dear. We can't stay a moment longer. Our carriage awaits us."

Joanna was shaking hands with Lady Marshall.

" Oh, it's been lovely, lovely, thank you so much," she was saying, but her thoughts raced ahead. " Oh, it can't be over. It can't be all over. It can't be that there's really nothing more to look forward to. The party. The lovely, lovely party."

She wanted to capture the image of that long room, and Lorna's bright dress, and the scent of the great pots of azaleas, and the young people, and the sense of well-being, and rich, easy, delicious life. She wanted to hold them for ever.

She told herself, " I had my hour. Life cannot touch it. It's mine, mine, mine for ever."

Thrusting her arm through Teddy's, because he looked as though he might faint at any moment, she walked slowly out of the long room.

§ 4

From Lindersdale Hall to Scatterthwaite is a drive of about four and a half miles. Teddy and Joanna, wrapped like cocoons in rugs, balanced themselves awkwardly on the sliding seat of the milk-float.

There was a bright moon, and the wind blew white clouds like great albatrosses across the dark blue sky, and leaves like little birds about the pony's ears. Its hoofs made a soft closh, closh on the muddy road.

At the end of the village, past the churchyard, the road turned sharply to the right and began to ascend the Fell. For two miles the pony climbed steadily, planting its small hoofs firmly on the soft track, its fat haunches straining against the traces. The smoke from its back rose to heaven under the moon as from a midnight sacrifice.

The dale slid down and down into a silver vapour, till suddenly the road rounded the crest of the hill, and for mile after mile before them, showed the vast rolling ocean of the moors.

" Supposing this were sand," reflected Joanna. " I am on my camel. Soon we shall come to the caravanserai. For miles and miles we have watched the distant hills, taking the lonely road to Isfahan."

The moors poured down their darkness into the hollow cup of Scatterthwaite. Joanna had to climb out to open the gates. Teddy, apparently asleep, sat rolled up in his rugs.

They entered the yard, the pony making, as usual, straight for the stable door, unable to understand, even after repeated experience, that he could not enter it until he had been unharnessed.

" Stop! Whoa, whoa! " cried Joanna. " Teddy, I shall have to widen the stable door. My arms will be pulled out of their sockets in trying to hold Ezekial from his supper."

Teddy did not answer. Very carefully he was unrolling himself from his rugs, trying to cheat the pain that lurked waiting for him if he moved incautiously.

Joanna felt the darkness of his depression beat against her heart.

" My poor Teddy. Are you tired out completely? Go straight in and I'll come and heat the milk. We'll both have lots of whiskey in it. My dear, what an adorable moon."

She felt her silly words dancing and posturing before him, like unwanted dancers, seeking to seduce him from his misery. He took no notice.

Then from the gaping blackness of the stable door came a low rustle of movement. Two small figures rose from the straw and ran towards them.

" Oh, Mummy, Mummy, poor Mochen Dee. Mochen Dee's dead."

" All dead, but not gone to Jesus, because though I tried to lay him out, he only came all bloody. Look! "

Pamela, beneath the moon, her winter coat buttoned across her flannel dressing-gown, and small hands and face dabbled with blood, was indeed a hair-raising spectacle.

"Mrs. Thorley said ' Go to bed.' But we crept out again because I wanted to see Mochen Dee go to Jesus. An' you said that you'd left us in charge, and then I remembered that he couldn't go to Jesus until he was laid out properly. And we did our best. Really, we did, we did, Mummy."

"Oh, children, run in quick, quick. Your bare feet. Oh, Pamela! "

"You must come first and look. Mummy, you must come and look."

Patricia was shaken and convulsed by sobbing. Joanna wrenched the lamp from its socket and followed her daughters into the sty. There indeed lay the great black pig on its side, quite dead. The ivory-handled bread-knife beside it and the two silver salt cellars testified to Patricia's good intentions of laying him out properly. From a jagged scratch on the hairy hide, dark blood was oozing slowly.

"He was too tough to lay out properly," explained Pamela, obliging and cheerful even in disaster.

"Oh, Mummy, never, never go out again," sobbed Patricia. "You never came and you never came. And we've waited for hours and hours, and it's been so cold. We prayed and we prayed. I prayed to Gentle Jesus and Pamela tried the Prince of Wales, though I told her it was blasphemy. But nobody came. Nobody came."

"Oh, come indoors, children, quickly. Never mind Mochen Dee. We will get Thorley to lay him out in the morning. Ah, what's that? "

"That " was the ominous sound of Teddy being very sick in the stable-yard.

§ 5

"Is this grief and tribulation, Mummy? " asked Pamela with interest.

It was indeed grief and tribulation.

Mochen Dee, it appeared, had died of swine fever. The other pigs were consequently condemned to a tragic slaughter of the innocents, which meant complete disaster for Scatterthwaite, though it saved the district.

Teddy took nearly a fortnight to recover from the party and the catastrophe, lying in bed and wishing that he could die, and betake himself from a world in which he was good for nothing.

Both the children had caught heavy colds, but Patricia's developed into a sharp attack of pleurisy.

Mr. and Mrs. Thorley both declared that such goings on were too much for them altogether, and gave a month's notice. "Which is just as well," said Teddy. "It saved us the trouble, because we really can't afford them."

Joanna, whom calamity exhilarated after it passed a certain pinnacle of disaster, ran from room to room, from house to yard, comforting Teddy, nursing Patricia, pleading with the Thorleys.

She felt as though she would never stop running in this world again.

CHAPTER FIVE

YOUNG TAM LIN

§ I

AFTER a month of bitter weather, when the sleet blew across the moor and the gale attacked the roof of Scatterthwaite, plucking at its loosened tiles and wrenching from its hinges the unused granary door, the first day of March came sunny and mild.

Joanna went to the yard gate to await Teddy's return with the children. Whenever well enough he drove with the butter and eggs to dispatch them by train to Clarington market. But since Joanna's attempts at dairy work were not invariably successful, and since he often felt too ill to go, the days when a healthy Teddy and satisfactory butter coincided were infrequent, and the dairymen of Clarington had no love for Scatterthwaite irregularity. And though it was known that Joanna alone milked the cows and made up the yellow pounds of butter in grease-proof paper, people murmured that they did not want butter and milk from a consumptive's farm.

Altogether things were so difficult that if Joanna had ever enough time to think about them, she might have given way entirely. Patricia had recovered from her pleurisy, but was still very delicate. The Thorleys had gone, and Teddy and Joanna had somehow to run the farm between them, "Or, rather, it runs us," Joanna explained to Mr. Boyse, "and sometimes it runs us off our feet." During that winter she had lost the glow of her rich comeliness. Her face was thinner, her complexion coarsened. One desperate day she had seized a pair of scissors and cut her thick hair short. She never had time now to mend her clothes nor to keep her nails trim. There were new lines about her mouth.

This afternoon, as she leant across the gate, her arms and back ached almost unendurably.

From the three fields came a confused plaintive cry of lambs seeking their mothers. The little black-faced ewes scampered no more on the moor, but galloped heavily round the roofless shelters of straw built by Teddy for lambing time. Joanna was holding a lamb now absent-mindedly, leaning the arm which held it against the damp wooden bar of the gate. Its stiff legs stuck out like match-sticks, and its agile tail wriggled extravagantly as the willow catkins in the dale. It was one of a triplet, whom their mother had found too many to feed, and Joanna was rearing it by hand. It sucked at Pamela's old bottle with an expression of wise concentration on its small black face.

"He must come soon," thought Joanna. She ought not to loiter there, with the crockery still in the sink and the beds unmade. But a dull lassitude had fallen upon her because she had been up till nearly one that morning acting midwife to a ewe in difficulties. She felt an amused and tender regard for these little women with their great puzzled eyes and burdened bodies.

Its bottle emptied, she set the lamb carefully on its

unsteady legs. It wabbled like a badly constructed toy, fluttering its ridiculous tail, slid into a muddy puddle, splashed out again with an aggrieved baa-aa, then trotted off on to the short turf.

She watched it skip with a deliberate affectation of playfulness, as though reflecting, " I am a lamb. Lambs skip. Therefore I skip." It skipped conscientiously till it grew tired, tried to nibble a clover tuft, sneezed at the cold wetness, then turned its back reproachfully on Joanna and set off down the hill.

" Well, well, my dear," said Joanna. " Don't blame me because the grass is damp. The Lord made the weather, though He seems to have expected me to make most other things." She looked ruefully down at her bulging shoe. " I cant make boots, though. I wish He'd hurry up and make Aunt Helen write."

Things had come to a pretty pass before Joanna had applied to her aunt for assistance. Ten days ago Dr. Hutton had driven over to Scatterthwaite on what he declared with hearty over-emphasis to be " a friendly visit. A purely friendly visit to snaffle a few of Mrs. Leigh's brown scones."

There had been, of course, no scones for him, though Joanna spread the best cloth of Teneriffe embroidery and cut thin bread and butter. For during the dreadful winter she had never had time for making things, scones nor dresses, nor marmalade. The dust lay thick on the piano. The fires were laid on top of yesterday's ashes. Pamela and Patricia usually washed the dinner things, splashing the floor and themselves with greasy water.

" It's hardly surprising that he says the children must go away," observed Joanna to a small inquisitive ewe who came sniffing her skirt. " They need a holiday. As a matter of fact, my dear, I need a holiday, too. Teddy, you see, won't go to a sanatorium, and the doctor says that he's better here than anywhere. But as a matter of fact, you'll know when you've had your family as long as I've had mine that though you love them frightfully, you don't always want them about. I mean that holidays are good for everyone."

She dropped her head on the top bar and looked sideways at the wise little ewe. " You see, my dear, — damn these shoes, they do let the water in — Patricia's cough is really rather serious, though the doctor does say that her lungs are all right. But it is getting on Teddy's nerves. What I mean is, that you don't have the complication of a husband, my dear, to your family. And a farm and whatnot. You see, Teddy's getting careless about infection. He's tired of being ill. And Aunt Helen, on the other hand, has a garden and a car and five children and heavenly nurseries, and really it couldn't be any trouble to her to take Pamela and Patricia for a few weeks. She must say Yes. She must."

And then she threw up her arms and began waving wildly because she saw the cart crossing the brow of the hill. Before the pony had stumbled down the steep road, the children had run down to her.

" Mummy, are there any more lambs? "

" Mummy, have a peppermint? "

" Mummy, we nearly missed the train with the milk."

" Mummy, the Finns have come."

75

" The what, darling? "

" The Finns. You know. The Finns. We met Sir Wentworth Marshall on his new pony; it's all dappled, fourteen hands, an' we nearly missed the train with the butter because Daddy stopped to hear all about the Finns an' they've got a camp on Mallow Fell an' they had special conshesuns from the Home Office, an' a Nungarian interrupter."

" Interpreter, silly, an' . . . "

" Oh, Mummy, do let's go and see them. They eat horseflesh. . . . "

Teddy had arrived. He smiled at his wife. " I say, Jo, the blasted buckle bust on the beastly belly-band. Isn't that sweet alliteration? Honest, though, we nearly had an upset."

Sir Wentworth or somebody had evidently driven away his black mood of the morning, when he had threatened to cut all their throats and end their troubles for ever if another lamb died before he could sell the lot to Fatty Paxton.

" Any letters? " asked Joanna, her heart in her mouth.

She had not told Teddy about her appeal to Aunt Helen. He would have said, " I hate whining. I won't have charity." But she knew now, looking at Patricia's fragile face, that the children must go away and go quickly.

" Letters? Letters? " Teddy slapped the pockets of his British Warm. He had still an air of slender elegance on the days when he felt well enough to shave. He produced three envelopes.

" Bills, bills, bills, yes. Here's a pukka letter, and
for you. What is it? "

Joanna glanced carelessly at the envelope. " Aunt
Helen. Her cook's given notice again, I expect. Don't
you pity the poor rich, Teddy? They have such frightful trials."

Her heart said, " It will be all right. It must be
all right." She cried out, " Come, children. I'll race you
to the house. One, two, three! "

They were off, hilariously, laughing and panting,
while Teddy, erect in the milk-float like a racing-
charioteer, pounded past them and in at the yard gate.
Joanna went into the kitchen with her letter. She felt
a little sick, but smiled determinedly. She opened the
envelope.

" MY DEAR JOANNA," she read.

" I hardly know what to say in answer to your letter.
I should, of course, if I had only myself to consider be
only too glad to have your little girls to stay with me,
though I have not been at all well myself lately, having
had several goes of lumbago and your Uncle Arthur
has had influenza twice this winter. He has a very delicate chest. I am worried about Ronny, too, who may
have to have his tonsils out — so very trying in his
last year at school — but you know what I feel about
infection and how careful we must be though I did go to
a very interesting lecture on Christian Science, which
says that Mind overrides Matter, which I well believe.
Though one must not take risks. But if you had thought
a little more I am sure that you would have seen that

you were putting me in a very difficult position, for how can I have Patricia and Pamela at home when Wendy and Jean are here and attending school and must have absolutely no risk of infection? I am sure that you are very wise to stay in the North Riding. The air up there cannot be bettered and all the milk and eggs and healthy farm life. As a matter of fact, we have had to change our milkman because the last lot was so very poor. And I am sure that altogether your farm life is much more healthy than down here, which is really very enervating. Marshington is really too damp for us and we are looking out for another house. You do not mention your husband. I hope that he is keeping as well as can be expected. Your aunts Emily and Kate seem in a poor way, I fear. I suppose you heard that the Transvaal Platinum Shares which Mr. Burdass bought for them have turned out very disappointingly, so it means that your Uncle Arthur is practically having to keep them. But he is very good and hardly ever grumbles.

"With love to you all,
"Your affectionate aunt,
"HELEN."

"Well," said Joanna. "That, I suppose, is that." And she tore the letter into little pieces, thrust it between the bars of the grate, and went to make the tea.

§ 2

She did not know what to do.

Her fears had become abominable, affecting every

78

thought and action of her day. Dr. Hutton was a placid kindly creature who knew from long acquaintance with the makeshifts of poverty that a little infection more or less makes small difference to a world where everyone has to take his chance and death is the certain end of all. But Joanna found herself watching the children with a new sickness of heart, fussing over them, scolding Patricia if she went out without her goloshes, petulant when Pamela touched her father's cup or towel.

She found herself watching Teddy with suspicion. He must not touch the children. He must not touch her. He must keep himself apart. Hating herself for her anger, she found a new terror in life lest she should hate him for his disease.

" It's my nerves. They're getting the better of me, and that's silly. I've kept on top of things all this time. I'll get on top of this. I can. I will. The children shall go away."

She made the bread and milked and sewed in a quiet fury of thought.

She did not answer Aunt Helen's letter, but turned over every other source of a possible loan. She might try Agnes.

" That's a good idea," Joanna told herself. She was ironing late one night in the kitchen, drawing warm comfort from the lamplit room, the glowing fire, the cheerful clink of iron against the stove and the pleasant smell of hot linen.

" Of course, I'll write to Agnes. Friends always help each other in real trouble." She tried to imagine Agnes, witty, gentle and absent-minded, entertaining young men in the Customs Commissioner's House, or riding a white pony about the sunlit rice fields. Perhaps Lorna Lavine had called upon her. Perhaps she had gone to Africa to join Rachel. Perhaps at this moment they rode into the opalescent twilight of an African evening. The soil baked red and the tawny grasses faded into the ghost of a round brown hill. The molten red of the kopje flowed into the clear water of the sky.

Her hand moved gently as she set down the iron on its stand.

The black cypresses blew across the stars. They were mourning nuns in sable weeds. They were reeds afloat in the clear water of twilight; they were slender fingers beckoning to the moon; they were swaying dancers having their feet set firmly, firmly on the harsh red soil. The little dark cypress fruits weighed down their branches, curving them outward away from the tree with compelling gesture. " Back to the earth," they said. " Back to the dark mortality of earth."

Her head bowed down. It lay on the half-ironed tablecloth.

Down the burning rocks of the great fortress kopje the aloes marched, like warriors with flaming spears erect. Aloes on the march, left, right, left, right, spears uplifted, red and orange, down the jagged ironstone of the hot terraces. Ironstone, beloved of lightning, aloes like the forces of flame on the Hills of Mars, Mars' Hill, Jove's Hill, Vulcan's Hill. . . .

Her thoughts drooped away with the marching aloes. She slept.

§ 3

Upstairs in his room Teddy lay with a jaeger jersey drawn over his blue and white striped pyjamas, reading Dostoievsky's *Idiot* by candle-light.

His room was the most comfortable in the house. Here stood his Cambridge desk and the two arm-chairs and the beautiful oak chest which had been his mother's and which he would not sell. Here were bookshelves with orange-bound classics and cheap translations of German philosophers, and theologians and histories, and popular treatises on economics and pacifism and abstruse journals on philosophy and politics.

Here too lay the yellowing pages of his manuscript of the " Life of Christ," which he would never finish, because he could obtain no access to the conclusions of modern research, because he felt at last that he had nothing new of his own to say; and because, any way, it was too much trouble ever to finish anything.

He had felt indignant all day because Joanna was so sharp-tongued and preoccupied, " vague " he called it, so fussy about the children, so much unlike herself. Good God, if she changed, what was there in life left for him? Had not health, fortune, a career, the possibility of being useful deserted him? He had made his sacrifice when it was demanded, and in return had received the corrupting futility of idle sickness.

He wanted to serve. He wanted to be good. He wanted to lose his life in order that he might save it. He was sick of the distress and stupidity of the world, its high causes defeated, its sanity diseased. He felt that if only he had been well, he might have had a message for it. He was entrapped in his sick, futile body. Once he thought that he had escaped. Once, when the army doctor passed him for active service, he had known liberty and hope. But the War had robbed him of all it had once given. He saw himself growing daily more bitter, more exacting. Joanna was too good to him. He did not want her goodness. He did not want to be under an eternal obligation to her. He did not want to be a debtor to people. He wanted them sometimes to be under obligations to him.

He must have some reassurance of his manhood, some comfort in his intolerable weakness.

By his side, Joanna had left a little bell, lest he should feel ill in the night and want her. He caught it up now and rang it furiously.

Its thin tinkle died away in the darkened house.

She must be still downstairs. Damn it, and it was nearly midnight. She had no sense.

Taking up a stick, he tapped, once, twice, three times on the floor, growing more and more frantic with a blind panic of desire.

Then she was coming.

He heard a chair screech, a door open. She was running up the stairs. She was stumbling along the passage. She stood in the door, her face rosy with sleep, her bright hair tumbled, blinking in the candle-light.

He smiled at her alarm.

" Are you never coming to bed? "

" I was ironing."

82

" At this time of night? My dear woman! Can you never get to bed at a decent hour? You're getting so plain. Other women . . ."

He began to cough.

" Oh, my poor Teddy."

He turned wearily away. He did not want her compassion. He wanted her love.

" Come and sit down," he panted.

Slowly she sat beside him on the bed, her warm vitality beside his wasted body. The coughing ceased. He ran his hand up her bare arm. It glowed almost cherry-coloured from the heat of the stove.

" Nice warm arm."

" It's the ironing. I must go back, Teddy."

She bit her lip and turned her head aside. He began to play with the buttons on her faded blouse.

" Nice warm Joanna."

" I must go, dear."

" Freezing Joanna." The seeking, creeping fingers moved softly. " Cold Joanna, cold as the moon."

The burning colour flooded her cheeks, but she sat passively. Outside the wind hurled itself across the moor. It blew the short checked curtains in at the open window.

" Don't go down again, darling. I can't bear this wind."

" I must, Teddy."

" Stay here. Stay here. I need you. I'm frightened. Everything's gone so wrong with me. Sometimes I can't bear it because I think you've changed to me. Joanna, darling, don't leave me. Don't be so cold and hard and

managing. I can't bear it if you change to me. I can't
go on living. I can't."

This was not what he had meant to say. He had
meant to be strong and dominating.

She gathered his thin body into her arms. He lay like
a child against her warm comforting breast.

"Darling, Joanna, darling. Don't go. Don't leave me
to-night. I need you."

He turned his face against her woollen blouse.

"Darling, I must go. I must. The doctor you know.
. . . He said. . . . We're not to . . . the children,
you know."

"Oh, damn the doctor, you're my wife, aren't you?
You're my wife? I need you. I can't go on living without you. I can't bear it, Jonnie, I need you."

"Oh, my love. . . ."

He began to cough again. Joanna slowly let go of his
racked and shaken body. She stood looking down at
him with wide anguished eyes. He fumbled for her
hand. His seeking fingers were like old Mr. Crowle's,
old Mr. Crowle's.

Joanna suddenly snatched her hand away and ran
from the room. The stir of her flight blew out the
candle.

Teddy lay back on the pillows. His coughing ceased.
He was quite alone, staring into the darkness.

§ 4

Joanna could not sleep that night. Next day she was
up at dawn, trying to kill her remorse by furious work.
She could not make up her mind who needed her most,

Teddy or the children, and she knew now that it was impossible to serve them both.

Towards evening, going into the coal-house, she saw that the supply of sticks was almost exhausted.

" Mummy, there are heaps and heaps on the top edge above Mallow Fell," said Patricia. " An' you can look down from there on to the Finnish Camp. It's frightfully lovely."

" Yes, and Pat an' I met such a nice funny man there the other day. We went to look and he gave us sweets, but he didn't talk properly at all, an' he didn't seem to know what we said."

" He took me on his knee," said Patricia proudly.

Joanna looked apprehensively from one little girl to another. What was happening to her that she saw danger everywhere?

" Well, let's go and gather some sticks anyway," she said.

It was a windy evening, and even while climbing out of the top field on to the strip of moor between the farm and the Fell, they found that the gale had torn off branches and fir cones, and scattered them at their feet.

At the edge of the moor the Fell dropped suddenly down into Lindersdale. Two steep miles below in the valley lay Letherwick, grey as a ghost city in the mist from Linders River. Half-way down the scarred and despoiled surface of the Fell, on a small plateau, like black hobgoblins, crouched the low huts of the Finnish Camp. Three fir trees, black as the huts, lifted their aristocratic protest of silence against this desecration of their solitude. Beyond them, across the dale, red and

85

menacing, flared the vast enchantment of the setting sun.

The men had left off their work for the evening. Some had climbed down the winding path to the village. Some stretched themselves before the smoking fires. One, two, three, four fires, Patricia counted. The scent of wood smoke mingled with the damp heathery smell of the moor, and with the soft murmur of sound from the camp, like the humming of summer bees.

Suddenly Joanna felt herself seized by tremendous excitement. The men down there were strangers, foreigners, Finno-Tartar, queer, wild, mysterious men with hidden lives passed in far, foreign lands. They were Mongolian. Their language was an old wild language. They had known incredible loves and dark adventures and the twisted streets of alien cities. They had known the green breaking waves of the sea, and the green aisles of the silent forests. They had known war and death and fierce, cruel elation.

Fairyland had opened at her feet, not the gentle fairyland of a child's picture-book, but the grim dark fairyland of the ballads.

" It was mirk mirk night
        There was nae star light,
      They waded through red blude to the knee;
    For a' the blude that's shed on the earth
      Rins through the springs o' that countrie."

Why was her head ringing with the sound of spears? Steel clashing on steel and wicked cries of savage pleasure? Fairyland opened at her feet; the fortresses of the earth were broken; its defences were down. With a blast of trumpets and the red banner of sunset streaming across the sky, the hosts of faerie came riding through.

Standing against the sunset, shivering with rapt excitement, she did not see the young man who climbed the narrow path till he came face to face with her.

He was dark and picturesque and shabby. His ragged shirt lay open at the throat, and above it he wore a loose sheepskin jacket. His black hair waved back from a fierce unhappy face, pale, with high cheek-bones and large melancholy eyes.

So suddenly he appeared, and so strange he seemed, that Joanna would not have wondered had he turned into a deer or a hare before her eyes.

> " She had'na pu'd a leaf, a leaf,
> A leaf but only twae,
> When up and started Young Tam Lin,
> Says ' Ladye, thou's pu' nae mae.' "

But Young Tam Lin looked at her and at her children with morose displeasure, as though they unduly troubled his solitude. So disconcerted he seemed that Joanna found herself laughing at his dismay. He glanced at her once with hostility, then turned and plunged again down the Fell path whence he had appeared, crushing the fallen pine needles as he fled.

" I know who that was," said Pamela. " That was the Hungarian interrupter."

"Interpreter," Patricia corrected her with patient weariness. "I'm cold, Mummy; let's go home."

But Joanna did not hear. She was looking down into the Finnish Camp with a smile of enchanted pleasure, curiosity and bewilderment.

CHAPTER SIX

HUNGARIAN NIGHT'S ENTER-TAINMENT

§ 1

SIR WENTWORTH MARSHALL looked mildly at his wife across the breakfast-table. He very rarely looked in any way mild. If it had been a matter of air-power, of sugar refining, or of Simplified Latin Syntax, he would have looked quite fiercely; but this was merely a matter of a person, and persons are, after all, numerous, imperfect and not very important things to people like Sir Wentworth.

"My dear," he said, "that young man distresses me."

His wife pursed up her little round mouth over a belated nursing subscription. "It would take a Hungarian to distress you," she said, quite smartly for her. "I am always being distressed and by quite ordinary Yorkshire people."

"He was at Cambridge, you know, and used to stay with the Nethersoles in Warwickshire. Nethersole's a decent fellow. He's got one of the finest irrigation systems of any man I know. The streams up from the level canals are driven by water-power from the . . ."

" I told you that I have no use for Hungarians. They fought against us, and though we may overlook that, you can't expect them to be popular."

" As a matter of fact, I gather that Szermai did not fight. He was a prisoner in Russia or somewhere. And he's a clever chap. He knows more about larch settings than Betterton from the agricultural college. Can't you think of anything? "

The question was a clarion call to Lady Marshall. She lived in a happy world where there was always something to be done for every human affliction.

" Well, let me see," she said, helping herself to marmalade. It was, of course, she who would see a solution. Beatrice, her eldest daughter, was apparently thinking too. Recently, Beatrice had shown signs of taking too much upon herself.

Lady Marshall's mind suddenly delivered itself of a great thought.

" The Leighs."

" The what? "

" The Leighs. Let him go to the Leighs as a paying guest. They'd be glad of the extra money. As a matter of fact, it would be a tactful way of doing something for them. I am afraid that they must be in rather a poor way. I saw Doctor Hutton and he says that he's afraid that the elder child's lungs may be affected. Captain Leigh ought to be put in a sanatorium, I said, but apparently the military discharged him before, and he does not want to go, and the doctor says that he is just as well playing at farming. It's all terribly sad. But certainly though their house is sure to be in a huggermugger with that Mrs. Leigh, it would be better than nothing. I shall write to Captain Leigh to-night."

" What about the infection for Mr. Szermai? " asked Beatrice.

" To a Hungarian a germ or two, if they are germs, which I for one doubt, can't matter very much. He must put up with what he can get, and the house is very near the camp. It's not as though he would be welcome in every house himself."

She went off to her desk in high spirits. No form of sport was more congenial to her than the killing of two birds with one stone.

" DEAR CAPTAIN LEIGH," she wrote.

" I wonder whether you and your wife would undertake a most kindly action. There is a young Hungarian acting as interpreter to the camp for foresters which my husband has built on Mallow Fell. He is an educated man, the son of a count, I understand. In fact, I believe that he is possibly a count himself, though those terrible Bolsheviks have taken his land and he calls himself Mr. Szermai. He talks perfect English and was educated at Cambridge. He may even have been there at the same time as you were. He will only be here for a short time, because we have only a limited permission for these men to remain in the country. But Sir Wentworth and I feel most distressed about him as he ought to be in lodgings and not in the camp, but the village is too far away and he wants to be near the spot. We wonder whether you and your wife would consider taking him as a paying guest. My husband says that he would be delighted to pay two and a half guineas a week for him, and he might be good company for you in the evenings. " Do let me know what you think about it.

" Yours sincerely,
" LETITIA MARSHALL."

§ 2

What the Leighs thought of this, was, of course, not to be contained in the polite note of acceptance written in Teddy's small Cambridge handwriting.

It meant two and a half guineas a week. It meant that Joanna could pack off the children to Scarshaven in the care of Aunt Emily. " Though I need a holiday more than they," said Teddy, " but nobody ever considers me." It meant that there would be somebody else in the draughty malicious house during the long dangerous spring evenings. It meant that for the first time in five years, something really fine and unexpected had happened, " Except, of course," said Joanna, " Mochen Dee's prize. We mustn't be unfair to Mochen Dee, though he did let us down so badly in the end."

It was a trifling matter to air the mattress of the big east bedroom, to carry the Morris chair from Teddy's room and the washstand from the Thorleys' deserted bedroom into the new guest-chamber, to iron faded curtains and a clean bedspread. Joanna ironed and the children fastened hooks on to the curtains, and Teddy smoked his medicated cigarettes with smiling pleasure. He was growing soft in this eternal company of a woman and children. It would be good to have a man again to talk to in the evenings.

Joanna's competence rarely matched her good intentions.

When Teddy had driven the milk-float down by the low road to fetch Mr. Szermai's bag from the camp, and the beef-steak pie for supper was in the oven, Joanna suddenly found that she had no potatoes. "We must have potatoes. It's not late dinner without potatoes." They were to have late dinner as the supreme acknowledgement of the arrival of their guest.

She slid a coarse apron over her tidy dress, and thrust her feet into Teddy's old farm boots, and ran through the yard with her basket and fork, singing,

> "Oh, I forbid you, maidens a'
> That wear gowd on your hair
> To come or gae by Carterhaugh
> For Young Tam Lin is there."

For she was very but quite unreasonably happy, and had been so ever since she had seen the moor open and let in fairyland, and the eldritch knight start up through the undergrowth and flee away glowering. What if fairyland were hostile, since it was really near, since there was something else in the world but making beds and peeling potatoes and turning the churn when the butter wouldn't come?

She began to dig. The first bunch of potatoes was rotten; she dug again.

> "She hadna' pu'd a leaf, a leaf,
> A leaf but barely twae,
> When up an' started Young Tam Lin
> Says 'Ladye, thou's pu' nae mae!'"

"Joanna, this is Mr. Szermai. Szermai, my wife," said Teddy.

Joanna stuck her fork in the earth, tossed her short hair out of her eyes, dusted her earthy hand on her coarse apron. She looked up at Young Tam Lin.

His appropriate and dramatic appearance made her want to laugh again, but she restrained herself as the young man brought his feet together on the muddy soil of the potato patch, and taking Joanna's grimy hand, brushed it lightly with his lips.

"What beautiful manners," thought Joanna. "It will be rather difficult to live up to them, but a pleasant sort of difficulty."

"I expect that you would like your tea," she said aloud. "You know we are awfully glad to have you. Did my husband get your luggage? I hope you know that we live in rather a muddle here, but we shall try to make you comfortable."

"I wish that he hadn't seen me in my apron," she thought. "I really look quite nice in my blue frock. However, I can take off the apron and tidy my hair and come into tea looking lovely."

The young man bowed unsmilingly again, "My bag is indoors already, thank you. And please do not concern yourself about the tea."

"But I've finished here." She began to throw her potatoes into the basket. The young man said, "Allow me," and picked it up for her. She walked into the house before him, knocking the earth off from her clumsy boots as she walked, and thinking, "He makes me feel like a princess."

As she made the tea, Teddy and Patricia came into the kitchen. " Mummy, mummy, you never told that he was Young Tam Lin on the moor," cried Patricia.

Teddy looked up sharply, " What's that? Have you seen Szermai before, Joanna? "

" I — I," stammered Joanna in confusion, suddenly shy of her childishness in thinking a young Hungarian a fairy.

§ 3

Next Saturday the children departed to Scarshaven, Teddy travelling with them as far as Follerwick. He returned to a sitting-room swept and tidied, to Joanna in a resurrected gown of dark green silk, and a supper-table carefully arranged.

" Hullo, my dear, you are smart."

She looked up happily. " Oh, Teddy, such fun. Paul Szermai sent two darling men to help me from the camp. We've got stacks of wood and one of them fed the cows, and milked, and he's coming every morning to milk before he goes to work. Mr. Szermai says that he's a Lithuanian and a peasant and he's home-sick for his farm and loves doing it. Do you think we ought to let him? "

" Szermai's a decent fellow. He seems to know his men. What he says goes, I imagine." Teddy unwound his muffler and came forward to warm his hands. " I must say that you're a devoted mother. Aren't you going to ask about the children? "

Joanna flushed. " I supposed that they were all right. You put them into their carriage, didn't you? I'm not.

really an unnatural mother, and I expect that I shall miss them frightfully after a day or two, but I've been so busy cleaning the house and making friends with a Lithuanian. My dear, you haven't a notion how easy it is to make friends with a Lithuanian. You just make clucking noises like this and waggle your head and show it the cows and give it great slabs of cheese-cake, and it eats out of your hand! "

" I hope it doesn't," laughed Teddy, but he was looking at her uncomfortably. To tell the truth, he had always regarded Joanna as a devoted mother, cherishing a thought common to many men that mothers possessed a standard of values unknown to husbands and spinsters which made the presence of their children essential to their happiness, even if it involved continual work and supervision. He was just a trifle shocked at Joanna's manifest delight in the prospect of a period of less work instead of more maternity.

He was, however, deterred from making further comment by the entry of their paying-guest.

Paul Szermai had taken his place at Scatterthwaite with remarkably little fuss. Not that he was in any way a sociable or accommodating young man. On the contrary, his morose detachment encircled him like a private dwelling. He did not mind where he slept nor what he ate nor whose company he kept, because he lived quietly invulnerable within the shelter of his self-absorption. His beautiful manners were superimposed by social habit above complete indifference.

Teddy liked him because he was a man, a sportsman, a gentleman and had been to Cambridge. Teddy was

himself temperamentally a high-brow, but he enjoyed
the satisfactory conventions of gentlemen who made
England what it is. He felt that Szermai would have
made England what it is had he enjoyed the fortune of
being born an Englishman. According to Szermai, however, that young man had had unluckily no hand in
making Hungary what it was, otherwise it might have
been a better place. It was difficult to tell exactly what
his past career had been, except that he had in some
mysterious way avoided fighting in the War, and had at
some time been all round the world. He had also a
healthy hatred for Bolsheviks, Czechs, Roumanians,
Jews, and Socialists. He disliked the League of Nations, however, which Teddy felt to be disappointing of him. "A Quaker imposition," he said. "I
cannot tolerate this humanitarian softness. Pah! "
He really did say "Pah! " with a violence that
fascinated Joanna. "We grow over-civilized and
soft."

"You don't," Joanna teased him. "You really like
to sit on the edge of chairs, I think, and to eat off tin
plates, and to wash in springs. I believe that you're
quite sad that we uprooted you from your glorious discomforts on the Fell."

He would, however, listen with polite interest while
Teddy held forth about strikes, Trade Union tyranny,
the British Legion, colonial preference, and the optional
clause of the Permanent Court of International Justice.
Teddy was a Tory Democrat, who thought Lord Cecil
the first statesman in Europe, and read the works of
Dean Inge with sad conviction; but who conceded

enough to eccentricity to call Gandhi a saint, though deploring his interference with politics.

To-night Teddy had brought back with him his envelope of little pamphlets from the League of Nations Union, and Joanna was inspecting the gay covers.

" I wish that the maps had names on them," she said. " There's nothing lovelier than names, and I like maps to have the routes of steamers marked in dotted lines crossing the seas." She repeated privately to herself, " Bagdad, Lahore, Bermuda, Dar-es-Salaam," while Teddy and Paul Szermai became involved again in their usual argument.

" But you can't deny that war is one of the greatest evils of our generation? "

" For myself," said Szermai, " I think that men only look dignified when they are fighting. I prefer a generation of soldiers to a generation of clerks. We talk too much. I prefer that we should act. The world is filthy. Only cowards and traitors prosper in it. But who cares nowadays about fidelity or treachery? We ask only comfort and happiness and an old age pension. We clamour to the State to make us safe because we dare not risk our own adventures."

" It's not the danger, it's the futility, the lies of war," Teddy began.

" And do you not think that there are lies in peace? I see no reason to think one system better than another. We make reforms. We build institutions. The greed and the cowardice remain. Look at my country. Look at that degenerate, that imbecile, Karyoli. He thought that it would be fine to be a Liberal Count. He was a stupid boy with a hair-lip. My father knew him. He yielded to the flattery of Jews and panders. And look what happens. He sells his country to.Russian Jews and Roumanian robbers."

"You really believe in force, then?"

Teddy delighted in exposition, but felt that he failed in argument. Somewhere he was right and the young Hungarian wrong, though there was no denying that Szermai had the greater eloquence. "Perhaps even if I had been strong, I mightn't have been a great man," he thought tentatively; but he could not really believe it.

"Force? Believe in force? I am no fool. I know that force destroyed my country. I know that force tore my estates from me and killed my father and my elder brother. I know that the force of your armies holds Germany disarmed and is driving the Riffi into the hands of Spain and . . . Is not the whole world organized by force? 'All right,' says Wilson to Masaryk. It was the only word the Czechs could understand. 'All right,' says Smuts to Roumania. 'All right, you sneaking, thieving little countries. Crawl in between our legs and despoil our noble enemies.' See how the strong take pity on the weak. See how the conquerors respect the conquered. All right. All right. We use force and we acquiesce in its results, yes? And by force, I tell you, I tell you, they take my friend in the Parliament House. He stands with his hands in his pockets, mocking the Bolshevik. They say, 'Mock no longer! Take your hands from your pockets.' But he is no coward. He will not accept the dictation of force. So they take him and say, 'All right.' They cut pockets in his thighs and thrust

his hands into them. And he laughs till they shoot him.
Of course, I believe in force. Such things happen."

" Oh, by jove, is that true? "

" True? Am I a liar, Captain Leigh?"

It was all very terrible, thought Joanna, going to
bring in the supper. Yet somehow one could feel no
compunction for the Hungarian. He was so fierce and
so articulate.

" He really has no heart at all. It's rather like keeping a dragon about the house. He's not a real person, I
believe. He's an eldritch knight. He's young Tam Lin.
He does not belong to our world at all. He comes from
the land of Green Ginger."

She was delighted by this reflection, and brooded
with a little secret smile over the pancakes that she was
making for supper.

When she returned with the dish, Szermai sprang up
to open the door for her, and then continued his argument.

" My men here are fools and poltroons. In Hungary
the peasant is like a prince. He is a magnificent fellow.
My estate when I returned after the War, I found in the
hands of the Roumanians. My peasants say to me,
' Shall we fight for you? ' I say, ' It is useless now.'
They ask me, ' Was not the Holy Stephen a fool, when
he made us turn from the old gods and give our hearts
to Christianity? What has he done for us, this Christ
of the West? There is no justice in Him. Henceforth we
look to the East.' I tell you, these are proud men. But
those fools in the camp, Finns, Ruthenians, Russians.
I spit on them. I despise them. They would get drunk

before their grandmothers and cut each other's throats for a few kronen."

"What's the matter?" asked Joanna.

"Two of Szermai's young hopefuls have been getting into trouble down at the pub," said Teddy. " They got drunk and began to pull their knives from their sleeves. We aren't used to such habits in sober Letherwick. And I gather that some of our young women find their charms too fatal. Our people are a trifle sore. Can't you restrain them a bit? "

" Why should I? What are a few throats? I have seen better throats cut than those of a few peasants. I have seen . . ."

His gloom was so intense that Joanna suddenly found herself wanting to laugh. She had the same intense desire to giggle as she had sometimes known in church. " Such a bloodthirsty young man," she told herself. " What a change to have a bloodthirsty young man about the place. He is just what Teddy would call a he-man. I don't wonder that we both find him exhilarating."

" Why not try to keep them in the camp in the evenings? Can't you find anything to amuse them? What about concerts and things? We used to have awfully jolly shows in the army behind the line. Look here, I've got a scheme. . . ."

Teddy was happy. He was always happy when he could live again in those days when he had been a man as other men, not an invalid, but a popular subaltern with a charming tenor voice, whose place on concert programmes was assured. It was illogical, of course, this wistful memory of the army as of the happiest period in his life, when his intelligence assured him that the greatest curse of modern civilization was the menace of war. Teddy realized his lack of logic. It distressed him, yet it remained. In the army he had been somebody who counted for something. Life had been simplified for him by authority. It was no longer necessary to see both sides of any question. The army and the Roman Catholic Church, thought Teddy, were the only institutions that gave a man perfect assurance. His questioning mind might rest, and his eager heart snatch from the life made sweet by hourly peril of death, such gifts of fortune as might come his way. He remembered a concert party at Abbeville in the queer little crowded theatre, that had ravished his soul as though by perfect art. The rows of upturned faces gleamed pallidly from a khaki shadow out of the smoke-filled atmosphere. He heard laughter greeting his mild, simple jokes. He felt the warm comfort of applause. When the mind is freed from questioning, the nerves and senses may devour with happiness such easy tributes.

"Why don't you let them get up a concert for us? My wife and I could come to the dress rehearsal, and censor your jokes. Luckily jokes in Lithuanian or whatever your people speak would have to be very broad before they shocked Letherwick."

"I do not suppose that they would give a concert. But they often sing among themselves. Will you not both come down one evening, on Saturday next, say, and I will ask them to sing and dance?"

"Ooh, wouldn't we just?" cried Joanna.

She had never learned how to curb her enthusiasm, nor to accept invitations with the proper degree of diffidence.

§ 4

The plateau hung suspended in fiery light between the black wall of the Fell and the black pit of Lindersdale. In the centre of the huts roared and leaped an enormous fire, scattering ephemeral constellations of sparks along the dark air beneath the fir trees.

Before the fire Joanna sat perched on a throne of piled logs covered with a sheepskin. Teddy, huddled in two coats and a muffler, for the April air was chill, sat at her feet, drinking coffee out of a jam jar. Paul Szermai lay full length on the turf, his chin on his slender brown hands. Sometimes he watched the flames dancing and shivering across Joanna's radiant face. Sometimes he watched the half circle of men. Ruthenians, Poles, Finns, Lithuanian Jews, an odd assortment of vagabonds, but all good foresters, crouched on their haunches or sitting on the prostrate trunks of trees round the great fire. Sometimes his sombre eyes only stared into the crackling furnace before him.

The coffee had been handed round with sandwiches of a remarkable kind, thick slices from a long loaf, buttered and sprinkled on one side with chopped nuts, cheese, pickles, scraps of bacon, nutmeg, salt fish and cold sausage, all most savoury and strange. Joanna ate one after the other, unable to face the risk of missing some queer suggestive combination of flavours.

Szermai called to a slender boy with pink cheeks,

pretty as a girl, who rose in a business-like way and stepped forward to sing. He had a clear high tenor voice, and sang with robust enjoyment a wailing melancholy tune, evidently about a lady called " Sonia." Joanna, who understood nothing but the often repeated name, found the contrast between the composer's passionate despair and the singer's sensible relish deliciously piquant. Szermai lay staring into the fire. The foresters smoked, spat, and wished that the party had included beer as well as coffee in its elaborately prepared menu. They knew all about young Sonia and her tragedy, since it was the only song that the Ruthenian boy sang, and he sang it every evening. There were twenty verses, each with a refrain of six lines, sung slowly to a tune of indescribable melancholy yearning. The fire crackled bravely.

But even twenty verses have an end, and having concluded, the singer shut his mouth abruptly, bowed and retired with modest self-satisfaction. There was no applause from the foresters, and Joanna and Teddy heard their feeble clapping die away in the disconcerting silence.

" You would not understand the song," said Szermai gravely. " It is about a lady who loves a demon knight and is betrayed by him to her husband. But though she tries to kill him in revenge, he is immortal and eludes her. It is very sad indeed. We shall now watch a Cossack dance performed by a peasant from Galicia. He has never seen Cossacks except in a Berlin music-hall, but he is quite a good dancer."

With a wild whoop and a leap, a fantastic figure

sprang from the shadows, hurled itself into the circle of firelight and began to spring about, making strange grimaces and uttering weird cries. The dancer wore tall boots of scarlet cardboard and a paper cap, a jacket turned inside out and a red sash. He folded his arms and danced with bent knees, like a grotesque dwarf. He flung out his arms expanding his chest and leaping into the air. Shrieking like a maniac, he swept down upon the fire, caught a smouldering branch and whirled it round his head till it burst into flame. Holding one foot, he hopped in staggering circles, flinging his arms and legs wide apart and closing them again, he flashed like a pair of gigantic scissors, cutting the air. The foresters began to clap as he leapt higher and higher, flinging out his legs wider and wider till sometimes he hung suspended between the horizontal bars of his arms and legs. He was possessed by a demon of movement. He was drunk with an ecstasy of rhythm. Suddenly, clapping his boots together, he began to spin round and round, his arms extended. The audience yelled its delight. He spun almost into the fire, like a whirling salamander, then out into the shadows and was lost to sight.

" Ooh! " sighed Joanna. " Ooh! "

She was completely entranced with pleasure.

" He is not in the least like a Cossack," remarked Szermai, " but he is quite energetic. All dancing is, however, degenerate nowadays. They will now sing in chorus."

They did, with such unbearable melancholy that Joanna wanted to run away and cry. In the sweeping despair and grandeur of the rhythms lay a dark power, unknown and dispossessed. She heard all the sorrows of exile, all loneliness, all the undying poignancy of the disillusioned, of the defeated cause.

Teddy grew very white and quiet. Joanna let the tears trickle childishly down her cheeks. Paul Szermai never moved; but when the song was ended, the singers wiped their moist foreheads cheerfully, and coughed and spat and cleared their throats and called to each other for more food and coffee.

" That song was about Finland. Most of these men only know Finland as a place in which they have worked, but it is a good song." Szermai paused to light a cigarette. He waved the match with an impatient gesture till it went out. " You found it sad? "

" Why is all folk-music so sad? " asked Joanna.

" How should it not be? " He appeared to reflect. " Yet, perhaps you are right. Why should we bother about life, you mean? It does not really matter."

Teddy, watching them, felt a sudden stab of unreasonable pain. These two really shared a secret sympathy. They were invulnerable, akin in their belief that after all, it mattered very little. A phrase came into Teddy's mind, something remembered from his reading at Cambridge, " These ignorant and brawling fanatics who vex me with their pother about liberty . . . " Absurd. It had nothing to do with the case. There was no case. Yet somehow he felt it to be an indictment of his anxieties, his futile, painful ambitions to be of some use in the world, to do something. Life mattered to him, because of all that he desired to do. Joanna was different. She had no fundamental preoccupation of pity. Life was a show to her. She only desired to see more of it. Her thirst was for sensation, the sober, exquisite sensation of watching new places form and assume colour and solidity before the eager vision. She was eager for life; Szermai disdained it; yet somehow both shared this aristocratic indifference to its fortune. They made their own world. They were akin, and now, perhaps they knew it. Joanna, Joanna. With horror he saw her slipping away from him. Indeed, he thought, " She has never been mine." She would fall in love with this Hungarian, this creature who lacked the bowels of compassion. Even though no thoughts of love might yet have entered her unquestioning mind, Teddy, staring at Szermai's slim figure, knew that he saw her future.

"We shall now watch the Dance of Four," said the Hungarian. " It is a folk-dance of Lithuanian origin. It is not sad at all, Mrs. Leigh."

The foresters began to settle themselves comfortably, and the young Ruthenian who had sung about Sonia, hummed the first bars of an accented refrain.

" Tá-ra, tá-ra, La-la-la, La-la-la, Tá-ra! "

The others clapped to emphasize the beats. From the group two middle-aged men detached themselves and came forward with linked arms. They rocked swaying from side to side, their feet quite still. Then as the singing grew louder, they began to move, backwards and forwards, throwing out their feet.

" Tá-ra, tá-ra, La-la-la, La-la-la, Tá-ra! "

The music swelled with the voices of the chorus. The clapping doubled its time. Two other dancers sprang up and joined the couple, all four swaying with linked arms in a line. " Tá-ra, tá-ra," throwing out their feet to the rhythm.

" Hie! " shouted the dancers. The two men outside swung together, locked arms, and formed a circle, which spun round and round, inside and out, tossing heads and bodies, swinging heavy boots.

" Tá-ra, tá-ra, La-la-la, La-la-la, Tá-ra! "

It was a wild gallop of sound, a crazed frenzy of dancing.

Then, abruptly, with a shriek, it stopped. The circle broke, scattering the dancers, panting, laughing, shouting, on to the turf, where they rolled like drunken men.

From the darkness beyond the firelight there came a shrill titter.

A voice cried, " Oh, go it, Charlie! "

" Shut up! "

" Look out. The bogy man'll be after you! "

" What's that? " asked Joanna.

" Girls from the. village, I expect. My friends appear to have an irresistible fascination for them," said Szermai contemptuously.

" By jove, that's pretty rotten, isn't it? Can't something be done about it? " Teddy asked, in his orderly-room manner, remembering bothers with camp followers in France. He disliked " all that kind of thing " intensely.

But Joanna did not seem to listen. She was sampling

the effect of grated cheese, sausage and nutmeg on a slice of bread, handed her by the young Ruthenian, and enjoying herself very much indeed.

The entertainment over, the three walked back to Scatterthwaite, Joanna with head erect, her fair hair silvered in the moonlight, striding happily across the springing heather, Szermai silent and stiff, Teddy stumbling behind them. He was tired and cold and irritated with himself because of his unreasonable apprehensions.

At the house Joanna turned on the Hungarian and thanked him enthusiastically. " It's been the loveliest, loveliest evening," she said. " Thank you a thousand times."

He bowed.

" It doesn't mean anything," Teddy told himself. " I'm behaving like a fool. He never looks twice at her nor she at him. She's just a trifle too exuberant in her manner. She always was." Aloud he said heartily, " Come and have a whiskey and soda before you turn in, old man," although he knew that there was hardly any whiskey in the house, and that he was so tired that he could hardly stand.

They drank each other's health in the chill sitting-room.

§ 5

For the following week, the excitement of the entertainment wrapped Joanna in a warm cloak of pleasure. Life had become incredibly brilliant and surprising. Spring had come. The daffodils opened golden faces in the cottage gardens down in Letherwick. The lambs followed their mothers out on to the moor, adventuring farther and farther from the three fields of Scatterthwaite. The larches lit their small, vivid green torches, every branch burning steadily with green flame.

The hollow cup of the farm seemed no longer to Joanna a prison that shut her off from a wide lovely world. The world was coming to her. As she washed the supper dishes, she would seek one excuse after another to return to the sitting-room that she might catch the phrases which pierced the veil of her ignorance.

" No, the scenery from the Irriwaddy is, as a matter of fact, quite remarkable. . . ."

" We only touched at the Philippines."

" Personally, I prefer Mexico."

He had been everywhere. He had seen everything. Tantalizing, exasperating Young Tam Lin, who knew so much and said so little. Her head rang all day with the sound of lovely names like tattered fragments of forgotten songs.

Every morning the little peasant with scared brown eyes collected the cows and milked them for her. Every evening a pile of firewood lay at her back door. The troughs for watering the beasts were filled as though from heaven. The largest Finn mended the pony's bellyband. The letters from Scarshaven told her that Pamela and Patricia were growing rosy and plump.

She went out to the evening milking, an old cap of Teddy's covering her hair, swinging her three-legged stool and whistling,

" Tá-ra, tá-ra, La-la-la, La-la-la, Tá-ra! "

She settled the stool in the straw, her bucket between her knees, and her forehead against the cow's broad flank.

" Ping, ping! " came the fierce little spurts of milk against the side of the tin bucket.

" Tá-ra, Tá-ra, La-la-la, La-la-la, Tá-ra! " hummed Joanna.

No one had told her that unless you have a strong head it is unwise to sing while milking.

She began to see through half-shut eyes Lithuanians dancing on the deck of a moving ship. Above them swung a single lamp. The sea was still. The large pale moon hung suspended above the slowly swaying mast.

" Tá-ra, tá-ra, La-la-la, La-la-la, Tá-ra! "

Her hands began unconsciously to tug in time to the beats. Faster, faster, louder, louder, sang the song in her head, faster span the wild monotony of rhythm. Faster and faster moved Joanna's hands.

The cow, resenting such violent, rhythmic assault upon so intimate a part of her person, with quiet dignity raised her hind leg, and pushed Joanna, bucket and all into the straw.

She cried out with surprise and indignation rather than with alarm. Paul Szermai, passing the shed on his way down from the camp, came in at her cry, to see his hostess, covered with milk, rolling helplessly below a large, benign-looking cow.

He sprang to her assistance, but only those who have experienced entanglement with cows, buckets, three-legged stools and straw, know the true difficulties of extrication. Joanna was still on her knees, shaking the milk out of her hair, when Teddy, who had also heard her cry, came in.

He saw Szermai holding his wife's hands, and Joanna kneeling shaken with helpless laughter.

He stopped quite still in the doorway.

Joanna saw him and cried, " Oh, Teddy, isn't Cowslip a beast? I feel like crying over the spilled milk."

But Teddy stood looking from her to the young man as though he had seen a ghost.

CHAPTER SEVEN

KNIGHT-ERRANT

§ 1

IF the Leighs had been villagers born and bred; if they had not been isolated from their neighbors by two and a half miles of bad road and the exacting despotism of agriculture; if they had learnt the gossip of the Dale more quickly; if, indeed, Bessy Bottomley had not fallen off her bicycle right on top of Joanna's Lithuanian, then at the end of May the foresters' camp might have been quietly demolished, and the Finns, Ruthenians, Poles and other aliens have folded their red-spotted bundles and silently stolen away.

But these things all befell quite otherwise.

Joanna, unlike Lady Marshall, had never given a thought to Bessy Bottomley. There was, perhaps, no proof of her isolation from the village more complete than her ignorance of Bessy Bottomley's existence. Bessy, though she had failed to rise above Standard Three at the Church School behind the yew trees, was no fool. She knew that bold brown eyes, hard as polished wood, red cheeks and a ripe, comely figure have their value, and that promiscuous maternity, unlike virtue, is not necessarily its own and sole reward.

Her two babies, having been born in the Clarington workhouse infirmary, were bred in the dark parlour behind old Mrs. Bottomley's shop. But Lady Marshall, who regarded the wrongs of unmarried mothers as one of the rights of the benevolent, interested herself in Bessy's case with such energy that two maintenance allowances were weekly handed to Bessy by the clerk of the Petty Sessions Court at Clarington.

Bessy used to cycle into Clarington once a week to collect her money. " An' we all on us know who's paid for that there Humber," said the Village, watching from a cluster round the pump on the Green her flaunting progress. Her bright jersey and her red straw hat, flopping down at one side under the weight of a huge rose, proclaimed her shamelessness. The Humber had a bell with a clear, echoing ring, " a warning," said Mr. Dalby, to all young men of " t' danger coming round t' corner."

That year, however, Bessy had had, she considered, " the luck of a lousy calf, girls," and felt as downcast as Lady Marshall felt elated by a brand obviously snatched from the burning. Her bicycle bell might ring as loudly as her broad thumb could twitch it, and her green jersey flash along the leafless lanes. Danger had lost its spice since young men knew that their charmer, though buxom, was businesslike. A bit of a lark, with no harm done, was as far as they would venture. And Mrs. Bottomley, who had so loudly bewailed her daughter's falls from grace, now secretly lamented at her virtue.

It happened, however, that on one Saturday morning, just before the camp entertainment to which Teddy and Joanna went, the Lithuanian peasant was walking down the road to Clarington, lonely and miserable, hating his exile in a foreign land. He was a shy creature, who found the gregarious life of a camp intensely trying. He missed his wife and his children; he wanted some human and simple consolation and more kindness even than the cheesecake bestowed upon him by Joanna. He had been praying quite vaguely to the Virgin for comfort as he trudged listlessly down the road on a holiday less acceptable than work. And as he paused by the bridge over Linders River, Bessy, sweeping round the corner on the bicycle, ran straight into him, and fell with him in a tangle on the wet bank, scattering dewdrops from the hedge on to her red straw hat, and covering the shoulder of her green jersey with soft dark mould.

The Lithuanian picked himself up and gazed with wonder upon the splendid, plump gipsy who had thus, apparently, descended from heaven. The implications of the encounter appeared quite clear to him, and he thanked the Blessed Virgin for her promptitude.

The implications of the encounter were also quite clear to Bessy. She shook the soil out of her skirt and brushed her hands together and stared at the short, but well-set-up young fellow with an appraising smile. She knew no Lithuanian, a difficult tongue to learn, in its roots not unlike Sanskrit; but she spoke a language more universal even than Sir Wentworth's simplified Latin, and found that the forester understood it too.

They continued their pilgrimage to Clarington, cheered by each other's company, and the Lithuanian held Bessy's bicycle when she went in to fetch her money from the collecting officer. Before the day was over, she had received three yards of blue crêpe de Chine from the Bon Marché, a shilling tea at the Clarington Creamery, and two small tawny ports at the Lindersdale Arms, in the Parlour Saloon, where there are plush seats and aspidistras, and a young gentleman can take his young lady without feeling ashamed. For these mercies she returned thanks duly, with a little pleasant dalliance under a haystack near the Letherwick Road.

It was therefore Bessy who, a week later, urged Eva Thurtleby to go with her to Paul Szermai's concert, and whose inopportune laughter had disturbed Teddy so much. It was Bessy who told young Brindle, who told Sam Buggins, who told the world at large, that Mrs. Leigh had sat drinking and laughing beside the fire while those foreigners danced real indecent. It was Bessy who thus became the indirect cause of a conversation in the Smoke Room of the Coach and Cushion, when Chris Paxton protested against the injustice of foreigners who, having come to plant trees, remained to cut firewood and milk cows at Scatterthwaite.

" What I say is, if we must have a pack o' foreigners to teach us how to plant trees an' our grandmothers how to suck eggs, let 'em get on with it. But when it comes to turning good men out o' their jobs, it's a different matter altogether. Owd Thorley and Mrs. Thorley were the real good owdfashioned sort, as couldn't stand the doings up at Scatterthwaite nohow."

" What sort o' goings on? "

" Why, nowt above board, as you might say, though

queer goings on up front ways. Captain Leigh's no more a farmer than my owd mare. Though I wouldn't say he don't know a thing or two. Thorley tell't me that when t' prize pig died o' swine fever, they all tried to cut t' corpse intid bits, an' bury it in t' garden, for all the world like a murder tale in t' *News of the World*. To save notification like, he thought on."

" That's a criminal offence, a criminal offence," cried little Mr. Grig, who knew everything. He was an ex-schoolmaster who had drunk himself into being a cobbler, but who retained the habit of instruction. " Non-notification of swine fever is a criminal offence. So is improper employment of aliens."

"Ah know nowt about their employment being improper, though Bessy Bottomley knows whether their ways are."

"Bessy Bottomley's a bad lot," said Dick Dalby firmly. "So's them Lithuanians and Finns, an' for all I know, Mrs. Leigh's a bad lot an' all. We'd be well shut on 'em."

"What's she done with her bairns, I'd like to know? "

" Gotten 'em out o' the way of her carryings on with that Hungarian."

"If you ask me, if you ask me," exploded little Mr. Grig, almost dancing up and down in a frenzy of self-assertion. But nobody did ask him. They never did.

" Settin' like a heathen idol on top on a lot o' fire-wood."

" Nameless orgies, nameless orgies," chirruped Mr. Grig.

"Loose lot, all on 'em," decided Dick Dalby. "Thanks, my boy, I will have another," and Chris Paxton paid for his drink, and they all fell to talking of wireless and aerials and the Major's prophecy for to-morrow's selling plate.

§ 2

Meanwhile, the promoter of nameless orgies stood before a great earthenware bowl in the Scatterthwaite kitchen, kneading dough and thinking, with a worried line between her brows, about her children. Joanna should not, of course, have been baking after tea, but one of the failings of a " loose lot " lies in the inability to do the right things at the right time.

So she buried her hands in the soft flour, and poured in the milk and water, and reflected how Pamela loved to watch her " stirring the miller." Pamela was such a darling. She knew all about pleasure. She had a fine, rich zest for life, adventurous in seeking sensations, gallant in disappointment. She was healthy too. Never from the first day of her life had she given Joanna cause for anxiety, being a happy child, so different from poor Patricia, who was always delicate and always a little sad.

" I wonder if some mothers just think about their children as their children," pondered Joanna, punching the cushion of dough and turning in to the centre its ragged edges. " I wonder if I haven't really got any mother-love. I can't help wishing that they'd grow up and talk to me properly. Real companions never have to be protected from your dark thoughts. How can people say, ' I'm never lonely when there are children about? ' I'm lonely, I think, because I'm always having to edit my thoughts so carefully. Teddy mustn't be upset. The children mustn't be frightened. Is nobody ever really able to say what they think? "

Agnes and Rachel had, of course, been friends of that kind. They had scolded and teased and petted and understood her. Did friendship only belong to school-days? When a woman married, was she always having to consider people ever after?

" The matter with you, my girl," Joanna told herself severely, " is that you know so few women. You always live among men, and although they may be darlings, they just won't *do*. Not as friends. Men are always wanting to be listened to. They feel tragic and want to be comforted. Then they feel humiliated and want to be grand again. You've all the time got to be nursing their vanity, poor dears, or they can't get along at all. Oh, dear. I wish that I knew how people ought to feel. I'm sure I'm all wrong to love Pamela more than Patricia, and to wish that I sometimes had a woman friend to talk to when I've got Teddy. And Paul Szermai's awfully exciting when he's just a Hungarian, but I wish that I didn't feel all the time afraid that he was going to turn into a man and want comforting and admiring and made to feel dominating again."

She set down the bowl by the fire, and spread a cloth above the fragrant dough.

Pamela loved the dough. She always wanted to poke her finger in and make a burrow. " Jus' one tiny mouse's hole of a burrow, mummy, just my littlest finger." Patricia rarely wanted to experience these irrational sensations of pleasure. Nothing pleased her in which she did not play an active and appreciated part. She had her father's sensibility to her own achievements.

"I suppose that I ought to be with her. She's so awfully vulnerable. I ought not to feel relieved when somebody else has to deal with her. Oh, dear, I suppose that this is really frightful of me. Why did nobody ever teach me how a real mother ought to feel?"

It was no good. The times would come when all that Joanna wanted to do was to sail away, either alone or with a real friend, whose feelings she did not have to consider at all. She wanted to open her port-hole one morning and see against the sky the faint outline of an island, iridescent as a bubble on the grey water. She wanted to lean out above tossing blue-green waves, and catch the end of a string thrown to her by dark, smiling men, and haul up from baskets bananas pulled that morning on the green island. She wanted to climb terraces, frothing over with purple bougainvilia and splashed with scarlet hibiscus, and scented with magnolia.

She wanted to walk round the deck of a ship, and to bend over the stern rail, and see the phosphorous flashing with great green stars in its wake.

Paul Szermai, she considered, was not good for her. His company awoke in her far too many ruthless desires, as the torchlight of his experience illumined now an almond tree in Florida, now the tortuous street of a Chinese city, now the vaulted darkness of a Persian bazaar, fretted by golden wires of sunlight. Joanna could see them all, but sight with the mind's eye was inadequate.

"I want to go, I want to go," she whispered. Then the rhythm of her thought reminding her absurdly of the refrain, she hummed

"I want to go right back to Dixie,
    Where the hens are doggone glad to lay,
    Scrambled eggs in the new-mown hay . . ."

So she was singing when Teddy came into the room, newly shaved, and drawing on his brown leather gloves.

"My dear, you are all dressed up. Whither away?"

"I'm going down to the British Legion," said Teddy, looking at her with a queer, strained smile, yet at the same time, somehow pleased with himself, as though he had suddenly thought of something rather clever. "There's been trouble. If somebody doesn't do something soon, there'll be a real row about those foresters. When people like these village chaps get an idea into their heads, there's no knowing who can make them see reason. Perhaps nobody can. But one has to have a shot at it, anyhow."

"But are we . . ." Joanna was going on to add. "But are we the right people to stand up for them, we who are obviously deriving benefit from their presence, who are ourselves strangers compared to these real inhabitants of the Dale? Shan't we be resented more than ever?" But she did not complete her questioning, for she saw that Teddy had made up his mind to do something rather important. Whatever was in his mind, it was a fine thing. It made him feel noble and strong. He was about to make, Joanna felt certain, a fine gesture, though exactly how and why, she could not guess. Invariably, of course, she had somehow to pay for his fine gestures, but that, she supposed, was how providence arranged its justice. Whatever it was, she had no right to interfere with his adventures. If he felt it to be the right thing to stand up for the foresters, he must go. " But I hope you won't be back too late, dear. You'll be so awfully tired."

" It's hardly the sort of occasion to consider whether I shall or shan't be tired," said Teddy. " Besides, I think it's a good thing to keep in touch with the young farmers. You never seem to find time to call on their wives. Somebody has to dispel the illusion that we are hermits or lepers."

Gently putting Joanna into the wrong, he strode out of the kitchen, and she, with a sigh, went to get her old cap and stool for the evening milking. Poor Teddy, he had been so difficult lately. The interest in Szermai's company seemed to have waned. So often he was like this, enchanted by people for a week and then tired of them.

" But he really mustn't get tired of Tam Lin, because I don't know what we're going to do without the money. And even that has to come to an end in May or June or sometime."

He was difficult about other things too, amorous and resentful by turns, threatening suicide or suddenly buoyant. " This really is no place for the children," thought Joanna. " What are we going to do? "

She went across the yard to call the cows in from the paddock, and found Teddy leading the pony Ezekial, out of the stable.

" I suppose that I shall have to lift the shafts myself? " he asked.

" Oh, my dear, I'm so sorry," she said, remembering the doctor's orders that he was not to strain himself by lifting things.

She lifted the shafts and stood while he backed the pony between them, then tugged at the traces and belly-band, fastening straps.

" I suppose you thought that I was going to walk to the village, that I was a young giant, like Szermai? Unluckily, Providence which kept him out of the War, was not so kind to me. I am only sorry that you should be penalized by having to remember to help me to yoke up the pony."

He looked at her across the pony's back, his unhappy grey eyes heavy with hostility.

" By the way, where is our guest? You won't forget to give him his supper, will you? "

Then he climbed into the cart and drove away.

Joanna looked after him with apprehension.

" So that's what's wrong. He's jealous of Tam Lin, because he at least is healthy. He's always getting jealous of people who are quite well. Pat's like that too. Oh, my poor darling, fate isn't kind to you, and you're not very kind to yourself either, are you? "

She went off to milk, and to tell herself a lovely letter which ought to have come by post from Agnes that afternoon, but which reality had inadvertently failed to deliver.

" My darling," wrote Agnes in the letter which did not arrive.

" Are you alive or not? Are you ill or well? The reason I don't write oftener is that there is so much to say. I am living in a temple with fifty golden bells that ring all day in the wind, and the little monks in grey robes come to their part of the temple as quietly as the small sheep on your moor, and as inobtrusively. I have three dragons guarding my house, and a yellow horse called Ancient Glory, and a new husband. Did you know that I had a husband? I forget when I found mine, but I expect that he is much the same as yours, so really there is little need to bother you with the details.

" The reason why I write now is that I met a woman who has discovered the fourth dimension. So really we can spend week-ends with each other now. All that you have to do is to step out of the world and take a ticket for China, and here you are. I have got the spare room ready, with hot water and a tin of biscuits by the bed, and *Home Chat* to read and a fire in your room every night. You may have the yellow kitten, but I insist upon the blue Persian for my room, because he goes with the curtains. I have a lovely padded silk kimono for you, embroidered with scarlet dragons. They have eyes of green and gold. Do come and wear them. And, by the way, I had a dream about you that you were not well, and that you came to me and brought your cuckoo clock and the little silver clock by your bed and the tall grandfather clock that stood in the corner of the stairs in Park Street, and that you made a happy presence in my house. Then suddenly you said, 'I must go home,' and vanished. Oh, my dear. For the Lord's sake, be happy. I will send you a lovely poem to put you to sleep and to remind you of my sentiments when I am deserted.

"Now she is gone, but all her clocks are ticking
    With gentle voices, punctual and polite,
Their thrifty hands the scattered moments picking,
    Tossed from the careless bounty of the night.

"Oh, foolish clocks, who had no wit for hoarding
    The precious moments when my love was here,
Be silent now, and cease this vain recording
    Of worthless hours, since she is not near."

Joanna knew that Agnes wrote poetry, but, being no poet herself, she found it difficult to supply the necessary verses. Fleeing her incompetence, she darted on to her own letter.

"I have a dragon guarding my house," replied Joanna. "His name is Young Tam Lin, and he comes from your country and has seen all the world. He is fierce, but very polite as dragons go. I am afraid that he may be only a prince in disguise. So very disappointing, I always think, don't you?"

But by this time, the milking was ended, and Joanna had to go to put the hens to bed. They were less exhilarating than monks or dragons.

§ 3

Teddy drove down to the village with a set smile of heroism upon his face. For what he contemplated was an action of great magnanimity, and all the more magnanimous because no one would ever know what it had cost him. For now he was perfectly sure that Joanna and Szermai were in love with one another.

Some subtle intuition had first told him, the delicate sensitiveness of the invalid, whose perceptons were more delicately attuned to fine shades of emotion than were those of the common man. Ever since Szermai had first come to the house, Teddy had recognized it as inevitable. He should have acted before it was too late, for he had seen what must happen, even before Szermai had seen it. Even before . . .

He was still uncertain of how far Joanna understood her own position. He suspected that she deceived herself. Dear, strong, beautiful, dense Joanna, whose insensitiveness had so often jarred upon his finer nature, and yet who thought herself so loyal and good, who meant to be so loyal and good. He must be fair to her.

He should have known that fate, which had marked him down as a victim of misfortune, would never leave him the rare consolation of domestic happiness. For long enough he had deceived himself, thinking that out of the wreck of his life he might preserve this one legitimate treasure. But now it was time to open his eyes, to realize that he must ask from misery no quarter. Some people were born to be unlucky, and he was one of them.

" It isn't fair, it isn't fair," he had cried in his heart

again and again, lying wakeful at night, and thinking in his folly that long rebellion against the injustice of fortune might receive ultimate recognition from the gods. But now he knew that such rebellion was useless. The assignment of human griefs and satisfactions had nothing to do with justice.

Driving through the green twilight down to the calm valley, he looked back into his brief, unhappy history, and saw himself estranged from the invigorating joys of youth, frustrated in the ambitions of his manhood, pursued from the beginning by disappointment. How false, how stupid of him to expect any release from the hounds of misfortune dogging him to his grave.

Sorrow was his birthright. His father, Martin Leigh, a pleasant, ambitious, moderately athletic youngster, had fallen passionately in love with Gertrude Wise, the daughter of a poor clergyman. Directly he had risen in the provincial bank where he was working, to the position of cashier, he married her. Teddy was born in the second year of marriage, but his mother, instead of sensibly recovering from his arrival, and going about the duties of motherhood and housekeeping, declined instead into a lingering consumption.

Her illness became the predominating influence of their fortune. Martin Leigh, distracted by grief and anxiety, turned himself from a man into a machine, constantly engaged in the addition and subtraction of immense columns of figures, which were somehow to restore his wife to health. Teddy had memories of him as a lean, forbidding grown-up, who passed his time between the bank and the back sitting-room, with his short-sighted eyes continually bent over large ledgers, cherishing a fierce resentment against noise, callers, or similar disturbances.

When Teddy was eight years old, his father became manager of a branch of the bank at Grimsby, but the driving fury of his desire to succeed, to make more money, to provide every possible cure suggested for his wife, goaded him on, as far as Teddy could remember, from branch to branch, from little town to larger town, each move meaning a new Bank House, only partially furnished, a new housekeeper, a new grammar school. Wherever they went, they were accompanied by the same furniture: the dining-room table with fat, bulbous legs covered with nobbly carvings, the bookcase full of bound volumes of the *Gentleman's Magazine* and back numbers of *Punch,* and strips of stamped leather stretched along every shelf, and Teddy's own bed with the brass nobs, and the beautiful lace curtains and chintz-covered arm-chair, always kept for the one lovely place in the house — " your ma's room, Master Teddy," the housekeepers would say in a hushed voice, or " your poor ma's room, my dear."

And from time to time his mother would descend on them, lovely, fragile, with the light ephemeral gaiety of her kind. And then her room would be bright with a fire, and Teddy's father, unwontedly extravagant, would bring home huge bunches of flowers, roses at fivepence each, or shaggy chrysanthemums, and there would be tea-parties, and iced cakes and the daring anticipation of perfect pleasure. To Teddy these home-comings were all the Christmas and birthdays that he had ever known. They were marred only by the knowledge, slowly and painfully acquired, that upon such occasions his father seemed to resent his presence altogether. Later he understood the husband's jealousy for a son who in some way usurped the precious, exquisite attention that should have been his alone in the short moments of their life together. Later he understood something, too, of his father's tragedy. Having transformed himself from a man into a machine, in order to provide comfort for his wife, he found it more and more difficult, during the brief hours of their companionship, to turn himself back again from a machine into a man; so that Gertrude Leigh, before she died, preferred to play with her tall, solemn son, to talk delicious nonsense to him, and even at times to praise him, teasingly, to his grave taciturn father.

Her death, when Teddy was fifteen, robbed life of all its charm and colour. He had always been delicate; his pilgrimage from school to school had prevented him from forming friendships among other boys; he was vaguely called clever, and had won two essay prizes and a reputation for being a good classical scholar. The truth was that he had no marked ability, but spent all the time when not actually in school browsing in free libraries and reading. He had so little else to do.

Before his mother's death, his naturally devotional nature concentrated all his warmth of feeling and his adolescent dreams upon her. When she died in a sanatorium in Switzerland, it seemed by a quite natural transference of thought that he turned his attention from her to God. He must, it seemed, worship something. *The Confessions of Saint Augustine*, found in a dusty binding on the back shelf of a Kingsport library — they moved to Kingsport just after his mother's death — brought him his new determination, to be a priest.

" Great art Thou, O Lord, and greatly to be praised; great is Thy power and Thy wisdom infinite. And Thee would man praise; man but a particle of Thy creation; man, that bears about him his mortality, the witness of his sin, the witness that Thou resisteth the proud; yet would man praise Thee; he, but a particle of Thy creation."

Right from the beginning, it had spoken straight to him. Had his mother's mortality, which she had so obviously borne about with her, indeed spoken of God's resistance to pride? Had his father's will, the proud, despairing will of a man who fought against the eternal sentence of mortality, indeed fought against God? Was that the meaning of the shadow that darkened their household, Martin Leigh, fighting with Mammon against God for the life of his beloved? Why had this horror of desolation seized them? What had they done, father and son, to be so greatly visited by sorrow, estranged from one another and from the world by this fierce menace of disease?

" I will seek Thee, Lord, by calling on Thee; and will call on Thee, believing in Thee; for to us hast Thou been preached." " Oh! That I might repose on Thee! Oh, that Thou wouldest enter into my heart, and inebriate it, that I may forget my ills, and embrace Thee, my sole good. What art Thou to me? In Thy pity, teach me to utter it. And what am I to Thee, that Thou demandest my love, and, if I give it not, art wroth with me, and threatenest me with grievous woes? Is it then a slight woe to love thee not? Oh! for Thy mercy's sake, tell me, O Lord my God, what Thou art unto me. Say unto my soul, I am thy salvation. So speak, that I may hear. Hide not Thy face from me. Let me die — lest I die — only let me see Thy face."

Surely here was the end to his questing. Here, if he could only find, was the goal for which he sought. " Now are my years spent in mourning." That was true enough, in the chill bedroom of the Kingsport bank house, the bedroom never more to be decked with roses, never more to be lit by the dancing firelight, by the little rose-shaded lamp, by the gay smile of his mother. All light, all colour, all glory had vanished from the dark city. The trams clanked dismally outside. The rain dripped from the chimney pots.

When should he say, " And Thou, O Lord, art my comfort? " Nobody was now his comfort, neither the form master who had praised his translation of the Eclogues that afternoon, nor the slatternly housekeeper who made him toast for tea and worried kindly about his cough, nor, certainly, his father, drowning sorrow in a stream of compound interest. " But because Thy lovingkindness is better than all lives, behold, my life is but a distraction, and Thy Right Hand upheld me."

He had seized his school cap and run into the darkening street. His feet mechanically took him along the road which led to the Grammar School. Down one street, round to the left, past the row of lighted shop-windows, up to St. Saviour's Church. The door was ajar, but the big building was empty and dark, except for two candles glimmering on the altar, and the electric light behind the curtains that shut off the vestry. Teddy had knelt down in a side pew, waiting for revelation.

And the revelation had come.

St. Augustine had found peace through dedication. " O Lord, I am Thy servant; I am Thy servant and the son of Thy handmaid, Thou hast broken my bonds in sunder. I will offer to Thee the sacrifice of praise." Was not this the solution? Why not, with one fine simple gesture of self-abnegation, renounce the world, the flesh, and the devil and surrender himself to this eternal Lover? Might not peace be found in the Church? Why seek for the affection of his father, when the love of the Eternal God awaited him? Why mourn his mother when his true mother, the Church, beckoned to him with outstretched arms?

It had seemed then so simple and so comforting. Always Teddy had desired to make by one complete irrevocable decision, the sacrifice that should set him free. " O Lord God, give peace unto us. The peace of rest, the peace of Thy Sabbath, which hath no evening."

The peace had come. Even as the verger shuffled out of the lighted vestry to extinguish the altar candles, Peace laid her hand upon Teddy's shoulder, Peace was given to him, a Peace that passed all understanding. He dedicated his life to the Church.

It must have been that evening that he caught the cold which turned to pneumonia, and from which he recovered only with great difficulty. On the whole, he had been very happy in that first illness, perfectly content to die immediately and go straight to his Lover. But God had decreed otherwise. The doctors reported that he was threatened by the same disease of the lungs which had killed his mother. He was sent to Switzerland.

Even now, driving the fat pony down the steep muddy road, he could feel again the horror of those two years at Davos. He knew the hushed monotony of the cure; the atmosphere of the sanatorium, with its artificial cheerfulness, the careful superficiality of conversations, when everybody tried to suppress the subjects interesting them most, weight, coughing fits, hæmorrhages, and those filthy, terrible little black flasks. He shuddered.

Always since then, the possibility of return had haunted them. Whenever he felt ill, whenever a violent fit of coughing threatened hæmorrhage, he sweated with fear of the living death awaiting him. While in Switzerland, his religion had provided him with a spasmodic consolation. He had at times known ecstasy. On the other hand, he had known desolation, and the death of Karl von Petersdoff, the German boy who became there the first friend that he had known, had driven him to savage rebellion.

His partial cure, his return to England, his father's grudging permission for him to go to Cambridge, resulted in two years of alternating happiness and misery. The prospect of going to college had delighted him. In his gratitude he had renewed his ambition to be a priest.

But the Church offered no simple solution of life's difficulties. Nothing, it seemed, was easy and clear-cut in this world. Theology itself was not an uncontroversial science. Kind hearts had been exposed by the Fabian society. Simple faith was compassed about with hideous alternatives. Teddy, who sought to empty himself of selfish desires, to walk clad in a rich nakedness of self-surrender, found the path of sacrifice beset by economic and theological snares. The inebriation with the love of God, which St. Augustine had besought, appeared at Cambridge to be as undesirable as any other form of inebriation. Modern Protestantism demanded hard thought, not only about the Trinity and the doctrine of personal survival, but about economics and sociology and the psychology of youth. To empty oneself until one had nothing seemed too short a cut to the possession of all things.

Almost, Teddy had become a Socialist, under the influence of Jefferson of Trinity. But the War had saved him from that. Jefferson had become a Pacifist, and Teddy knew that this was a war to end war.

At a recruiting meeting in the autumn term of 1914, he had found the peace of mind for which he had prayed so long. Here was the perfectly clear and simple issue. Here was the sacrifice no longer chosen with hesitation, but demanded; here the self-abnegation, no longer tainted with the possibility of ridicule, but august and honourable.

He had set about, carefully, cautiously, knowing the difficulties of his past record, to enter the army.

It was just after the surprise of his acceptance, the intoxicating knowledge that at last he had been recognized as a man, part of a real man's world, that he had met Joanna. His marriage had been part of his new manhood. He had found his true self at last.

And he had been cheated. Here, as ever, fate had robbed him of satisfaction. There had been no splendid sacrifice, no simple and sufficing act of courage. He had hoped for an honourable return, or for a poppy-covered grave, a simple cross, and his name living for ever more. He found himself imprisoned in a military sanatorium.

He had been cheated, cheated, cheated, singled out by fate for humiliation. Neither the Church, nor the army nor marriage nor health would claim him. Even Joanna now had failed.

Should he not have seen, when she hung about the sitting-room in the evenings, listening to the glib tales of that young Hungarian? Should he not have known that youth must beckon to youth and health to health, that a normal, vital woman needs satisfaction, a strong, vigorous lover, no puny invalid? Had he not seen her, like Desdemona, listening, wide-eyed to every word of Szermai's enchanting tales? Why had she been so reluctant with him, who was her husband? What had made her shrink from him lately?

Good God, Good God, hadn't he suffered enough? Had this final humiliation to conquer him? Must he see the disease which had robbed him of his vocation, his manhood, his possibility of service, now rob him also of his honour? Was there no time when a man might say, " Thus far, no farther! " to the pursuit of sorrow?

He must purge himself of all desire. He must face death empty and naked, leaving the world as he had entered it. Perhaps then Joanna would realize all that he had surrendered. Perhaps men might in time to come treat the afflicted with greater dignity, because one man had had the strength to gather up his afflictions on to a funeral pyre, and light with them a flame to illumine weakness and disease for ever.

Teddy was driving to the British Legion Club to make his defence of the invading strangers. Then he was going to tell Joanna that he would not stand in her way any longer. She might marry her Hungarian.

Then he would die.

Always, failure had dogged his footsteps. But now he would fail, he would be weak, no longer. It was a far, far better thing that he would do than he had ever done. Now, with so grand a gesture, death would be proud to take him.

He turned the corner into the village street, and came upon Sir Wentworth Marshall riding his beautiful bay thoroughbred.

" Oh, I say, Marshall, I wanted to speak to you."

He felt quite strong and sure of himself.

" Good-evening. Oh, it's you, Leigh. Not seen you about for a long time. Fairly fit? "

" Splendid, never better," said Teddy, who had been awake all night, who knew now that he must have a temperature. Joanna had been careless about taking his temperature lately. Of course. Her thoughts had been otherwise occupied. He recognized this without bitterness. " I wanted a word with you about the foresters' camp. I'm afraid that there's going to be trouble in the village. The British Legion are organizing a deputation or something, I hear, asking for them to be deported. I'm going down there now to see if I can do anything. It might be awkward if they really got rampageous."

" Oh, really, good of you, Leigh. By the way, have you seen the notices of the new British Institute of Biological Studies? To bring statesmen and doctors and business men and so on into touch with — Whoa, girl, Whoa, steady! " The bay was fidgeting. " I've been riding over to Bartondale. It's later than I like to be out on horseback. Whoa, there! I'd like you to have a look at the syllabus, Leigh. Quite interesting. My wife doesn't approve of the artificial limitation of families, but I always said that contraception. . . Whoa there! " The bay mare in the fading light began to waltz steadily round the plot of trampled turf. " Biologists," jerked Sir Wentworth, facing Teddy. His next words were lost in the twilit tangle of thorn bushes. " Birth-control, you know," and he was off again. " Population question." The mare began curveting gently down the road. " Sorry, I can't hold her. She's getting cold. What I meant was a parliamentary committee on contraception. . . ."

He was lost to view, cantering like a child on a hobbyhorse, down the shadowed lane.

This was about all the reasonable argument that one could ever expect from Sir Wentworth.

The sign was all the more clear. Teddy alone must face the burden of an unpopular decision. If he were execrated in the countryside, that was nothing. Popularity was one of the lesser joys of life which such as he must forswear for ever. He must choose the hard road uphill all the way to the final sacrifice. What matter? One day Joanna might understand all the nobility that she had disregarded. One day she might regret her blind insensitiveness.

The village street closed in upon him. He passed the Coach and Cushion and chose the road to the north of the green, past the low school-house, and the village shop where old Mrs. Bottomley dozed against the counter, her head resting greasily on a box of Liquorice All-sorts.

" I shall pull this off," he told himself. " I shall have power."

He left the pony as usual at the Shepherd's Arms, and walked slowly up to the converted Army Hut which formed the Club House of the British Legion.

The bar room was empty except for Dick Gunning, ex-ploughboy and corporal, who had lost a leg in Palestine with Allenby. He was now employed as bar-tender and caretaker by the British Legion.

" Good evening, Gunning."

" Evening, sir. What'll you have? "

" Whiskey and soda, please. Anyone about? "

" It's a bit early yet. There are one or two playing billiards."

" I hear that they're talking about a protest against the foresters' camp. What do you think about it yourself, Gunning? "

The bar-tender scratched his head.

" Well, sir, it's like this. Some on us here have seen summat of the world. I've been to France, an' I've been to India, an' I've been to Palestine an' Mespot, an' what you can tell me about foreign parts won't go on a sixpence, as the saying is. They call Palestine a land flowing with milk and honey, an' all I can say is, it got dried up somehow before we arrived. And what I feel about it is, give me Letherwick. Mind you, as foreigners I won't say nawt about them. Though mark my words, sir, the Turk's as good a gentleman as the Arab any day; more. And as for the French, I'm fed up with 'em."

Teddy nodded judicially in his orderly-room manner. He was happy here. This was a good man's place, this bar with its scrubbed wooden tables and new green paint and the atmosphere of beer and tobacco and carbolic soap. And Gunning's company was a refreshment after Joanna and the Hungarian.

" An' I've had my bad luck, the same as you've had yours, sir, if you'll excuse the liberty. An' all we've got left, as you might say, is old England. But when they go an' fill it up with a lot of Hungarians an' Finns an' God alone knows what else, then that's what I call coming a bit too thick on us. What I feel is that a chap likes a bit of privacy. It's a question of principle."

" It always is," thought Teddy wearily. This was a decent fellow. Why should he put himself outside the pale drawn by all decent fellows between what things were done and not quite done?

"Yes, thanks, I will have another little one," he pushed his glass forward. Perhaps this had not been a wise night to choose for his adventure. He felt so damned tired. He had been sleeping so badly. He'd never slept properly since Joanna withdrew herself in that absurd way into the box-room. As if there were any fear of infection, especially now that the children were not in the house. It was all part of a put-up job, of course. But it wasn't fair, that he should lie awake night after night, pestered by beastly dreams, beastly dreams, because his wife harboured a strange delusion that she must sleep in the box-room.

"A question of principle," he said slowly. "It's always a question of principle. That a man should keep what he's got. That he should live comfortably at home with his wife and not be overlooked by a pack of beastly foreigners."

It had been all so admirably clear in his mind that morning. He had been putting a new door into the side of the hen-house and planning out just what he should say about toleration and free-trade in labour, and the best work being done by the best people for the job. Now he was growing confused. His head ached so damnably and the room was full of fog.

He felt a little sick. Another whiskey might clear his head, perhaps. He mustn't take too much, of course, but just as in the army he had found it a help when he felt too tired even to breathe, so now it might lift him from this gulf of lassitude into which he was slipping.

The door from the billiard room opened and Brindle, the red-faced young farmer, came in with Chris Paxton. Brindle was a worthless fool. He drank too much and gambled away the capital needed for his farm. Teddy disliked him. He was gross and vulgar. If only it had been anyone but he. . . .

" That's good, by gosh! That's good. I say, Gunning, heard this new one of Paxton's? Hullo, Leigh? By Jove, you are a stranger! How's things, eh? Come on, what are you going to have? Gin and bitters? "

" I mustn't antagonize him right away," thought Teddy. " He's one of the ringleaders in the anti-foreign move. I must make friends with him and get him to see reason."

" M'thanks. That's awfully good of you. You must have one on me afterwards then."

" You're the very man I was wanting, Leigh. Look here. This rotten dance we're getting up. Funds low and all that, you know. I've promised to sell tickets. Five bob. Rotten show. I'm no dancing man. Game o' billiards suits me better or a hand at poker. Can't you take a couple or so? You've got a wife. Come on."

Two tickets. Ten shillings. One fifth of what was paid him every week for harbouring the enemy who had destroyed him. Ten shillings, two tickets. He would send Joanna and Szermai. That would be fitting justice.

" I'll take two." He fumbled for his note-case, but his hands somehow would not keep steady. He could not pick the ten-shilling note out from its fellows. Damn it all, they would all be laughing at him. His nerves were in such a rotten state. He could feel his heart pumping violently. Only somehow it pumped just below his temples.

His heart had shifted. It had, perhaps, being broken, disintegrated already. What a joke! Teddy found himself laughing quite naturally.

The room seemed to be full by now. Everyone was laughing. He was making, perhaps, quite a social success, a gallant gaiety before the darkness closed over him.

Somebody was telling of how Bessy Bottomley had clicked with a Lithuanian.

" I don't want any of their damned souvenirs kicking about our village. When we're shut on 'em, let's be shut on 'em, I say. Let Bessy go back with 'em an' all."

" There'll be a fine crop of Finno-Tartars before they take themselves off. Let 'em get back to their own women."

Teddy set down his glass very carefully. His mind seemed now to be perfectly lucid. He had come to say something to these vulgar fellows, something very important. He was their intellectual superior, an educated gentleman. It was right that he should instruct them in ethical values. He wiped his little military moustache with a silk handkerchief and leant across the table to young Paxton.

" That's just what I say, exactly. Let them get back to their own women. We don't want them here messing about with our wives. Joanna's a good woman, a good woman, but very — stupid." He nodded with emphatic dignity. " A good woman. Very stupid." And bowed his head down, down through the black rushing waters, through the deep, swirling, engulfing waters, down into intolerable darkness.

He lay with his head on the wooden table, among the little damp rings where unwiped glasses had stood.

The young farmers looked down at him for a moment in silence. Then Brindle burst into a loud guffaw of laughter.

CHAPTER EIGHT

FINNO-TARTAR

§ 1

JOANNA was growing anxious. Teddy ought to have returned an hour ago. She walked up and down between the back door and the yard gate in the mild spring evening, trying to summon her friends to bring her consolation. But neither Rachel's practical assurance, nor Agnes, with her whimsical affection, nor Sir Walter Raleigh, dashing and romantic, could combat her foreboding.

A round moon spilt pale silver on to her fair hair and tall figure.

"I'm wasting time," she told herself. There were socks to mend, and the curtains in the sitting-room were still frayed at the bottom, and she ought to write to her aunts. "I wish he would come home," she thought. "Perhaps I worry stupidly. My nerves seem to be all on edge these days. I may be missing the children." But this she doubted. Much as she loved them, the thought of their arrival, and the constant necessity for looking after them, brought her no joy.

She had forgotten about her lodger. A miserable certainty that both she and Teddy were approaching the end of their endurance robbed her of peace. He was so wretchedly unhappy. "I can't get near him nowadays."

She knew really why she could not get near him. " I can't bear him to be so unhappy," she told herself, but she could not bear either the remedy that he proposed. Besides, the doctor had forbidden it. Any emotional or physical excitement might destroy him.

She moved forward slowly along the road, out of the yard and into the first field. Black pools of shadow lay below the ash trees. The stone wall dripped black shadow on to the grass. The road curving to the brow of the hill was empty.

" He'll be coming over the hill in a few minutes," she told herself, and returned into the yard, following the wall as it dipped along the uneven ground, then resting her elbows on it, watching the dark hillside.

A movement in the shadow just below her on the other side of the wall startled her. " Oh, who's that? "

It was Paul Szermai, sitting with his back against the stone, his hands clasped round his thin ankles.

" Good gracious! I'd forgotten all about you. I'm so sorry. Why ever didn't you come in for some supper? "

She felt quite cross with him.

For once he did not spring politely to his feet. " I want no supper, thank you," he said, and the tense misery of his pose struck her almost with the force of a physical blow.

" I forgot you," she went on, feeling that explanations were necessary, " because I'm a little worried about my husband. He ought to be back by now."

" It is a fine night. And it is early. It is not yet half past nine. He is enjoying company."

Joanna found her irritation increasing. What did he

mean by being so miserable? Wasn't there misery enough in their house already? She wanted him to be inhuman and exciting. She was so tired of the pervading misery of men.

"Have you been here all the evening?" she asked.

"Yes. Since I came in at five o'clock."

"Oh, then you've had no tea. You must be starving. You're not ill, are you?" She couldn't do with him if he were going to be ill. Really she had had more than her share of illness. She was so tired of a world dominated by physical things.

"No. I am well. I was remembering only, and one should not remember."

"I call that ungrateful. If I were you I should want to do nothing at all but remember. You're ungrateful for your luck. Think of the heavenly places that you've seen and the things you've done! Why, if I'd travelled as you've travelled, I'd never want to be done with my remembering." She shut her eyes and saw the sudden delicate flowering of a city into domes and spires. Black cyprus trees pointed away from it up to the evening sky. She stood in the blue dusk of Fiesole, looking down upon Florence, and knew the joy of a lover when after many days he sees his mistress.

"Why," she cried hotly. "You've got no business ever to be miserable, you who are so rich in memories. You're like a spoiled child. Oh, I've no patience with you. You've done all the things I ever wanted to do. You've seen everything. I only wanted just for a minute, a minute, really to see one island, one really foreign city, and I've had nothing, nothing, and you've had them all. You've been all round the world and you're not grateful."

" You tell me to remember," he said harshly. " You think that that would be very agreeable for me, do you? Well, I tell you then that I do remember." With his hands still on his ankles, he rocked gently to and fro. " I do remember."

" Oh, dear, now I've started him off, and he'll want to tell me all about his troubles," sighed Joanna. " I have heard enough troubles in my time. I don't want any more. I want to hear about happy things."

Aloud she said, " You never told me about your home in Hungary. Which part did you come from? " " Homes are by no means necessarily happy things," reflected Joanna, " but men generally seem to like to talk about them."

" My home? Ah. That was in Transylvania."

" I know where that is. That's to the East of Hungary, and part of it belongs to Roumania now, doesn't it? And it's full of forests. Oh, is that why you know so much about trees? "

" My father was of the nobility," continued Szermai, without reference to her interruption, which suddenly seemed to her to have been rather gauche. Perhaps one did not mention Roumania to somebody from Eastern Hungary. It might be like mentioning sausages to a pig, or red rags to a bull, or . . .

" We were of an old family and had large estates, though until my father's time they had been neglected and the family had not been rich. My father was something of a genius. Yes, I think so. He was a Liberal, and in more ways than one. We are not, as you seem to think in this country, all barbarians there. By no means. I have seen Hungarian estates run in such ways before the War that everything I have seen about here seems most primitive in comparison. My father was a practical man. He saw that if we would continue in the old ways we must continue poor. And that did not please him. He himself studies irrigation, and we have, when I was quite a small boy, a system of dams and drains from the river down to the valley that regulate the water supply. You must know that after 1867, Hungary is often very advanced. Very. We had a model dairy too, and my elder brother was sent to Denmark to study electricity applied to agriculture. When he returned we were to have cows milked by electricity, though the peasants do not like this at all. By no means."

" Had you many brothers and sisters? "

" Two brothers and one sister. My sister married when very young. I have not heard of her for years. It was a commonplace marriage. My brothers were educated, one in Vienna, one in Paris, and I went to the university at Cambridge. As you know. When I left Cambridge I travelled round the world. My father had plenty of money then. He thought it a good thing to do. We have always been wide travellers, we Hungarians. I came home in 1913."

" What did you mean to do? "

" To marry. I fell in love."

" O-oh." Somehow Joanna had not quite expected this.

" She was the only child of some near neighbours of ours and heiress to an estate, not so large as ours, but quite considerable and of a very good family. Her name was — never mind. What does it matter to you what her name was? She was very beautiful. Much of her time she spent in Buda and in Vienna. She had a lovely voice. She — ah, but what is the use of trying to describe to you my countrywomen when you have never seen anything like the grace, the elegance of them? There is a soft brown bloom on them, and a brightness unlike any other women. My love was tall, like a princess, slender and beautifully made. There was not a moment of her life which she did not make exquisite. And she was alive, alive, in a ball-room, playing tennis, riding down the long forest paths, talking, singing. She was full of eager life. She loved living."

Joanna's attention strayed off to the hill and to the road along which Teddy must drive. She hardly heard Paul Szermai's story.

§ 2

" My father tells me that if I will go for one year to Finland to study a new system of forestry there, I may come home and have a small country-house which belonged to the estate near Jobbágytelke and in return I shall give advice about the afforestation of the country. We were all determined to make this Hungary of ours most beautiful and prosperous.

" Well, I did not want to go, but my love says to me, ' Go. It is only a year. When you return, we will be married. We will have Jobbágytelke and a little house near the Vervoshy Útsca in Buda. I will wait for you. I will write to you every week. The time will soon pass.'

" So I went north, in the spring of 1914, with letters of introduction to a family called Faushufrud, with whom I was to stay in Helsingfors and who were to show me all that I needed to see. They also had estates up in the country, near one of the lakes, and forests there, and very advanced knowledge of forestry.

" There was a son, Henning Faushufrud, and he and I soon became friends. They were not of the nobility, you understand, but of the higher bourgeoisie and rich. Also they were people of culture. They carried on a large timber trade in England. The old man owned a line of boats that went to Kingsport. Henning was a fine young Finn, a great patriot, and they all shared a hatred for the dark chaos of Russian barbarism over-shadowing their country.

" Until this time I had thought little about politics. I knew of course something of the noble history of my own land, and of how Hungarian civilization had marched step by step with English civilization, since the thirteenth century, when the Golden Bull of our King Andreas II was promulgated fourteen years after your Magna Charta. I knew that my countrymen had stood as the outpost of Western civilization against the Turk, but until I went to Finland I had never seen the fruits of injustice, the stirring of savagery, no, not even in Mexico, nor in China."

His voice dropped. He seemed to be gathering to-gether his memories of injustice. Joanna wished that she had a watch. She did not like to interrupt him and ask the time. It seemed so rude.

"At Cambridge I had read law, though I did little work there. I preferred riding and visiting and sport. But I had learnt enough to see that your English legal school is one of optimism. An evolution of order. Liberty flowing easily through precedent into coherent form. Yes. I was dancing and having a good time, but when I thought at all, it was to see the constitutional development of a state growing slowly and easily as a tree grows, almost apart from any human effort.

"I saw in Finland at once that this is not so. You have never lived in a country on the eve of revolution. You do not know the swift secret goings and comings, the letters hastily dispatched, the travellers by night, the house where no door opens but heads are lifted in anticipation. You do not know the nameless unrest invading every trivial act of life.

"But I know. I saw. My friends, Henning Faushufrud and his father, did not feel the pressure of Russian imperialism as a distant menace. It was there, about them, an ever-present evil. And they were good patriots. They saw too that their own common people, the peasants on their estate, the working men of Helsingfors, had been deceived by the friendliness of the Russian malcontents, even as our workers were afterwards deceived in Hungary. They confused Russian conditions with those of Finland. They thought that salvation could come from a general upheaval, from destruction of property, from short-cuts to Utopia. But my friends knew that Finland, even as Hungary, had laws and justice and a trained sense of freedom; that all it needed was political independence to enjoy the rights which were its heritage and to develop internally along its own national lines. There were in Finland then two hopes for the future, the Red hope of revolution united with Russian Socialists, the White hope of national independence."

" All this," thought Joanna, " would be very interesting if he were giving a university extension lecture. As it is, I want to know whether Teddy is all right. I wonder if I could interrupt Tam Lin and ask him to walk towards the village to see if he can see any signs of Teddy? "

But Paul Szermai's voice swept on remorselessly.

"Look, your husband is always talking about the need for political action, the Red Menace here, and the brotherhood of those who were in the fighting forces. But he has never seen revolution. I tell you, I tell you there is something exciting about political revoluton. It makes one alive. A man is conscious of life when at any moment a door may open and a hand be laid on his shoulders and he marched off to a wall to face the rifles. There is noise, and movement, and the motor-cars dash about, and telephone bells ring, and there is no time for proper meals, nor leisure; but we all have revolvers, yes, and mass meetings, and talk, talk, talk until the daylight. Ah, then one feels that something great is surely at hand, because there is never time to eat a proper meal. It is the fine gamble for life, the rich adventure that seems so good. For a time. It is when death is close at hand that life tastes most sweet; and that is why those who, like your husband, seek to stop wars and to make your pacifist Leagues impose peace upon us, why you will never succeed. You rob man of his precious heritage of danger.

" My friend says to me, ' But never mind. We will drive out to the forests.' I never now see larches and Scotch firs, but I remember that drive on the soft country road. We stopped continually to notice the setting of the young trees. The car could sometimes hardly move for the mud, but we cared little. Henning was telling me of how his father had been refusing to obey illegal Russian orders which ran against the laws of his own country. And I, look, Mrs. Leigh, I was indifferent. I thought ' This has nothing to do with me.' I wanted to get back to Hungary, to learn my lesson and return to my love. I nearly lost patience when I heard on the road behind us horses, galloping horses, coming to arrest my friend because he and his father were guilty of illegal practices, contravening the Russian law.

"We drove back to Helsingfors accompanied by a mounted guard. Two Russian police were in the back of the car with loaded rifles. Well, it was nothing new.

" But the old man, who was in the Finnish Landtag, had not had time to destroy his papers, and the house was full of police. Then there was a trial. A mockery of a trial. Tsarist or Bolshevik, Russia has no sense of free justice, as in Hungary, or even in England, they have learned it. They sentenced old Faushufrud to Siberia, he, whom afterwards the working class in Finland were to call a tool of the Tsar, a butcher, an oppressor. Pah! There was no gratitude, no sense in those *canailles.* My friend, Henning, felt it dishonour to remain behind. Therefore he struck a Russian guard over his ugly face, and he also went, though not to Siberia. They sent him to prison in St. Petersburg, I beg your pardon, to St. Leningrad, under sentence of death for treason.

"He had been my friend. Before they take him away, he says, 'Wait for me. Look after my mother!' What could I do? It was a nightmare to me. I appeal to my consul. He says, 'Be still. You will only be suspect. You can do nothing.' The old lady asks me to go to Petersburg to be near her son. To get news. I apply for leave to enter Russia. But I am suspect. They know that I was with him when he was arrested. I am Hungarian. We all know what love Holy Russia had then for my countrymen. I write to my brother. He says, 'Come home.' But like a fool I stay, living with Madame Faushufrud, interviewing officials, trying to get into Russia, soiling my ticket with every one. So. That was in July. In August, you know what happens. Austro-Hungary is at war with Russia. I am an enemy alien in Russian territory, already suspected of complicity in Finnish national risings.

"What can you expect? I was packing my things. 'I will be off,' I said to Madame Faushufrud. 'I can do no more.' They arrested me for acting as *agent provocateur* for the Hungarian Government. Fools. Fools. And I? A million times a fool. Why could I not have gone back before? Why did I not go back? There was my love, tearing her heart out for news of me, and here was I tied by the heels by my own folly, folly, folly!"

154

He dropped his face into his hands, and Joanna, roused out of her inattention, looked down upon him pityingly. " Oh, poor young man. Poor young man." She knew already that this story must have a tragic end.

§ 3

" For four years," he said at last, very quietly. " For four interminable years. For four years I was cut off from all decency, all comfort, all equal companionship, all knowledge of the outside world. And do you know why I speak all these peasant languages so well? Why I am such a good interpreter? Because for four years my only amusement was in talking to my fellow prisoners. You have smiled at me because you say that I sit always on the edge of my chair, that I do not appreciate the admirable food you serve me. For four years I have slept on planks in a filthy hut. I have had no change of linen. I have known what it is to starve. You say that I look young. You say that my manner is sometimes the manner of a boy. I have lost four years of my life. I have been dead. I have . . .

" Listen. For four years I knew as certainly as I know now that there is no more peace for me on this side of the grave, that I must get back to Hungary. My love was needing me. That if I do not get back soon, it will be too late. I tried three times to escape before I got away. It is not wise to escape. No. No. If you are dead, better to lie quiet. To escape is like moving again after you have been cramped. It is like regaining consciousness after a blow on the head. It is agony after despair. Hope may be hideous. I tell you, I tell you.

"In 1917 the revolution came, and some of the prisoners were released. But I, do you see, had been clever enough to get myself suspect every way. I had talked in prison. Who was I to fawn upon these illiterate peasants? Who was I to keep still and see injustice done? Tsarist tyranny, Bolshevik tyranny, what were names to me? I wanted to go home. Ah, but my love lay in Hungary and I could not go to her!

"When I heard that the others had been allowed to go and that I was still a prisoner, I would have taken their oaths. I would have sworn black white and God the devil. I would have spat upon my mother's grave, I do believe, if they would have given me a passport through to Hungary.

"You in England who truckle to these men, who speak of toleration, who allow your members of Parliament to visit Russia, to receive hospitality, hospitality, ye gods! You do not know what it is like to lie night after night and know that I could have got through to Hungary and to my love if I had sold my honour — in time. Now, it seemed, that my honour had no market value.

"In April of 1918 the Red armies of Finland were being defeated by the White armies and by the Germans. Some of us were sent to a place called Tavastland to do forced labour for our Red captors, making earthworks for the fortifications, or working in the Valkiakoski paper factory producing paper for the lying pamphlets, which circulated reports to poison men's minds as bullets destroyed their bodies. A paper factory, that was an important possession, I can tell you. It was

the fifteenth of April. You see, I remember the details.
You may find all this on record if you care to verify
what I say. The woods on the way to the factory were
full of small flowers and the birds sang. My love had
said, ' I will ride in the woods and think of you.' Four
years ago. Four centuries. I do not even know if she
is alive. Ah, but I do! I do! I tell you I knew quite certainly that she was waiting for me, that she had kept
faith with me. Kept faith? Dishonour could not be mentioned in the same breath as that proud, honourable
woman. Ah, my dear!

" On the way to work, the Lenin-boys pick out two
decent, middle-aged men, employees at the factory, and,
for no reason that I ever learned, they shoot them, leaving their bodies in the wood. And suddenly I know that
this is my time. There was a stir among the prisoners.
One, a clergyman whom I disliked very much, for the
irritating sniff he had, and his vulgarity of address, he
broke rank and began to run. The group breaks. The
guards lower their rifles. And I run too.

" There were not yet leaves on the trees. Oh, how we
prayed for leaves, my clergyman and I. At least, he
prayed. But I did nothing but run and run. The earth
was marshy. It sucked at our feet as we ran. And the
rifle shots break little branches of undergrowth. The
twigs catch at our faces. Everywhere, everywhere, a
noise of shooting and calling and the fear that we may
turn in a circle in those woods — did we not know the
stories? — and find ourselves face to face with our pur-
suers. Yet always the cries grow fainter. The kindly
trees close in upon us. The sound of pursuit dies away.

"I was a week in those woods with that man. He caught a cold, and the sniff was worse than ever. Listen. We were hiding for our lives. For more than our lives. If they had caught us then, they might have tortured us. It was the fashion. And yet I could think of nothing but of the way that man sniffed and of his fat thick voice. And he was always praying and talking about the Deity. If ever you run for your life, remember to choose a congenial companion. We ate roots, and the little tender green buds, and rabbits caught in a trap, set perhaps by a peasant. Well, then I drink some tainted water, perhaps, or perhaps it is a chill. I take fever. That clergyman — the worst of it is that he was a decent fellow. He saved my life. He got me somehow into a woodsman's hut, and because he is a priest the peasants obey him. He nursed me and saw that they fed me. He had a way with him certainly. And when I was better, the revolution had ended and there was peace with Russia, and my friend Faushufrud's party was in power, and I was free to go back if I like to Hungary.

"But it was not so simple. I had no passport, no money, no name. I might be anybody, nobody. I get back to Helsingfors, yes. But where are my friends? Such a scarecrow as I, dead, you see, for four years. If you have no money and no name, you might as well stay dead. I begin to wonder, ' Am I indeed Paul Szermai? ' When people look at you with suspicion, when you have no boots, no jacket, who is there to say that you are yourself? And I was also ill.

"I would have gone to Sweden. But I had no money.

158

There is fighting on the frontier in Poland against Russia. There is excitement in Lithuania. Everywhere things are changing. One cannot say from day to day which country is at peace and which at war. It is a nightmare world. One cannot even say which country is which. I tell you, it took me four months to get to Prag. I say, 'I will go from Prag to Vienna and so to Buda.' Yes; but this is November and peace has been declared now with France, but there is a revolution in Prag and the Czechs say that they are now independent. A nightmare, I tell you. You no sooner reach a country but it has changed to something else. The very languages changed. In Prag, men will not speak German. Oh, it was comical, comical, if it had not been that in Hungary I knew my love was waiting and I must get to her.

"Delay. Delay. The Czechs do not love the Hungarians. I am suspect and put in prison again. I have grown so used to prison that if I came to a strange town, I would make for the prison almost by instinct now, I think. I, who have done nothing. But nothing. I did not even have that satisfaction. Well, it was all a mistake. They decide that though a Hungarian I may be harmless. I am released, after four months in Prag. So that is good.

"In February, I am in Vienna. Actually. In Vienna where I have friends and influential relatives and money and everything. Would you believe it? Is it possible that in man's history there has been greater chaos? In Vienna I find another revolution."

Joanna, wrought up both with the emotional strain of

the story, her own anxiety about Teddy and the cold darkness of the night began to giggle.

"Oh, laugh, laugh; funny, wasn't it? I think it the most humorous joke that was ever perpetrated. I get to Vienna. I go round to seek my friends. And lo, the humble have been exalted, the rich man has been sent empty away. The Kärtnerstrasse shops are all nailed up. The Hofburg is an office. Women in the streets, in clothes that have been bought in Paris, are selling trinkets and starving before your eyes. It is a city of ghosts. Well, I had some decent bourgeois acquaintances, their father had been a lawyer employed once by my father in a suit taken to a court in Vienna about some shares in an engineering company. I hear that Fraiserhof lives out near Schönbrunn, so I go. Would you believe it? Actually, he is there. It was the first thing that happened as might have been expected in the whole of those five nightmare years.

"He lends me money. No, he had heard no news of my father, my brothers. He fears though that my elder brother was killed in the early years of the War. But Hungary will be all right. They were not so short of food there as in Austria. Well, things are bad here. Bad everywhere. The world is coming to an end.

"I had money. I had friends and a name. That night I would take the train across the frontier. I was going home. Ah, but I have known happiness! After nightmare, to be awake again. After frenzy, to be sane. After namelessness and captivity to be a free man, to have a place in the world. They drank my health and my good fortune.

" Old Fraiserhof talked a little about Hungary. He said that Karyoli was not to be trusted. He might sell Hungary to the Russians in return for help against the plots of Czechs and Serbs and those Roumanians. He talked about Wilson this, Wilson that. I hardly knew this Wilson. What did I care for politics? I was a free man and I was going home.

" Besides, Karyoli was a gentleman. I had known him when a boy. A weakling, you understand, with a hare-lip. Degenerate, we thought him. He might have got into bad company, been flattered. But what did it matter? What patience had I with politics when in twenty-four hours I might see my love?

" I knew then that I had not dared to think of her, never dared in my long captivity to picture her face, to call her voice to my mind, to dream of our meeting. But now when we were so near, I dared to think of her. She seemed so near that as we approached the Hungarian frontier, at every station I put my head out of the window, thinking that by some miracle she might be standing there on the platform. Almost I saw her, with her lifted chin, and the grace of her slender body and her proud smile. I knew quite certainly, quite certainly, that she was alive and free and waiting for me. I felt her coming nearer and nearer. I tell you, it was not hallucination.

" It was the truth."

Far off in the dale a dog began to bark forlornly. Joanna shuddered. In the pit beyond Linders Fell the foxes answered him.

" At the frontier," said Paul Szermai very quietly,

" they stopped the train again. It was quite natural. I had expected it and my papers were ready. But they tell us that there has been another revolution. Karyoli has sold the country to the Russians, the Russians, and Belá Kuhn had declared a Bolshevik republic.

" They look at our papers and make us descend from the train. Some are allowed to get on again. But I am told that they must make inquiries. I must wait until next day. I saw the lights of the train swing off round the curve of the platform into the darkness and knew that my chance had come and gone.

" It was then that I lost my head. I ran down the platform. I tried to board the train that was no longer there. I fall and break my leg. Fool, fool, fool, fool.

" You may say that these things do not happen. What do you know? It was my folly that betrayed me. My own impatience. Now listen, you who think that I have only to remember to be gay.

§ 4

" I had been right. I had been right in the madness of my belief. My love was waiting for me.

" During the war she had nursed the wounded. She had suffered privations. A little. Not too much. When my father had died of influenza, she went to comfort my mother. When my elder brother was killed, she said to her, ' Never mind. Paul will return.' She was quite certain. They tell me that she grew more beautiful than ever — thin, a little, but gay, gay, with a sort of gallant courage.

" So. The Peace comes. The peace of villains and

traitors, though then we do not know. She hears that
Wilson and the French are going to sell our lands in
Transylvania to the Roumanians, to those little people,
peasants, who have always been servants to the Magyar
when they have not been slaves to the Turk. She, who
is so young and fragile, is undaunted. My father is
dead. My brothers are dead. But I am alive, and the
estates are mine. She had not heard from me, mind you,
for four years. She knew nothing but that Finland had
swallowed me up, yet she sets herself to fight for my
estates for me. She went to Buda. She interviewed
Karyoli. She sees military officers, French attachés, the
whole of the Liberal party. She guessed their corruption.
There was no help from them. She went to the royalists.
If there is a chance of a fight, she will fight too, for the
Holy Crown of St. Stephen, and for me, for my rights,
my property.

" This was happening when I was at the station. The
night when I leapt from the platform after the train, she
was driving from Budapest with her old mother and
father. And I — I was lying in a wretched school house
in a frontier village, and Karyoli had sold his country
to the Bolshevik.

" For my love knew that for a time there is no hope
in Hungary. I think that she had intentions of getting
to Paris and seeing President Wilson for herself.
Heaven knows what schemes were in her gallant brain.
I am sure that she did not despair, but she determined
then to leave the country.

" They cannot get passports in their own names, but
she sells what are left of her jewels and buys the pass-

port of an old gardener and his wife and daughter. Also a market cart and ragged clothes. She dressed herself and her mother and father in the old, filthy rags. She put on her body, which had only known fragrant silks the evil-smelling clothes of a peasant girl. Early in the morning they drive out of Buda.

"Her mother afterwards told me the story of that drive. Always they were being stopped. Always they had the papers, the old horse and the vegetables. Always they were going just to the next village along the road. Always she tells the two old people, 'It cannot be impossible. Paul is waiting for us.' She was as sure as I had been sure.

"You told me to shut my eyes. Well, they are shut now, and I can see them travelling. It is very cold, and the ploughed lands have the faint pink of turned earth, with a green haze of springing corn. The women in the fields, with their white handkerchiefs about their heads, glance up at the cart, then back again to their work. There are no towns. Only the scattered villages.

"The horse is very old and they go slowly. They stop one night in a filthy inn where the beds are covered with vermin. I do not know how long the journey took. Her mother's story was confused. A lifetime. At such times, hours have little meaning.

"Then late one evening the cart gets a wheel into a deep rut, and the horse stumbles and falls. My love was the gentlest of creatures. She had a most tender heart to all animals. But I suppose that she was half mad with anxiety and fatigue. She sprang from the cart, and fell and sprained her wrist. But she did not care. She shouted to the horse. She tugged at the bridle. And when it would not get up again, she seized the whip and she began to strike it.

"I think it very strange that it was this thing which destroyed her, this thing which of all that she did was the most unlike herself. Just as it was my own folly which destroyed me when I leaped after the moving train. We had both been so certain.

"A peasant comes up and scolds her for cruelty to the animal. And she, who is already in tears, horrified at what she has done to the old horse, turns on him and rends him with her tongue. She will not be spoken to so by a rude peasant. I can imagine how she spoke to him. And he, well, he walks in to the next village reflecting that there is something very odd about that party there with the cart. Something that does not smack of the class-conscious proletariat.

"But all night they sit there by the roadside, the old man asleep and the mother whimpering that my love is a wicked girl to bring them all here to die of cold by the wayside.

"And my love sat very straight, her mother told me. She was in pain from her sprained wrist, and she had cried a little over the horse when she found that it was dead. But now she did not look unhappy. Expectant, her mother told me, as though she was waiting for somebody.

"In the first light of the morning men came along the road. They were Red Guards. The peasant whom she had scolded had reported them as suspicious characters.

Do you know, they had sat all night so near the frontier that if they had set off to walk, they could have walked over. Quite easily! Straight into the village where I lay in the old school house, another suspicious character, of course, with my leg in a splint.

" They were taken to the village headquarters, in the customs house, I think it was, and examined. The old man would not stand such impertinence and gave himself away completely. They disposed of him easily enough. They took him and shot him against the wall. I remember from time to time that I heard shots. I cannot tell if this was one which I heard. It may well have been.

" They said to my . . . they said that a pretty girl had no business to play such tricks. She said, ' If you will let my mother go safely across the frontier, I will play you a prettier trick than that.' They ask, ' What do you mean? ' She says, ' Let my mother go, and a fine fellow like you should have little more need of questions.' She told her mother quickly to do as she said. That it would be quite all right. That she would follow. She looked, not unhappy nor desperate at all, but excited, eager, as though she were playing a game in which she could not lose. She seemed so confident that her mother, dazed and terrified as she was, allowed herself to be led away. Of course, they cheated her. They only brought her to the old school house, where in the boys' department, I lay a prisoner.

" They put her into the girls' department with other women captured on the frontier, suspicious characters. When at last I saw her, the Roumanians were entering

Hungary from the east: the Allies were threatening from the west. The Lenin boys no longer kept guard on the frontier for Belá Kuhn. I had begun to drag myself about on crutches.

" It was she who recognized me. I should never have known her. ' Of course,' she said, ' we knew that you would come. She always said that you were waiting. We had better go into the village and find her. Perhaps she has played her pretty trick by now. A clever girl and brave, but very headstrong. You'll find her a diffi-cult wife to manage, Paul. We gave her too much of her own way.'

" It was bright summer, August, when I at last en-tered the village. I could walk quite well again. The revolution is over. We can, they say, all go home if we like.

" I made inquiries. But there had been so many girls. Yes, the innkeeper thought that he could remember one, a stranger. Dressed like a peasant. They said that she was a countess or something in disguise. No, that was the actress from Lintz. Everyone was confused. But some woman, anyway, had been shot or had shot herself, and been buried in the ditch at the back of the customs house, and an officer of the Red Guard with her. They rather thought that she had shot him first and then herself. It was difficult to remember. So many such things happened.

" That night I took a spade and a lantern and went to the ditch behind the customs house. The place was over-grown with coarse weeds, dock and darnel and cow parsley, and great cobwebs netted over the little thorn bushes. A rank, evil place enough. The villagers threw their broken pots and bits of old ironware down there.

" I began to dig."

" Did you, did you — find her? " Joanna asked tentatively, when the silence had lasted so long that she could bear it no longer.

" I do not know. I do not know. I suppose that I shall never know. For that happened in March and this was August, and the place was very damp. They used no coffins. By the third night of digging I had found four bodies, not buried very deep. You could tell by the stench of the place that it was a burial-ground. And I do not know if one of the things that I found was my love's body.

" Well, I went back to Buda. I learn that both her estates and mine are confiscated. By the Roumanians. It is quite funny. I forget what offence I have committed. Something technical, I fancy, done without my knowledge. My mother, at any rate, is with my married sister. The woman who never became my mother-in-law was with her relatives in Austria. And I — there was no place for me in Hungary. Not yet. Not yet.

" But I know that I have a sacred duty. One day I will render back evil for evil. I will avenge. Wherever I learn that there is action to be taken against Russia, there will I go. When I heard that in Finland there was to be a great White offensive against the Bolshevik I went to Finland again. I have been here, there, everywhere. I wanted to return to England, but I had no money. I wanted to learn if it was true that yours was the only country where Bolshevism had gained no power. I hear of Sir Wentworth's forest scheme. Well, here I am. You say, ' Remember.' Tell me, Mrs. Leigh, do you think it is likely that I shall forget? "

" Oh I am sorry. I am so very sorry," said Joanna.

" I do not want your sorrow. I do not ask for pity. Why should you be sorry? Are you not thinking while I talk, ' But I have my own troubles? Why should he burden me with his? ' You do not want my memories. You are not sorry. You know nothing, nothing at all." He had sprung up and climbed across the low wall to her. " It is perhaps all lies that I have told. Just a good tale. These things do not happen. The ingenuity of fortune is stupid and clumsy but not devilish. Not like this. Ah, you . . . you do not understand at all."

" Beg pardon, but is that Mrs. Leigh? "

They spun round to face young Brindle, standing sheepishly in the yard behind Joanna.

" I'm sorry to intrude, but we came back with your husband, Paxton and I. Drove back up the low road. I couldn't find you anywhere. Door open, too. Thought you must have flitted maybe."

" Is — is Teddy ill? "

" Oh, nothing to worry, a common complaint, you know, after a bit of a gay evening. He'll be all right in the morning except a headache, maybe."

Young Brindle's sympathies were all with Captain Leigh, whose wife was now so plainly proved to be no better than she ought to be.

CHAPTER NINE

THE SCARLET WOMAN

§ 1

MR. BOYSE had made up his mind that something must be done about it. He was, after all, in spiritual *loco parentis* to the Leighs, since his Rector had absorbed himself completely in tracing Phœnician settlements on the Cornish coast, an admirably appropriate pastime for a Yorkshire clergyman. But when you have a large private income and a good curate, Mr. Boyse reflected, you must be permitted certain latitudes. Only the Rector's absence did at times involve Boyse in awkward situations.

Everyone in the village was discussing the Scatterthwaite Scandal, the rumour reaching quite enviable proportions, and revealing an ingenuity of observation and deduction, worthy, one might have supposed, of higher things. Mr. Boyse thought it all most regrettable — most.

First, there was the harbouring of the Hungarian, not necessarily an unwise, and certainly not a disreputable action. Besides, Lady Marshall herself had suggested it. But then there was the episode of the Lithuanian who had seduced — well, no, considering her record, hardly that — but had at least misconducted himself with Bessy Bottomley. And Mrs. Leigh chose him, of all people, to attend to her cows when he ought to have been working on the Fell.

There was the Concert. Exactly what had occurred there, it was hard to tell, but Mr. Grig's word of "nameless orgies" went echoing round the village. What orgies were like when named, Letherwick never paused to ask.

And Captain Leigh's extraordinary behaviour at the British Legion. So very unlike him to take too much to drink. "He must have been driven to it, poor chap," Mr. Boyse considered. Feeble health and a bad wife were evils with which the least imaginative could sympathize. And finally, there was young Brindle's discovery of Mrs. Leigh and the Hungarian practically in the act of — well, really. Far be it from Mr. Boyse to cast the first stone, but at the same time, Mrs. Leigh, you know. It was going a bit too far.

He knew now that he had been right in his judgment of her as a trifle odd. It was not merely because she wore green stockings, and said smart, uncomfortable things, and brought up her children badly, and proved herself to be no housekeeper; but because of that dangerous levity of manner, that impression which she created of temporary and incomplete adjustment to circumstance, as though she had never managed to settle down in life, as though her business of being a wife and a mother were somehow not quite real to her. Almost it seemed as though she were playing at being herself, and not quite serious.

Well, that was hard luck for her husband. As far as Mr. Boyse could gather, poor Leigh had collapsed pretty badly, been in bed ever since his unfortunate break at the British Legion. Somebody ought to take her to task, to pull her up before matters grew any worse.

Yet Mr. Boyse, sturdily climbing the steep road up to Scatterthwaite, wished the business well over and himself back with his troop of Boy Scouts, who were, for all their stolidity, jolly and decent and easier to manage than the complex problems of domestic and national ethics.

The dip of the hill showed him Scatterthwaite, its quiet grey stone buildings poured, as it were, into the cup of the paddocks. In the green fields, lambs played and cows were lazily feeding, warm in the April sunshine. Mr. Boyse had always before thought of the farm's isolation as of something a little sinister. But now, when he knew it to be an abode of evil, he saw it for the first time as homely and reassuring.

Yet here was the wall, surely, beside which Brindle had come upon Mrs. Leigh and the Hungarian. Three fat ducks now slept below it, their orange beaks buried in creamy feathers. The curate's approach aroused them; they uncurled their necks and regarded him with round, beady eyes, disapproving. With one accord they rose and waddled, cackling, towards the pond. It was hard to imagine scandalous passions in connection with creatures so innocent and comical.

Mr. Boyse, disarmed by rural placidity, almost wavered. Conscience, however, spurred him on, past the pigsties, where Rumour said that the Leighs had conspired to cut their black pig in pieces and bury the

corpse, to save notification of swine fever. He avoided
the little paved yard, where Joanna's household wash-
ing hung limply from lines, or straddled over into the
strip of garden, decorating the gooseberry bushes there.
Skirting the tangled flower-beds and the weed-grown
path, he found himself in front of the door, on which
Pamela's fat forefinger had squashed the paint bubbles
as far as her arm would reach.

Pausing outside to consider suitable openings for
his delicate topic of conversation, Mr. Boyse started at
a sudden noise. The door was torn open with a grinding
screech of warped wood on the bare tiles, and Mrs.
Leigh herself stood before him.

"Oh, Mr. Boyse, angels and archangels alone have
sent you. Never was man more welcome. Come in, come
in, do."

It was, he considered, hardly a suitable greeting from
a sinner to her spiritual pastor and master — not that
Mrs. Leigh had ever come to him in the past for spiritual guidance, but still she was in his parish, and she
was a clergyman's daughter, and had always welcomed
his visits. And that was how she ought to regard him.
Mr. Boyse wavered continually between his vision of
personal relationships as they should be, regulated by
his office, and the same relationships as they too often
were, regulated by his personality. That was where
Rome scored. A priest was a priest.

He followed Joanna apprehensively through her
shabby hall into the sitting-room. The sunlight revealed its poverty. There was no fire; and matches,
flower-stalks and apple-cores decorated the crumbling

ashes in the grate. A discarded meal lay on the table. An overturned work-basket had been left with cotton reels and darning wool strewing the carpet.

Joanna whisked a couple of shirts and some socks out of the chair and almost thrust the curate into it.

" Listen. You've got to help me," she said, half laughing, half desperate. " I'm at my wits' end. Dr. Hutton is up there with my husband now, and he's told me that he'll have to stay in bed at least for two months, perhaps six. His heart's gone all dicky. Now I can't, I simply can't manage the farm and the house and the dairy and nurse him properly. It's day and night, you know. I've got to find a couple who'll come in and look after the farm. I can take the nursing over then. You've got to help me."

" I — what — I mean — how can I be of use? "

Even in his embarrassment, he could not help noticing her remarkable appearance. Her short skirt was spattered with chicken food, her feet thrust into men's thick boots; but this day being the warmest of the spring, she had discarded the green jumper for an affair of orange silk, once made from an old petticoat and embroidered in a frivolous moment with blue and purple and bright scarlet birds. Her thick fair hair had grown from the orthodox bob into a wild and not unattractive mane, which stood out round her haggard, smiling face. In the last few months she had become quite outrageously thin. Her hands were red, and roughened with dirt. She spoke with vehement cheerfulness, as though things had become so bad that they could not

possibly be worse, and so might reasonably be expected
to turn for the better.

"Wait a second. Is that Dr. Hutton coming down?
No, it's all right, I think. Well, first of all, if you are
really going to be a dear, you might help me clear away
the breakfast things. You see, I have to have breakfast
properly, because of Mr. Szermai. That boy would eat
absolutely nothing if I didn't thrust the food down his
throat. And seeing he pays three guineas a week now,
though it's robbery, I simply have to see that he gets
something. No, carry the cups, will you? and I'll take
the coffee-pot." She was piling the soiled dishes together on to a battered tin tray. "We'll all have tea
together in Teddy's room if I can get these things
cleared up. It cheers him so much to have company."

He followed her into the disordered kitchen, and
before he knew quite what he was about, found himself
standing beside the crowded sink, drying the dishes
which she almost threw at him in a fury of conversation
and activity.

"This kitchen's a disgrace, isn't it? But what can I
do? You know, it's really awfully funny. I no sooner
get Teddy settled than Mr. Szermai wants something,
and as soon as he's supplied, the cows want milking or
the hens want their supper. You've no idea how I'm
getting to hate those hens. Didn't the ravens feed Elijah
or something? Can't you possibly train modern fowls
even to feed themselves? Degenerate age we live in,
don't we? And if the camp on the Fell breaks up next
month, I simply don't know how we are going to manage.
We're living on our lodger at the moment. And nobody

else could ever get people to come and milk for me, or to run in to the chemists at Clarington for Teddy's medicine. . . . No, you needn't bother to dry every prong of the fork. Just do anything with them. That is why you've got to find me somebody. Oh, and they must be able to drive the pony into the station. We've sent no butter to market for weeks."

" Mrs. Leigh," interposed Mr. Boyse, faint but valiant. " It was really as your spiritual . . ."

" Please. That coffee-pot goes on the shelf. It's all right, my cups aren't babies that you're baptizing. They won't cry if you pinch them. Yes, it was as a clergyman that I wanted you too. Teddy wants to have Holy Communion one morning. Could you arrange it? I know that it's a frightful drag up here. And, look here, Mr. Boyse, can't you persuade him that it's quite all right really to have a cup of tea and some bread and butter before the service? He wants to have it fasting, but you know, he can't stand it. He gets frightfully exhausted as it is, and is ill all day afterwards, and the iller he feels, the more depressed he gets, and really it doesn't do him any good. You'd have to come up awfully early; but of course, I'd love to give you breakfast afterwards. It might help him. I don't know. He seems to be terribly down in the mouth. Oh, damn that potato knife. I always forget that Tam Lin sharpened it for me."

" Have you cut yourself? "

" Er — Um." She stood with her thumb in her mouth, regarding the curate with an amused despair.

It was a deep cut. Mr. Boyse, expert as a Scout Master, looked round for a clean rag.

176

She produced a medicine chest of unexpected efficiency.

" Fortunately, I have most things for invalids," she explained, and when Dr. Hutton came down into the kitchen, he found his hostess sitting on the table while Mr. Boyse stood in front of her, bandaging her thumb, and breathing deeply.

" Hullo, hullo, has there been an accident? "

" Yes. A frightful one. I've cut my thumb off. But you're too late. Mr. Boyse has stuck it on again. Do you want tea? Look in the tin over there and see if we've got any cake, doctor."

The curate bent over his knots, tucking them in most carefully. For some reason or other, he blushed.

There was no cake, but half a dozen ginger biscuits, a little soft but otherwise none the worse for wear, lingered from the children's tea three months ago. Anyway, they won't break our teeth," said Joanna. Within ten minutes, a procession trooped up to Teddy's bedroom, carrying trays and bread and butter and a teapot.

Whatever other impression of squalid misery the rest of the house might convey, Teddy's room was bright enough. Great branches of young green decorated the tall vases. " Paul Szermai brought them for us. Aren't they lovely? " asked naïvely the woman supposed to be Paul Szermai's mistress.

Teddy, frail and facetious, propped upon pillows, hardly played up to the part of injured husband. The open window, Joanna's laughter, the cheerful clinking of cups and saucers, all defied the knowledge of imminent tragedy which haunted Mr. Boyse as it probably haunted the others. Captain Leigh was very ill, but he was holding forth at some length on the educational value of crossword puzzles. Joanna was probably guilty, yet she ate bread and jam with a childish appetite, and inquired wistfully about the preparations for the British Legion dance. Dr. Hutton, who probably knew more about the Scatterthwaite household than anyone else, simply enjoyed himself.

Mr. Boyse found it all very difficult.

Half-way through the hilarious meal, the stairs creaked again, the door opened, and in walked Paul Szermai. The curate had never before seen close at hand the young man around whom so much gossip centred. Now that he saw, he was not prepossessed. A dark, slender, morose person, with a slightly contemptuous manner, and a cold beautiful voice, which talked good English with occasional curious lapses of tense, Szermai seemed courteous enough, but not much interested. He drank his tea from a cracked cup, staring broodily at his hostess, and never smiling.

" You are, I hear, going to impose a ban upon my foresters in the village? " he asked at length.

" I — er — were you speaking to me? " stammered the curate, wishing that he would not. He did not know what to make of the situation, and wanted to escape without committing himself.

" Well, don't you know? or is it only a rumour? " The Hungarian looked almost as though he were despising him. " Are you frightened that we shall corrupt your morals, or is it because we may be Bolshevik? I assure you that these peasants are very harmless people. A little childish. But so few. Numbers alone are dangerous. You could dispose of us all in a few hours if you were so minded."

" But we, we don't want to dispose of you. Only, I think, a little narrow-mindedness, perhaps, you see, this isn't a continental village. Our fellows aren't used to foreigners knocking about. And then, one of your chaps hasn't behaved too well in the village, you know." Mr. Boyse was growing bolder. He would not be suppressed by this interloper, count or no count, this shabby Don Juan. Already he pictured himself doing battle for the morality of Letherwick, and for all simple decent English things, against a dark foreigner who never ought to have come at all.

" No. Ah, morality. That is very interesting. But you know I had thought that my peasants needed protecting. Fortunately they do not call upon my services as interpreter during their private intercourse with the village, but if I were you, I would tell your congregation not to take too much for granted. It would be awkward if we had knife-play here. My children of nature are a little crude."

" Paul dear, don't pretend to be sinister," said Joanna. " You're scaring Mr. Boyse." So it was "Paul dear " now, was it? The curate glanced at Captain Leigh to see how he took it.

He, apparently, took it for granted.

" I think you're making mountains out of molehills a bit, as far as the village is concerned, aren't you, Boyse? " asked Dr. Hutton.

" I hardly know what to say. There certainly is a lot

of strong feeling. If we are to get through this month, we shall all have to be careful. What do you think, Doctor? "

" A lot o' stuff and nonsense. We've got plenty to do in Lindersdale, without bothering about our neighbours' nationality."

" It must be all right. It must be all right," Mr. Boyse told himself, his wish begetting a small family of thoughts. " Dr. Hutton's an old cynic, but he knows everyone. Captain Leigh may be an invalid, but if his wife were really playing fast and loose with him, he'd hardly lie there so calmly and let that young Hungarian lay down the law in his bedroom. Mrs. Leigh's a bit queer, but she wouldn't call that fellow ' Paul dear ' under her husband's nose if there were anything in it."

The question was, ought someone to tell them what the village was saying? Well, there was Dr. Hutton, who knew them far better than anyone else. He talked about mountains out of molehills. Surely, if it was anyone's business, it was his. The clergy should not be scandalmongers. Scandal was, after all, beneath their notice. The business of Mr. Boyse was to bring the Sacrament to Captain Leigh. And to ask about a farmlabourer, certainly. And that grocery list which Mrs. Leigh mentioned.

" Teddy, isn't it splendid? Mr. Boyse says that he'll find a couple for us? " Joanna flashed her brilliant smile on the poor man. " And when is Sir Wentworth coming home? Look here, do you think that the Home Office or whoever it is who does passports will let Paul stay on a bit in England until Teddy's allowed to get up again? Paul, I'll teach you how to make butter. What fun! what fun. You'll be nearly as clumsy as I was."

" It looks all right. It must be all right," thought the curate.

Walking back to the village, he asked himself what he could have done differently. " I'll see what can be done to stop people's tongues," he told himself. " All the same, I wish the Lady Marshall were back. It's inconsiderate of the Marshalls to go away just when all this difficult business is on. But Mrs. Leigh's all right. Jolly as anything."

Finding a clear stretch of turf, he began to run. Running put beef into him, and blew away uncomfortable uncertainties.

§ 2

The curate's wish fathered too sanguine a conclusion. That night Joanna and Teddy had a scene.

It had been blowing up, Joanna knew, ever since the night Brindle had brought her husband home to her. She did not know exactly what had happened. Teddy had gone to the British Legion Club room, ostensibly to champion the cause of the foreign camp. Instead, he had drunk three or four glasses of whiskey, an almost fatal adventure to a man in his state of health. Now he was really ill, and more than that. His former moods of despair had been trifling compared to this dumb stupor of misery. " If only he'd talk to me. If only he'd say what's wrong. I can't bear it."

He was all right in company. He was all right even

when Szermai was with him. He seemed anxious, in
fact, to have the Hungarian about him as much as possible and complained bitterly if during the evening he
walked down to the village instead of playing bézique.

"He's got something on his mind." That was what
Dr. Hutton had seen. "What is it?"

"I don't know. Really I don't. I wish to Heaven I
did. It's horrible feeling him so unhappy, turning something over and over in his mind. I believe that he's
afraid he may have to go back to the sanatorium. It's an
obsession with him, that fear, you know."

"You don't think that something has got on his
nerves, somebody?" suggested the doctor. He had
looked at Joanna curiously.

"No. No. You see, there's nobody, except me. I
think, you know, that I do sometimes get on his nerves.
We've been very happy together, but of course, I'm
clumsy and untidy and not frightfully efficient."

"That does, of course, sometimes happen with the
best of us when we're sick, but I don't think so now,
Mrs. Leigh. What about your lodger?"

"Well, you know, about a month ago, I might have
thought it. Even a week ago. But since he's been ill,
Teddy seems to have depended frightfully on Mr. Szermai. He's been so awfully good, you know. He was up all
that night when Mr. Brindle brought Teddy home. And
now my husband hardly allows him out of his sight."

Then Mr. Boyse had come downstairs again, and
there had been no more conversation, but when Joanna
returned to Teddy, she found him thoroughly cross and
tired.

" I wish you'd tell that brute of a doctor not to pummel me about in that rotten way. Great coarse bully. If we were in any decent place and not in this godforsaken hole, I might get a doctor who understood me. That creature ought to have been a butcher, not a doctor, though I pity the bullocks he slaughtered. I'm bruised all over. And why the hell did you bring all that crowd up to my room for tea when you knew I was tired to death? "

Joanna, penitent, went to fetch his Bovril; but when she brought it, he wanted egg-flip. It was time to put the hens to bed, but she asked Szermai to do that for her and brought the egg-flip.

He sniffed it suspiciously.

" Where did you get this egg? "

" It's a new-laid one."

" New laid? By the hen out of Noah's Ark, I imagine. Good God, have I to endure a farm and not even get a fresh egg? Where did you find it? "

" Oh, Teddy darling, I really can't remember where I find every egg."

" No. You never can remember anything important, can you? I wonder you even remember that I'm your husband. But perhaps you don't remember that always, do you? I suppose that the farm never gets remembered at all. Really, it's hardly worth while my going to bed. There's so much accumulated work to do when I get up."

" Oh, well, we leave some things, you know. And as for the house, I'm like Aunt Kate. She used to say, ' I couldn't bear to live with a duster behind the picture. I just draw down the blind a little when company comes.' And as for the farm, Paul Szermai helps me immensely. Teddy, I don't know what we shall do when that man goes."

"Oh, don't you? Don't you? When you only have me, what? Isn't it a pity that you didn't marry him? "

"Don't be an ass, my beloved." She picked up the glass, trying not to show the frayed edge of her nerves. "'I love no love but you,'" she sang, smiling at him.

"So glad to hear it. I suppose that Paul Szermai knows nothing of love, does he? "

"Oh yes, he does. Poor Paul. He knows too much. I feel, oh, I feel so frightfully sorry for him, Teddy."

"Oh, you do, do you? Well, don't make a hobby of being sorry for too many men, my girl. It might get us a bad name, you know. Pity you were sorry for me first, isn't it? "

"Teddy, don't be so ridiculous. I'm going to make you a new egg-flip with a fresh egg, if I have to lay it myself."

"Don't go downstairs. Is Szermai in? "

"Maybe. I asked him to go and shut up the hens for me. He ought to be finished by now."

"Ah, then please don't let me detain you. By all means go to him."

"My dear goose, I'm going to make your egg-flip."

"Can't Szermai beat the eggs for you? Can't he make flips? God, how do I know what you do when you're not in this room? How do I know how you're carrying on behind my back? A cheerful thing for me, isn't it, to have to lie here while you gad about everywhere, entertaining your friends, and being sorry for people? "

" Now you're just being stupid. I'm not going to listen to you. You're tired out and you're letting your nerves get the better of you. You're talking absolute nonsense. You know that I'm in and out of your room all the day. And as for Szermai, he's a terribly unhappy and tragic young man, who's been extraordinarily good to both of us, considering that he's our lodger, and we put upon him quite shamelessly. But when Mr. Boyse gets us somebody, we shan't be so badly off. And I shall have more time for you. So please, dear, be reasonable. You make yourself ill, worrying over nonsense."

" Nonsense, is it? That I have to lie alone hour after hour? I might die at any moment when you're out of the room. I might have a hæmorrhage. Why, you even sent the children away. You may not miss them, but I do. Any other woman would have got servants long ago and kept the children. It's massive selfishness. You may have no natural feelings as a mother, but I have some as a father. I want to see them again before I die."

" Teddy, look here. You're working yourself up into a state about nothing. It's awfully bad for you. I'm going downstairs to make you another drink, and when I come up again, I'll bring my mending, or I'll read to you if you like. Just as I used to do, until you go to sleep."

" I don't want any drinks. Everything that you make is filthy. Doesn't everyone know that the way you treat me has made me ill again? I was beginning to get better. I'd almost stopped dreaming of that damned sanatorium. And then you upset me, and it all comes back again. Any other wife would have cared whether I got better. You don't want me to get better, that's what it is. You'd like to be done with the nuisance of me."

But Joanna could bear no more.

" Teddy, be quiet. Do you think that I'm made of stone? Oh, be quiet."

She ran out of the room. She ran downstairs. In the dark kitchen she walked up and down, biting her lips and trying to choke the sobs that shook her.

" I can't stand any more. I can't. I can't."

The old spell of her childhood returned to her. " Nothing's ever so bad as you think it's going to be." It wasn't true. Things could be just as bad.

Teddy was perhaps going out of his head. People with tuberculosis sometimes did. " This is up to me," she told herself. " This is up to me. I won't let him. He's my Teddy. He's my darling. I won't let him hurt me. I've got to help him."

She sank down in the Windsor chair at the end of the table and assumed her favourite attitude, her hands covering her face, shutting out the unlovely sight of her present surroundings, enclosing her in the garden of her imagination. Now was the time, if ever she had known it, when Agnes must come to her, riding in her swaying palanquin. Now was the time when the green groves of the bamboo should shimmer with falling light. Now down the glades of her heart's El Dorado, should Beauty walk to bring her rest and comfort.

" On both sides of this river we passed the most beautiful country that ever mine eyes beheld; and whereas all that we had seen before was nothing but woods, prickles, bushes and thorns, here we beheld plains of twenty miles in length, the grass short and green and in divers parts groves of trees by themselves as if they had by all the art and labour in the world been so made of purpose, and still as we rode the deer came down feeding by the water's side, as if they had been used to the keeper's call."

That was Guiana. Sir Walter Raleigh steered their skiff down the placid river. Agnes said, " Come along. I should like to walk," and they all disembarked, and sauntered slowly through the enchanted country, " the deer crossing in every path, the birds towards evening singing in every tree with a thousand several tunes, cranes and herons of white, crimson and carnation, perching on the river's side, the air fresh, with a gentle easterly wind, and every stone that we stopped to take up promised either silver or gold by his complexion."

Then Sir Walter, who was an egoist, like all great and beautiful persons, said, " Now let us sing."

And Agnes, who was always kind and understood people, said, " Of course, we'll sing the Manoa song." Because she knew that this would please Sir Walter. So they sat down on the bank of the river and challenged the birds with gay and lovely voices.

" Then the blessed paths we'll travel,
Strewn with rubies thick as gravel . . ."

But they were travelling them. There was no need to wander further along the road. Already they had reached Manoa, El Dorado, the lovely city built without hands; for the trees arched its roof, the short sweet grass paved its streets, its citizens dressed in white, crimson, carnation and all the most beautiful colours, and fed in the evening beside the river, beside the still waters, sleepily flowing, under the gentle easterly wind.

> " Ceilings of diamond, sapphire floors,
>   High walls of coral and pearly bowers.
>   From thence to Heaven's bribeless hall
>   Where no corrupted voices bawl,
>   No conscience molten into gold,
>   No forged accuser bought and sold."

That bit was silly, but they sang it to please Sir Walter, because in the Lovely Land everyone is pleased, even by foolish things. Small vanities are considered there, even more than the great sorrows, for which, perhaps, men need less consolation. But since there are great sorrows, they sang softly,

> " Blood must be my body's balmer;
>   No other balm will there be given
>   Whilst my soul like quiet palmer
>   Travelleth towards the land of heaven."

Ah, quiet, quiet; cease, tragic ghosts and delicate, mocking wraiths, cease from your singing. Have we not touched the land where our hearts would linger?

> " Here will I kiss the bowl of bliss
>   And drink mine everlasting fill
>   Upon every milken hill."

Drink deep, deep, the cool, dark flowing water. Not Lethe here; we do not seek oblivion. We seek a richer joy and fuller memory. We seek to remember not those things only which we have known, but all the wonders of which fate deprived us. Remember now. Do you remember Italy? Have you not seen the Umbrian plain silent in silver disk of olive groves? Do you remember Venice, Laguna, Rome? Do you remember the Fisher's Bastion at Budapest, when the snow has stricken the city's life into shining tranquillity, when all the kingdoms of the earth lie stretched before you? Only remember.

" I shut my eyes and I remember . . . " A lantern swung from the stake of a broken fence, and a delta of yellow light spreading across the ground. Dock and darnel and rank evil grasses entangle the spades. A foul stench sickened her. " Ah! What was that? Not a stone that I struck in the shadow. My love, my love, my very little love, come to me! Open your eyes, my sweet, my dear, my beautiful."

Joanna sprang from her chair, panting, terrified.

" Ah, not that horror! "

Always she saw that horror. Whenever she dared to dream and to seek her kingdom, she found Paul Szermai waiting there, bearing with him his unbearable memories.

They pressed about her. They besieged her, the miseries of these men, they entered with their incessant demands the secret fortresses of her mind. She had no place of refuge from their clamorous sorrows.

" Oh, must I bear it all for you? I have made your

189

beds and cooked your meals for you. I have born your children and nursed your bodies in sickness. Is there no end, no end? Must you take my dreams? Will you leave me nothing, not even the untouched privacy of my imagination? "

§ 3

" What am I thinking about? " Joanna asked herself. " I must be going a little crazy too. Come, pull yourself together, my girl. It's all very well to go to sleep on the kitchen table, but what about that egg-flip? "

She began to bustle about the kitchen and dairy. The fire, as usual, had almost died away. She poured sugar recklessly on to the damp green sticks.

" What's wrong with me when I hear tales like Paul Szermai's is that I can't get used to melodrama," she said. " I always thought that Truth was grey and drab. I had grown quite accustomed to her homely countenance. I suppose that when people live mediocre sort of lives like mine, they come to think that only imagination wears glowing colours, and only imagination knows great tragedy. We reconcile ourselves to mediocrity, and rather enjoy battles and executions and great, terrific betrayals, and choose ourselves heroes like Sir Walter Raleigh, to whom almost every conceivable human evil happens. But when in real life we meet this wild, devastating fury, revenge and revolution and torture and cruelty, all the elusive fabric of vision vanishes. Their realism robs us of fantasy and we don't like it. Paul says that he lives for revenge. I don't like it. But because I've accustomed myself to gentler virtues, it does not mean that there's nothing in this fierce integrity, which believes in a tooth for a tooth and all the rest of it."

She began to beat up the egg in an earthenware bowl, and the sound of her fork prevented her from hearing a step in the passage. Paul Szermai, as though in answer to her thoughts, came and stood by the table, regarding her gloomily. She smiled up at him.

" Well. Are the hens in bed? "

He disregarded her question.

" Why did I tell you? " he flung at her. " I have delivered myself into your hands. It was a betrayal. I had told nobody. I had promised myself that I would keep her memory a matter for my own concern. Then I was my own master. What did you do to me? "

Almost alarmed by his violence, she said, " I have done nothing. I only wanted to be your friend. I hated my own inadequacy."

" My friend? My friend? " he railed. " You are a thief. You have stolen not what was mine but what was hers. I cannot forget you. I cannot tear you out of my mind. Your face comes between me and my thoughts of her. I hear, not her voice, but yours, yours."

She felt too much shocked even to answer him. She sat with the fork raised in her hand, and the egg streaming off its prongs on to the floor.

" How dare you make me tell you all about her? How dare you share my memories? "

" Oh, you're over excited. You're ill. You don't know what you're saying."

" Now you're going to be kind to me. You'll make me hot drinks and send me to bed, and I shall be cheated by all your treacherous kindness. You offer me comfort, comfort, so that I shall forget her. How dare you? How dare you? You're not beautiful. She was beautiful. You have no grace, no style. You have not elegance nor charm, nor wit. You are only kind."

" What — what do you want? "

" I want to go. I must get away. I must go at once. To-night. I can't bear it. I've been living in hell for a week. I live in torment. I can think of nothing but of how, when I seek her face, I see yours."

Hysteria was catching Joanna's throat. " Oh, p-poor Paul. How dreadful. No wonder you want to run away. But you can't go. We can't spare you. We'll never get another lodger. We're living on you. Oh, I've no pride, you see. We can't help it. We must have your three guineas, even if you have to put up with my ugly f-f-face."

" You see a joke? You see a joke? You laugh at me? You think that I am not in earnest? It must seem very funny to you that I am in torment."

" No. I didn't mean to laugh. I'm so sorry."

" Sorry. Sorry. Always you are sorry. You are sorry for your husband. You are sorry for me. You are sorry for Mr. Boyse because he is a plain, stupid man. We exist to be recipients of your pity. I do not want your sorrow. I do not want your friendship. I want to forget you. I want to remember her alone. To give her memory life."

" If there was anything I could do . . . "

His great dark eyes devoured her anxious face. He glowered at her with fury.

" Ah. Perhaps! " he said.

She rose slowly, frowning, and setting her bowl on the table. She was saying to herself, " Here's another situation to face. He's just gone off the deep end for a bit, poor boy. I don't wonder. I'd never be surprised at what he might do. Only I mustn't lose my head. I've got to help him."

He came forward roughly and seized her in his arms. Before she could grasp his intention, he had covered her face with angry, agonized kisses.

She felt no emotion, but surprised and sorrowful repulsion.

She did not even struggle. She lay quite passive in his arms until he released her, and stood, panting and smiling with a sort of defiant triumph.

She waited quietly until he spoke first.

" Well? Well? "

" Perhaps you feel better now," she said slowly. She was indignant with herself because her voice trembled. " And now would you please mind fetching me the brandy bottle out of the dining-room cupboard? I have to make Teddy an egg-flip."

She picked up the basin and began to beat the egg again with her fork. He waited a moment to see if she would speak again, then left the room.

Ten minutes later, he followed her upstairs with the candle.

" You've been a hell of a time," grumbled her husband. " What have you both been up to? "

193

" Paul has been telling me that I am very ugly. And so I am, by Jove! " Joanna set down the egg-flip and went to Teddy's shaving glass. The two men watched her scrutinize her face gravely. She picked up the hand-mirror, turned round to investigate her profile, then set it down again reluctantly. " Well, really I hardly blame you.'"

" Blame who? "

" Blame Paul for thinking me ugly and you for getting fed up with me. My dears. As a lovely woman, I think I've missed my vocation. Now, are you two going to play bébique? "

" Might as well," muttered Teddy. Without speaking, Paul Szermai went to the desk and fetched the cards. Joanna brought out her darning box and sat close to the lamp. Her eyes were so tired that they could barely remain open.

" Do you mind if I darn your grey socks with green wool, Paul? So tasteful, I always think, a little colour about the heels, don't you? "

The walls of the room swayed in front of her. Of course, the house was a ship, and the sea was swinging gently. Soon they would reach the islands, and Teddy would find there his complete nobility, Paul his revenge, Mr. Boyse his authority. But all that Joanna wanted was just the island.

The voices of the card players came to her from far away.

She put her head down on the undarned socks, and slept.

CHAPTER TEN

THE SACRAMENT

§ 1

TEDDY lay in the darkness awaiting the approach of Christ.

" Draw near with faith and take this Holy Sacrament to your comfort, meekly kneeling upon your knees." He would not kneel upon his knees, because Joanna was so fussy, and the doctor had bidden him lie in bed for at least six months. But he would sit up with the pillows behind him and the fresh morning air blowing the curtains in at the window, and the ample curve of the quiet moor assuring him of the steadfast comeliness of earth.

And so his Lord would come.

" O Friend, more desirable than my sweet human love; O Lover, pursuing fiercely, tenderly, my soul down the dark ways of mortal impotence; O Dignity, glorifying my humiliation, come to me."

" Hear what comfortable words our Saviour Christ spake."

" Yea, Lord, I hear and believe. Help Thou mine unbelief."

What, after all, is failure or success in this shadow world? These houses are only made of stone, this money of gold and silver, this body of flesh and bone and sinew.

The Teddy Leigh who sat in the British Legion Club-room was counted a fool among men. Mocked by physical weakness, by the wine which other men made their servant, his wife unfaithful, his honour abused, he reckoned each day his failure as a man. He heard whispering voices.

" Have you seen about the Leighs of Scatterthwaite? They've failed. I could ha' tell't on long ago. What's a college fellow know about pigs, eh? Or dairy work either for that matter. Eating their dinners up at the Hall is more their fancy, I reckon."

" He won't eat many more dinners up at Hall anyway. His wife's gone off with yon Hungarian. A pretty carry-on for a quiet village."

He could keep nothing, nothing. Not even his wife's fidelity, not even his self-respect.

Joanna, Joanna. The splendid strength of her; her dear, funny foolishness, her beautiful body. Was it really possible that she was false to him?

" O Christ, Thou art the true Reality. What are these shadows of the flesh, these toys of frail mortality?

" My son, these sorrows were sent to try thee as by fire. The souls of the righteous are in the hand of God. There shall no torment touch thee. The man whom you see here humiliated is but the weary mortal ghost of one who walks in honour in My perfect safety."

" Oh, but when she looks at him. When she calls him " Paul dear." I cannot bear it. When I lie here helpless and quite alone knowing that they are there downstairs together, I am shamed. I am shamed. I dare not ask her to stay here with me. I am ashamed to play the spy upon hcr. Why was I born a man with this pride of desire, with this will to power ·over the body of my love, yet only to be mocked by weakness and disease? Must I lie in hell when I am yet alive? Must I go down quick into the pit? What harm did I do? What harm did my father do, that I should suffer without hope of respite? "

" My son, this little phantom universe about you, these wraiths of teasing flesh, these pin-prick pangs of jealousy and desire, know that they are but nothing. In a breath, in the twinkling of an eye they shall be changed. The cool pastures of eternity shall heal your spirit. Beside the waters of comfort shall you be cleansed from your desire. Take My yoke upon you and learn of Me, for My yoke is easy and My burden is light, and in the world all other things are shadows. This phantom life shall pass as a watch in the night. Hold fast upon the only true reality.

" Lo, I come unto thee. At cock-crow, in the morning, when the sword of My spirit lies across the East, when the angels of My presence ride on the cleansing wind, Lo, I am with you always. My Body I leave with you. My Blood I shed for you. Eat, drink and be merry, for when men shall despise you most, your Lover shall come to you. When the long night is near and the door shall be shut in the street and desire shall fail, then cometh unto you a Lover, blood of your blood, flesh of your flesh, to give Himself to you and not to take, to strengthen, not to exhaust; to honour, not to betray. Behold, I come quickly."

" We do not presume to come to this Thy Table, O merciful Lord, trusting in our own righteousness but in

Thy manifold and great mercies. We are not worthy so much as to gather up the crumbs under Thy Table. But Thou art the same Lord whose property is always to have mercy."

"Well done, thou good and faithful servant. Where others have gone proudly, thou hast been abased. Where others were filled thou hast been an hungered. Where others have been rich, thou hast been poor. To thee in thy defeat, thy poverty and thy humiliation shall a crown be given. For having nothing, thou possessest all things. Thy nakedness was clothed in glory. The wedding garment was such nakedness.

"For the ways of God are not man's ways, nor are the ways of spirit the ways of the flesh. God hath put down the mighty from their seat and hath exalted the humble and meek. He hath filled the hungry with good things, and the rich He hath sent empty away."

"Glory be to the Father and to the Son and to the Holy Ghost. And to the Son, the Son, the Son . . ."

As though to greet Him, Teddy turned too quickly. The pain caught his chest. His heart knocked angrily. He began to cough.

A light wavered outside the open door. Its pale yellow glow pushed back the darkness.

Joanna in her blue dressing-gown hurried into the room.

§ 2

It was about four o'clock when Joanna returned to her bedroom and set down her candle on the dressing-table. Already beyond the window the moors lay dark against a silvering sky. Cocks crowed and were answered by a faint eerie echo from the unseen choir in the valley.

She dared not return to bed lest she should fall asleep again when there was so much to do.

Mr. Boyse had found a man for them, one Thomas Bidgood, a small-holder from Bartledale over the fells, a dour, pernickety, cross-grained fellow who, having been unable to make small-holding pay, exchanged his own for this vicarious failure, and came to a farm tottering towards the edge of ruin, as he reminded Joanna not once nor twice, but many times a day. He was himself a childless widower, with only one sister out in service, a lonely man, honest and conscientious. The vicar of Shepley-in-Bartledale had recommended him as a good churchman, but Joanna confessed that he hardly added to the amenity of Scatterthwaite. " It's like living with the day of judgment," she told Szermai. " I feel that Bidgood sees all our secret sins."

However, he fed the animals, helped with the milking and drove the float to the station whenever that was necessary.

On the chair by her bed lay a battered red exercise book containing Joanna's accounts. She had been sitting up in bed the previous night staring at figures which never amounted twice to the some total, but which always, with whatever total, proved disconcerting.

She had indeed the farm, but this was not her own, and in order to raise money on it she would have to consult Teddy. He had refused again and again to hear of a mortgage. A bank manager's son, he forgot most things belonging to his father's profession, but he was certain that mortgages were dangerous. She might just borrow money, but she was terrified of money-lenders, and already had run to the limit of the bank's generosity. It seemed hopeless to apply again to the Ministry of Pensions. Teddy had commuted the small pension due to him in order to buy the farm, and to raise the question again seemed to be asking for trouble, since there was a doubt whether his disability was attributable to war service at all. As for the British Legion, they had helped once or twice, but last time Joanna approached them, nervously under the fear of Teddy's indignation, the secretary had suggested that Captain Leigh would be far better in a sanatorium.

That was of course impossible. To Teddy, with his recollections of Davos and Wellingham, a sanatorium meant a living death, hell upon earth. The notion terrified him. A hint of the possibility made him ill for days; Joanna, agonized by his fear, determined that nothing would induce her to let him go, until his fear had changed or until circumstances forced her to do so.

"I must have money. I must have money. I must have money."

Day and night she had been repeating to herself this sad little song. She had to pay the aunts something for keeping Patricia and Pamela at Kingsport. She had to pay Bidgood his weekly wage. She dared not allow the chemists' bill to remain unpaid, though she was deeply in debt to the grocer and shoe-maker and corn-and-cake merchant.

Her only assured source of income lay in Paul Szermai's fee, the quite preposterous amount of three guineas a week, which he paid regularly every Saturday night, having raised his own rent without a word just when she most needed the extra money. She should not, of course, have taken it, yet at the time she needed new shoes for Pamela and malt and cod-liver oil for Patricia, and weighed against the delicacies of conduct her desperate needs and theirs. Paul cared little for life. He had no responsibilities. She had many. When she found that he had money, she took from him shamelessly.

Now in the morning, seated upon her tumbled bed and shivering, she turned over in her mind the enormity of her conduct.

"Of course, I might have the children back." That would remove the need for sending money every month to Kingsport. While they were there she could not allow her aunts to starve themselves in order that her children might be kept. Besides, the aunts were growing weary of well-doing. Patricia's health and Pamela's ingenious naughtiness harassed the Misses Entwhistle, who only asked of life a mild tranquillity, seasoned by tea-parties, church work, and other decorous amusements. They loved Joanna, but her children strained the cords of their affection.

" But I can't have them back while Pat's so delicate. She's just in the condition to take infection. I can't be sure that they'll not use Teddy's cups and towels, and he's so obstinate about thinking that there's no danger. He will keep calling them to his room."

She began to dress, reluctantly pulling off her

dressing-gown and pouring cold water into her small enamelled basin.

"If I were only certain of Paul."

Szermai indeed presented a problem to her, and one all the more confusing because of an offer which Sir Wentworth Marshall had made him. When the other foreigners had gone, he could, if he liked, remain for a time as adviser on forestry to the estate. When Joanna questioned him, he appeared to be uncertain of his own intentions. Since the scene in the kitchen he had gone about very quietly. He had indeed hardly spoken to Joanna. As for her, Teddy's urgent needs, the garden, the farm, the cooking and the dairy work had occupied her attention. She hardly noticed that when Szermai's working days were over, he wandered about the moor or remained in the camp until quite late.

Sometimes as she brought him his supper or passed him on the stairs, she became conscious of the tension of his nerves, as though he were caught in the grip of a vehement emotion. She could feel with a sensation of physical discomfort the concentration of his thoughts upon her. His large melancholy eyes turned to her with sullen intensity, as though he were about to speak, and then he looked away silently, or made some trivial remark which seemed to show her the folly of her imagined doubts. Because he came from a foreign country, because she had never quite forgotten her first impression of him as an eldritch knight, something not completely human, she could not apply to him her ordinary standards of conduct.

Now, dressing rapidly, she forced herself to face a

situation which became more puzzling the longer she regarded it. "Am I really a bad woman?" she asked herself. "Am I really making him stay and harming him, because I need the money and we never shall find another lodger? She bent down to fasten her clumsy, unbrushed shoes. There was a hole in her stocking, and Mr. Boyse was coming to give Teddy Communion. She ought to be tidy. Still, it was churning day and there was no time to waste darning holes. "It can't be helped." That was how she was coming to see it all.

She went to the mirror to brush her tangled hair. Seeing her face, she gave a little smile. For in the grey light she looked so wan and haggard with her weather-beaten complexion and her untidy cotton camisole that it seemed ridiculous to think of herself as a desirable woman, trading upon the passion which she evoked. But then she sighed again, thinking of Teddy and Szermai, and saddened by the inconvenience of life which binds flesh to spirit in so comfortless a union.

Then she pulled herself together. "He shall stay. I can manage. Things are never as bad as you think that they're going to be."

In defiance of fate, she pulled on her clean jumper and fastened a bright green bow at her throat, and went downstairs to light the kitchen fire, thrusting her arms into her old overall as she ran.

There was so much to do, so little time in which to do it. She could not stop to worry over complicated ethical problems.

§ 3

She was on her knees brushing the dining-room carpet when Szermai appeared silently in the doorway.

"Good morning, Mrs. Leigh."

She looked up, pushing back her hair.

"Good morning. Oh, look here, do you want your breakfast now? You didn't say that you wanted it any earlier. Mr. Boyse is coming at eight o'clock to give Teddy Holy Communion and they have to have breakfast afterwards, about half-past eight. But if you would like yours now, I'll get it."

She always felt that she ought to do as much as possible for his three guineas a week.

"I can return for breakfast. There is a fellow from Bartledale coming over about seedlings this morning and I shall have to go down now to explain. But please do not inconvenience yourself. I am not hungry."

"Paul," she sat back on her heels, her breath coming quickly. "Look here, there's something I want to ask you. Are you thinking of staying on here when the foresters leave? If so, do you want to stop with us, or to find other lodgings? Anywhere in the village would be twice as cheap and quite as comfortable."

"I should have thought that that rested with you," he said nervously, turning away from her and fingering the pewter pots on the dresser.

"Why with me? It rests with you, of course. I can't pretend that you're not made horribly uncomfortable here."

"Do you want me?" He spoke without eagerness,

yet with a morose excitement characteristic of his mood during the past week.

"Of course I do. You know that you have made all the difference in the world to us. Not only financially."

"You do not tell me that I have insulted you?"

"Why should I? You mean that scene in the kitchen? You were tired. You've had a rotten time. I know that nerves play curious tricks on people. If it was anybody's fault, I suppose that it was mine. I did not even feel insulted, only contrite and very unhappy. But it won't happen again. You've quite got over it."

And with practical vigour she turned back to sweeping the carpet, her brush moving so violently that the flying dust made them both cough.

It was a minute before she heard Szermai say in a muffled voice, "But I haven't got over it. I live in daily and hourly wretchedness. I am distracted. I cannot sleep. I cannot think. What have you done to me?"

"I have done nothing. You don't mean what you say."

"But I do, I do. I tell you, I want you. I must have you. You come between me and my love and I must have either you or her, I must touch you. Joanna, Joanna. Let me be your lover. Once. No more, I swear. What harm could it do? I tell you, I tell you. It is necessary. I shall go mad."

"Oh no, no. That's impossible."

"Then why did you give me hope? Why did you not send me away after I had kissed you? You must care for me a little. Your husband is sick. You cannot make me believe that he has been your true husband for

205

many months. I tell you that I must have you. You obsess me."

"You don't understand, Paul. It is my fault, if I led you to believe that I cared that way for you."

"Am I then so unlovable?" He stood with his back to the dresser, leaning against it and challenging her fiercely. "That is not true and you know it. I have been loved, I tell you, and by a woman far more gracious and more lovely than you could ever be. Why should you not have me? She would have done so, and she had half Hungary at her feet, if she had cared for any other save me. Why did you not send me away if I was hideous to you? You knew that the fools down in the village coupled our names together. You can stop it now, by making me leave the house. Why don't you? Why don't you? Doesn't a woman always say No when she means Yes?"

But Joanna only shook her head and replied humbly and sadly. "I deserve everything that you say about me, but I needed your three guineas. I still need them. I am in debt to you. Why need this have happened? Your coming seemed to me almost like a miracle. It was just helping me over the worst time. Are you quite certain that you have not been mistaken? I believe that whatever woman you were with you might just now feel the same about her. Can't you manage to pull yourself together?"

She looked at him doubtfully yet eagerly, hoping that because he was strange and foreign and had so wild a story, he might in other ways be different from the men whom she had known. But before he could answer her, Teddy's bell tinkled and she rose to her feet stiffly.

"Oh, please, Paul, think again. It is really possible that you may be mistaken. But if you can't pull yourself together, you must go, of course."

He looked at her, seeing her soiled hands and the dust on her face like a grey shadow. Even her splendid figure was hidden beneath her shapeless overall. She had no beauty, no grace nor wit nor breeding, only a vivid strength which had ensnared his senses. Exasperated, bewitched and angry he stared back at her.

The bell rang again, its feeble insistence summoning her.

"You see, I must go."

She fled past him and up the stairs.

He moved forward and turned her brush slowly with his foot. He felt no tenderness towards her, but a blind hunger. He had been for so long stunned to a shocked unconsciousness that now his awakening came only with angry pain.

From overhead sounded a low murmur of voices.

Suddenly Szermai kicked the dustpan aside with irrational violence and turned, striding bare-headed out of the house through the yard and up the fields to the Finnish Camp.

§ 4

It was nearly half-past eight when Szermai returned for his breakfast.

A cackle of hungry ducks greeted him in the yard. They had not been fed that morning, owing to the general disintegration of the household, and they waddled round the Hungarian, jerking their necks, opening their orange bills and staring at him with beady reproachful eyes. But he was feeling in no mood for clemency.

He went through the house straight to the dining-room where an unusually orderly meal was laid for three people. On the hall table lay a strange hat and a wooden box of unusual shape. Through the window he caught a glimpse of a motor-cycle in the front garden.

They must be upstairs. Stirred partly by curiosity and partly by the compulsion which made him seek Joanna's presence, he stole upstairs and stood silently in the corridor looking through the open door into Teddy's room.

The card-table, on which they had played bézique the night before, stood near the bed covered with Joanna's best embroidered tea-cloth. A brass crucifix and other utensils covered with rich silk material had been set on the table, and before it knelt Mr. Boyse in his surplice, his red honest face turned to the wall.

Bidgood, the labourer, conscripted to provide the necessary number of communicants, knelt against a chair. The nails on the upturned soles of his farm boots shone oddly, and the seat of his corduroy trousers had been polished by long use. Joanna knelt nearer to the bed. There was a hole in her yellow stockings and another right through the sole of her shoe. She was disgracefully untidy and not even beautiful in that ridiculous posture. As she knelt, only the curve from her forehead to chin was visible, and the long sweeping line of her back and thigh.

So they were at their communion service. A sacrament — good. " Perhaps she is praying for me," he thought grimly. It was long since he had attended any religious service, having been brought up as a Catholic, and having decided years ago that his Holy Mother the Church was simply irrelevant to the life of a gentleman. At Cambridge he had sometimes attended a Protestant service for entertainment, but he had never before witnessed a celebration of Holy Communion.

There was a movement in the room, and he shrank back into the shadow where he could neither see nor be seen.

" Ye that do truly and earnestly repent you of your sins," said Mr. Boyse self-consciously, for he would far rather have been conducting the Early Service properly in church, " and are in love and charity with your neighbours."

" Love and charity," thought the Hungarian. " I am in love with my neighbour, and much good it does me. Leigh is in love with her and hates me poisonously. Much good it does him. What a farce! "

" And intend to lead a new life, following the commandments of God, and walking from henceforth in His holy ways, draw near with faith and take this Holy Sacrament to your comfort."

" A new life? " thought Szermai. A new life for Leigh? He certainly needed one. With one lung gone and the other affected, he could not enjoy this life for long at any rate. Or a new life for Bidgood, the pessimistic, incompetent ex-farmer? He could perhaps do with one, poor fellow, though his sort never made much of a life, whatever they were given. A new life for Mrs.

Leigh? She who was drawing near without faith, though with charity, to take this Holy Sacrament to her husband's comfort, meekly kneeling upon her knees. Why not a new life for her? A free life, spent in travelling to the places she desired, a life without poverty or disease to trouble her. Might it not be amusing, even for one whose own life was well over, to live again through her, watching her eager face brighten with pleasure as she saw the outline of an island take shape in the calm evening, or the procession of strange men in flowing robes pass by her, up the steep street of a hot Eastern town? Might one not find in her unquenchable youth and courage a new life even for oneself?

Fool. Fool. He knew that he did not wish to watch her pleasure. There was no philanthropy in his desire. He wanted to experience her response to his awakened passion, to reach through her body the lost personality of a dead woman, and thus to forget Joanna for ever if he could, and remember only his dead beloved girl.

A new life for that Other? A life born from his memory? Was that indeed not possible?

The curate's voice boomed gravely, followed by Joanna's clear rather nervous enunciation and Teddy's harsh whisper.

"We do earnestly repent and are heartily sorry for these our misdoings. The remembrance of them is grievous unto us. The burden of them is intolerable."

There they were wrong. The burden of sin remembered is quite tolerable, thought Szermai. It was the inability to remember which could pass endurance. " I

am forgetting her. I am forgetting." Without his memory she had no life, he felt, and now he was killing her
for a second time.

"Hear what comfortable words Our Saviour Christ
saith unto all that truly turn to Him. Come unto Me
all ye that travail and are heavy laden, and I will
refresh you."

There was no refreshment for Szermai save in the
sight of his dead love. But whenever he closed his eyes,
he saw only Joanna. Joanna, the usurper, the interloper,
had trespassed in the sanctuary of his mind.

"Lift up your hearts," said the curate.

"We lift them up unto the Lord."

From the hungry ducks below arose a plaintive and
indignant cackle. They had not yet been given their
breakfast. Startled by the sudden commotion, Szermai
moved forward and stood where he could see Joanna
quite plainly.

Here, he saw, was reality, comfort and easement,
here alone.

"But Thou art the same Lord whose property is
always to have mercy."

Joanna had no god-like mercy. She was foolish, blind,
reckless and wilful as a child.

"Hear us, O merciful Father, we humbly beseech
Thee, and grant that we, receiving these Thy creatures
of Bread and Wine, according to Thy Son our Saviour
Christ's most holy Institution, in remembrance of His
death and passion, may be partakers of His most
blessed Body and Blood."

Well, what after all was reality but faith, and the

defiant imagination of men outsoaring a tangible, imperfect world, and demanding the Immaculate Conception? What had it to do with him that the bread and the wine remained only bread and wine? If Leigh through these humble instruments could taste his God, was it not true for him that God was there?

" But I desire only a human body. I cannot touch a memory. I cannot see a dream. Leigh needs the bread and wine that he may taste his God. I need that woman that I may recreate my love. The outward, visible sign of the inward, spiritual grace. We, who are men, must touch and taste and see. I need you, Joanna. I need you for my sacrament."

" And here we offer and present unto Thee, O Lord, ourselves, our souls and our bodies, to be a reasonable, holy and lively sacrifice unto Thee."

Why not? Why not? Should she not offer herself, her soul and her body, to be a reasonable, holy and lively sacrifice unto God, God who was Love and Charity and Mercy?

Her clear voice answered his feverish thought.

" Glory be to God on high, and in earth peace, good will towards men."

Had she good will, she whose body was made by the God of inscrutable creation a sacramental chalice for the wine of life?

" Thou that takest away the sins of the world, have mercy upon us. Thou that takest away the sins of the world, receive our prayer."

But what was sin? What were the sins of the world which Christ should take away? Were they not unfulfilment, folly and frustration, the cowardice which dies, not daring to live, the dull negation which denies the fullness and joy of life?

" The peace of God which passeth all understanding . . . "

A clamour of ducks rose wildly with passionate insistence, drowning for Szermai the rest of the Benediction.

He tiptoed downstairs and would have left the house, but he was too late. Joanna, running down to fry the bacon for breakfast, came upon him in the kitchen.

CHAPTER ELEVEN

LETHERWICK NIGHT'S ENTER-TAINMENT

§ 1

TEDDY had returned to earth again.

For a week since the curate's visit he had lived in a state of emotional quiescence, suspended between heaven and earth in an ecstasy of worship. The life at Scatterthwaite, with its routine of invalidism, had become quite unreal to him. Like Enoch he had been translated while alive, and caught up into a peaceful Paradise. He was convinced of the nearness of God. The torment of his jealousy seemed like a nightmare from which he had awakened, and if he thought of it at all, it was to wonder how such an obsession could have held him captive.

But this serenity had not lasted. For two days now, irritation had run like fever through his veins and nerves.

Everything went wrong. His bed was uncomfortable. The pillows were either too high or too low. The coffee at breakfast had been cold and Joanna, while carrying it upstairs, had spilled some into the saucer. That was so like her, slack and untidy and casual. She could never finish anything properly. No life could be lived beautifully without a sense of detail, and she had none.

Her shoes squeaked. She had not rubbed his back last night and he was sure that he would develop a bedsore. The toast was leathery. He dropped a book which throughout the week had lain unheeded on his table, but which now, lying on the floor, tormented him with a demand to be read immediately. When he rang for Joanna to come and pick it up for him, she was out in the cow-house, and did not hear the bell. Having shaken it at intervals for ten minutes, he heard her coming upstairs, and could endure waiting no longer, so that as she appeared at his door, he had just dragged himself wearily out of bed and was grovelling on the floor for the book.

He had become conscious of his illness again. He drew no breath without feeling the unsoundness of his lungs. He could hear the knocking of his heart, and lay awake at night in an agony, expecting to cough. He calculated how much better he ought to have grown in two months, if it was true that he should be well again in six. He kept the thermometer under his pillow and took his temperature about every half-hour.

What was the use of dragging on such an existence, he asked himself. Why was he alive at all? Whence came he? Whither was he going? He swung backwards and forwards between confidence and fear.

His faith told him that the principle of life was good, being God Himself, and that neither his bodily existence nor his death mattered in the face of that eternal certainty. It told him that, having faith, he could never be alone. He was bound in an inescapable companionship by the communion of saints, sharing with them their animation by one fiery stream of life. He was the heir of an immense tradition. In his veins ran the blood of the Cæsars and of dark Burmese slaves, of Northern warriors and of Eastern saints; because coolies had sweated beneath a trader's lash, by that measure was his heritage less fair; because in an obscure hovel one soul and faced disaster unafraid, he was by that measure the stronger, in potentiality if not in deed. What he was, so would posterity become, by this or that the richer or the poorer. He was the master, not only of his fate, but of the destiny of man.

Feeding himself upon glorious immensities, he would lie entranced through half a morning and then fall suddenly into black confusion. What if, after all, they were just words, words, words? He was alone. There was no one to tell him that these things were truly so. The doctrine of the Church was only one among the hundreds of creeds invented to hide the nakedness of men from their own eyes. And if one creed were true, how was it distinguishable from the false? Was there indeed one which had offered any true satisfaction to the sick man? Christ healed the sick, since that was all He could do for them. But when there came no miracle, when one lay alone, gasping for breath through the interminable nights, then what consolation was there for the maimed body, except the chill regard of the indifferent stars?

In his reaction to despair he tasted a new and passionate desire for achievement. If he must die like a dog, then he would live like a man. If his life would leave no mark upon the universe after his body had crumbled, then by heaven and hell, it should make some difference while he lived. The circle of his influence was small, but it should render him absolute allegiance.

He made up his mind that Joanna should go with Szermai to the British Legion dance.

She did not want to go.

" I don't like leaving you, Teddy," she said.

" What nonsense. As though it were not as safe to leave me here with Bidgood in charge than to go off for hours together as you do into the garden or up the fields when I am helpless in bed. Besides, we ought to take some part in the life of the village."

" But I don't suppose for a minute that Paul wants to go. He won't have a suit of dress-clothes."

" Well, I have one, and they ought to fit him. He'll be very pleased to go. He's talked enough about dancing, and I'm sure that we haven't provided him with much entertainment. I shall be bitterly disappointed if you don't go."

" But I haven't anything to wear either."

" Oh yes, you have. You can make something. Why don't you go and get the trunk from the box-room and see what you've got put away there? "

His face was alight with interest. She did not know what freak inspired his sudden desire to see her dressed again in evening dress, but she recognized its intensity, and went obediently to see whether she could find the box.

She did not want to go to the dance. She did not feel interested in her clothes. She despised herself for her inability to respond to his mood. She felt dull and tired because late last night she had faced an exhausting scene with Szermai, at the end of which she had told him that he must go, and now she felt limp and inert. She started at every unexpected sound. When she went down the stairs she glanced over her shoulder, fearful lest Szermai should be waiting for her.

" Bring out your things," said Teddy. " I'm going to dress you. Yes, you might put another pillow there. No, the other. Now, what about that thing you wore at the Marshalls'? "

He looked like a different person, when his face was illuminated by this new interest in life.

" I must do something to keep up his spirits. If this really amuses him," thought Joanna. " What else can I do? "

She dragged from the box-room a dilapidated trunk, and tugged at its rusty locks. It opened stiffly, emitting a smell of musk and camphor from the cloth-balls which she had thrown inside.

She pulled out a faded silk scarf, and then the black and gold dress which she had worn at the Marshalls', terribly crushed, its skirt smeared with the mud and blood in which she had knelt by Mochen Dee.

" It's ruined," she said dully.

" Good God, do you mean to say you put it there in that filthy mess? " cried Teddy in disgust.

" Pat was so ill. It looks like a bit of hanging evidence in a murder case, doesn't it. I'd better burn it."

" Ugh! Yes."

She picked up the gold tinsel slippers, tarnished and showing ragged lines along the soles, but still rakish and gay.

"These might do as a foundation," she said doubtfully, "but they need supplementing."

"Do they?" He laughed. "Do you remember when I bought them?" She blushed, remembering the day at Scarshaven on their honeymoon when after shopping in Hardrascliffe he had returned with the slippers wrapped in fine black tissue paper. When she had appeared from her bath, he thrust them on to her bare rosy feet in the hotel bedroom, laughing with gentle adoration as she pirouetted, half timid, half audacious, clad only in gold high-heeled shoes.

"They're all worn out," she said quickly, and put them back into the trunk, among its battered feathers, petticoats and silk.

"What's that shining thing?" asked Teddy.

"That's the evening cloak Aunt Helen passed on to me, after someone had spilled claret cup down it." She produced a garment of heavy, glittering silver and blue brocade, and sat smoothing out its rich folds. "If I'd thought of it before, I might have made something out of that." Her instinct for dressmaking asserted itself even through her misery and fatigue. She began to lay seam to seam, pursing up her lips and frowning.

"There's lots of time. You like doing things in a huggermugger at the last minute. Go and get your work-basket."

"Teddy, I can't. I've got a hundred things to do."

But he insisted, and she, only too pleased that anything could amuse him, sat down in his window and sewed through the warm May afternoon, cutting and stitching, and running over to the bed, so that he could pin a fold in place on her hip, or hang the tinsel scarf from her shoulder.

Then he said, " Sit down. I want to cut your hair for you."

She gazed at him dumbly, then went and fetched her pair of scissors and sat on the side of his bed.

"Kneel down. You're too high there for me. I want to cut it into a dear little peak in your neck. Keep still. Idiot. Darling, why don't you wash more carefully behind your ears? I can't do with a dirty wife."

Docile, she knelt before him. His hands played with her thick soft hair and the firm warmth of her beautiful neck.

"Turn your head a little. Don't fidget. Really, I missed my vocation. I should have been a hairdresser. Beloved, thou hast adorable ears."

Szermai had said, "You are ugly. Hideous. Why can't I forget you? Are you afraid of sin? This would be not sin but charity. Is charity a sin? "

"There. Turn round and let me see you *en profil*. Now full face. Why didn't we cut a fringe? Never mind. It's very nice. Now thank me prettily."

She bent to kiss him. Poor Teddy. Dear Teddy. She felt that she would give all she had to make him well again. He could be so sweet, so sweet to her. She put her arms round his thin shoulders and drew him close to her. He was so good, so patient, and she could give to him so little compensation.

Szermai, lounging upstairs to ask whether he should

begin to get the tea ready himself, as Mrs. Leigh
had not appeared, came upon this scene of conjugal
affection.

§ 2

Beatrice Marshall, acting as hostess for her mother
at the five-shilling dance for the British Legion, wished
that Eric had not vanished and left her all alone to face
these farmers and their wives. It was not that she felt
incapable of dealing with them. Being her mother's
daughter, the supervision of rural festivities brought
her great satisfaction. But she wanted someone to share
with her her amusement at *crêpe de Chine* dresses from
the Bon Marché at Clarington, at shy young auc-
tioneers and mud-students in tight gloves or at the dashing manners of Paxton and Mark Longden and Digby
Marrable. She could not remember all their names, and
though her brother would not remember either, he at
least could pretend to lend her some support.

But since the departure of Lorna Lavine to China, he
had been more perverse than ever. Well, there was certainly no one at a Letherwick dance to distract his too
much concentrated affection. Unless, perhaps, it were
that woman over by the cloakroom door.

Beatrice, smiling half-mechanically at Mrs. Settle-
ton, in green satin with black sequins, noticed a tall,
conspicuous young woman move from the little parti-
tion labelled " Ladies' Cloakroom " and stand with her
back to the heavy maroon curtains, lent by the Hall for
the occasion. She was obviously waiting for somebody,
but without eagerness, withdrawn, it seemed, into a sad
reverie, as though the dance and her expected escort

were only parts of an unhappy dream. Yet she should have come prepared for enjoyment, in her gleaming gown, with her fair soft hair and the dull silver roses on her splendid shoulders. She was not a Lindersdale woman, thought Beatrice. And yet she was strangely familiar. Even her air of lordly extravagance, and her dress, so much too grand for the occasion, reminded Beatrice of something just beyond the edge of her memory. She tapped her foot on the floor, trying to remember.

" Good evening, Mrs. Pitcock. So good of you to come all this way." No, the woman was not from Lindersdale, for she appeared a stranger. Nobody spoke to her as she stood waiting, leaning a little against the curtain as though she were tired before the dance began. Yet many people looked at her, and Beatrice could catch signs of whispered comment. " Good evening, Mr. Green. No, Colonel Atherton has not turned up yet. Too bad of him, isn't it? Perhaps his car's broken down. By the by, can you tell me who that woman is by the door? Yes, there in the blue and silver dress. I feel I ought to know."

The young man smiled nervously, uncertain how much local gossip might be known to a squire's daughter.

" That's — er — that's Mrs. Leigh, you know, of Scatterthwaite."

" Oh, yes, of course. How stupid of me. One sees her so seldom. Is that her husband? Surely not? "

For the woman by the door had just been joined by a dark, slender man, whose thick untidy hair and odd manner appeared most out of place in the school hall.

" Oh, no, you know. That's not Captain Leigh. That's the other fellow. The Hungarian chap."

" Oh yes. Of course," said Beatrice again vaguely. " He lodges there, doesn't he? "

" That's right," said Mr. Green, glad enough to escape from what he conceived to be an embarrassing situation, while Beatrice reproached herself for not remembering. She desired to cultivate the royal gift of " placing people." She had a sense of being herself not devoid of some small shadow of royal prestige and royal responsibility. She was no fool, although she was young and stiff and self-important, and she felt that somewhere in Mr. Green's embarrassment, in the detachment of Mrs. Leigh and the arrival of her escort lay the materials for a situation which might surpass even her abilities as a hostess. For the first time she began to wish that her mother had returned from Italy.

" Good evening, Mrs. Leigh. Good evening, Mr. Szermai." What a good thing that she remembered the name. " How good of you to come down. Of course, I know that your husband's awfully interested in the British Legion. How is he? "

" Oh, he's pretty well; I hate leaving him really," said Joanna with truth. " But he insisted that we should come."

" How nice of him. I can't say what sort of a show it'll be." Beatrice wanted to seem grown-up and blasé. She was uncertain how to take this Mrs. Leigh, who was no villager, and who yet was somehow not of her own world. But Mrs. Leigh showed no disposition to be "taken" in any way. She smiled with a quiet friendliness and walked on to a seat by the wall, not thinking of Beatrice Marshall at all, but of Paul and Teddy, and of how she was going to manage both of them and of how soon she could get away. For just before they had started, Bidgood returned from the village with the letters, and one from Kingsport told Joanna that Patricia was not very well again. She felt far too anxious to wonder what the dance was going to be like, and how Paul would behave. She was not even much surprised at his consent to come, although, instead of appearing eager to dance with her, he faced the prospect with unflattering gloom. For a man who declared himself to be in love with her, he behaved very oddly, so oddly that she ignored the more embarrassing scenes between them, and in her anxiety treated him with complete candor.

"Paul, I hate this dance. I don't want to stay. How soon do you think we can go?"

"I don't know," he said, sitting down beside her on a bench covered with a large Union Jack, beneath a map of the Colonial Empires of the World. "Is this the village school?"

"Yes. Look here, do you think that it would be possible to leave Teddy alone in the house for two days with Bidgood if I went off to Kingsport to see Patricia? I'm worried to death about her."

The Select Band from Clarington made a curious wailing sound intimating its intention to begin. A fat, middle-aged man, with a very red face and a white rosette, stepped into the middle of the room and announced, " Ladies and Gentlemen! Take your partners for the Onestep."

" What's that? " asked Szermai, without interest.

" The M.C. They always have them here." She looked with a sad wonder round the room at the little, pert girls, in their short taffeta dresses, giggling and running their feet along the powdered floor. She looked at the gauche young men and the middle-aged women, and thought, " Actually there are people here to whom this is a pleasure. This is a real party to them." Mingled with her misery of suspense lay the grief of her zestful heart, because she also could not enjoy the party. She felt no envy of the more fortunate, but a shadow of remorse, because the good things of life were so few that it was wicked to waste them.

" We'd better dance," said Szermai, and rose, offering his arm with a bow, the elegance of which even then delighted her. " It is better than sitting upon this seat."

It was better. Moving through the gradually increasing crowd of dancers, she felt better. Paul danced so beautifully; he seemed so certain of himself; she could for once resign herself completely to the guidance of some other will.

The sound of the tinny piano, the saxophone and drums came to her in a dream. She was hardly conscious of movement, but immensely pleased to find that she need think no longer. The dance came to an end far too soon, and she clapped like a child for the music to continue. It was impossible for her not to respond to colour and rhythm and the light and sound of the party.

After the third dance, he asked her, " Are you tired? "

" No. I feel much better. How well you dance."

" Yes, I do," he said, and relapsed into sombre silence.

" I suppose that you used to dance a great deal in Hungary,"

" Yes," he said, and the dumb misery of his face struck her with a sudden overwhelming compassion. He suffered so much. He was, on the whole, so good. She had been so unkind to him.

" Paul. Don't look like that. I can't bear it. Let's go home."

" I was thinking," he said, " of a dance in the Verbozći Utsca in Buda, just before I left for Finland. It was an old Turkish house, built round a quadrangle, and on the first floor there were galleries opening out one from the other. They were panelled with a light sort of wood which looked apricot coloured in candle-light. There was a band from Vienna."

She looked at the whitewashed walls, the maps and crude lithographs, the hanging festoons of scarlet bunting and flags and the flushed faces of the dancers, in the crowded schoolroom.

" Oh, let's go home," she repeated.

He shook his head. " That would do no good. We had better stay."

He rose again, and she obeyed him; only, as they moved round the room, she said, " I am so sorry, Paul."

He looked into her face, turning his great brooding eyes full upon hers. " No. You cannot be. We are each too sorry for ourselves."

About them swayed the solemn dancers, serious, yet excited; the Chinese lanterns dripped their hot wax in the warm May evening. Couples wandered stealthily out at the door, or stole by ones and twos into the cool darkness of the infants' school, to make their own amusement among the desks and blackboards. Young girls powdered their noses and chaffed their awkward, less adaptable partners. Two couples who had learned the Charleston while on holiday at Blackpool, exhibited this fashionable accomplishment before admiring friends. Everyone was so much occupied by their own enjoyment that in the dance room the excitement of seeing Mrs. Leigh arrive with her Hungarian had been forgotten except by a few older women, who found in it a welcome topic of conversation, that conversation which at a dance must appear animated lest it should seem that women sat and talked, not because they loved talking, but because they had passed their dancing days.

Even these ladies found that Mrs. Leigh was very smart. Whatever else they might say of her, she looked a lady. " Though a little fast."

" Her father was a missionary."

" Never! Well, I shouldn't have thought it. Somebody told me that she was one of those illegitimate children Lord Rallock scattered about here. There are plenty of them."

" Oh, Mrs. Pitcock! "

" Well, there's no knowing. It's hard to tell in these

days, I'm sure, who's got a father. I suppose you've heard about Bessy Bottomley, again."

" Yes. Isn't it disgraceful. I always said that that girl ought to be locked up."

" Girl? I should say that the man . . ."

They found consolation in the iniquities of their neighbours.

A little group in the refreshment room found less consolation. Paxton, Mark Longden, Brindle and young Digby Marrable were holding a council of war. They had brought a whiskey bottle with them, having learned that the dance, being held in the school, was to be Pussyfoot, a most ill-considered limitation. With this, and with the natural indignation of a committee which has been overruled, they were preparing themselves for battle against the alien invasion of their happy valley.

" My fiancée's here," said Digby, with a newly acquired squeamishness which aroused considerable mirth among his auditors. " And I'll be damned if I'll stand that foreign —— flaunting his mistress all over the room."

" I thought that the committee had agreed," observed Paxton, who was a stickler for etiquette, " that none of the men from the Camp were to be invited. What I say is, that the wishes of the committee ought to be considered."

" The latest I've heard, though, mind you, I wouldn't stake my honor on it," quoth Brindle, " is that young what d' you call 'im is going to stay on, if you please and by your leave, after the lot on 'em have gone. To teach our fellows how to do their business, I suppose."

He helped himself gloomily to another whiskey and soda. For the truth was that though he felt affronted, he did not know quite what steps to take in order to restore his dignity. Nor did his friends. They only knew that they detested the Hungarian, that they felt vastly indignant and self-righteous, and that they wished the Chief Constable would come and somehow or other assert his authority in removing the Scatterthwaite obstructions from their party.

The longer they conversed and the more they drank, the more certain they became of their own justification, of the Hungarian's immorality and of the rights of English gentlemen to do what they like with low aliens in their own village.

By the time the sixth dance was over, and Joanna, tired and distracted, announced that she would stay no longer, they had achieved a fine pitch of angry exaltation.

"You will at least have some refreshment?" inquired Szermai, concerned, in spite of his preoccupation, by her pale face and haggard eyes.

"Oh yes, some coffee," Joanna said, grateful for his consideration and for the kindness of fate which had wrought this change in him. She had not expected to find him so tractable and courteous. The dance had changed from a nightmare into a tedious interval to be endured until she could return to Teddy and discuss with him the possibility of her leaving for Kingsport to see Patricia.

The room had grown very hot. The white powder, trodden into the floor, gave out a faint, peppery smell.

The hands of the dancers grew more and more sticky. The wax from the candles inside the magic lanterns dripped on to the benches and the floor. Rising to find coffee in the class-room, Joanna for the first time became aware that the company seemed to watch her with special interest. She grew more and more uncomfortable, as on Szermai's arm she walked across the dance-room and through the curtained door. It was almost as bad as though her petticoat had fallen off, she felt.

The supper-room was empty save for a noisy little group of young men in a corner, who fell silent as she and Szermai appeared.

"Wait here. Will you have coffee or some of that stuff in a jug?" asked Szermai.

"Oh, coffee, if there is any."

She sank gratefully on to a chair just inside the door, and closed her eyes. She felt quite sick with fatigue and anxiety, wondering why she had allowed herself to be persuaded to come. "And suppose that Pat's really ill? What if it's pleurisy again? And she hates being ill so."

Szermai approached the trestle table, covered with cloths and decorated with bands of tinsel, trails of smilax, and dishes piled with trifle and pink jelly.

"I want two cups of coffee," he said to the woman who watched him with curiosity from behind the table.

"Then you won't get them," blustered Digby Marrable, coming forward. "Don't serve him, please, Mrs. Carliff. He has no business to be here."

"I beg your pardon?" asked Szermai, really surprised.

"We don't want you," Digby shouted, working himself up into a frenzy of wrath, "and we don't want your mistress. We don't want any of you damned foreigners here, and you can get out, see?"

Szermai looked with amazed disgust into the red, stupid face and then turned to his companions. "He is very drunk," he observed coldly.

"If he is," said Paxton, "what business is that of yours? He talks jolly good sense. You'd better go. We don't want you here and you should have had more sense than to come." He was less drunk than the others, and disconcerted by the situation.

"I hardly understand you, gentlemen. Do you intend to insult me?"

"No more than you've insulted us an' our sisters an' wives an' all the decent women here. It may be all right in Hungary or whatever damned country you come from to drag your mistress about under everybody's nose, but Leigh was a member of our club, and by God . . ."

Digby Marrable stod on tiptoe, swaying backwards and forwards. The blow which Szermai gave him was light enough, the Hungarian being more surprised than furious, and striking out only to spare himself from words which he felt would be inadequate; but it sufficed to send the unsteady young man sprawling to the floor.

Joanna was on her feet and half across the intervening space.

"What is it? What's happened?"

There were voices in the doorway, and the curtain swayed.

Mrs. Carliff cried, "My God. My God. My God!" in a small jerky voice, though really she was not seriously agitated.

Szermai turned to Joanna. He was not unfamiliar with such situations, and he was the only person not appalled by this one. He bowed to her slightly and said, "There has been an accident, Mrs. Leigh. I regret that I cannot offer you your coffee."

Digby Marrable was struggling to his feet. "Let me get at him! Let me get at him!" But Paxton had begun to realize that a dance was no place for a scene. He was not too drunk to see that he and the other farmers were at a disadvantage.

The classroom was no longer empty. A dance had ended and the men and women were pouring in, still half unaware of the disturbance in the corner. Not more than a dozen could see Paxton holding back the infuriated Digby. A girl cried suddenly, "Oh, I say, they're fighting!" and giggled.

Joanna looked round her with astonished wonder. She perceived the hostility of the crowd and the sordid ugliness of its curiosity. Concentrated into that moment she felt the intolerance, the anger, fear and jealousy of the dales' people against marauding strangers. She was compassed about by enmity and betrayal.

She held out her hand to Szermai.

"Paul, take me away, please."

She must get him out quickly, before there was any further trouble.

He stared at the farmers, and they stared at him, uncertain now quite what was the thing to do. Should they literally take and thrash him, or should they spare the feelings of their partners now flocking into the room? Paxton, hovering between two standards of etiquette, and Longden and Brindle restraining the tempestuous Digby, hesitated too long.

"Come, Paul," said Joanna.

Szermai came forward slowly, offering Joanna his arm, and together they walked from the room, the wondering crowd by the door making way for them, uncertain still quite what had happened.

By the cloakroom entrance they met Beatrice and Eric Marshall beside a policeman.

Eric came forward, excited and important.

"Oh, Szermai. The very man we've been wanting. I'm awfully sorry, you know, but this constable's just told me that there's a fire up at your place, and a sort of free fight, I think. Some of your fellows have got an idea it's been done on purpose. Will you go up at once, please, and see what's doing? Colonel Atherton's there. He was stopped on the way to the dance. But he can't make head or tail of what most of them say."

"I'm so sorry to take your partner from you, Mrs. Leigh," smiled Beatrice, but growing aware too that besides the excitement of the fire, something was happening at the dance.

"It is all right. I was just going in any case," said Joanna. "Is the fire bad?"

" I don't know. Look here, Eric, I want to go too. I'll drive our car," Beatrice did not want to miss anything. " Won't you come too, Mrs. Leigh? "

" No. No, thank you. I'll get back to my husband. He may be anxious. I hope that it's not too serious."

She seized her shoes and cloak and ran off into the dark road. The cool wind on her face revived her as she hurried towards the inn where the pony was stabled. Waiting for the ostler to yoke up the cart, she heard shouts and movements in the street. Motor bicycles were buzzing, cars hooting, and people calling to one another. The whole dance was breaking up. On the side of the Fell a red glow was spreading.

She drove through the yard just as the first party from the dance came up to the inn, shouting for their horses. A few dog-carts and gigs still remained among the ubiquitous Ford cars in the dales. A fire was more exciting than a five-shilling dance, however intriguing its scandals. Besides, in a dry May, fire might do endless damage on the hill-side.

No member of the party breaking and scattering through the dark village street recognized Mrs. Leigh in her rattling cart, driving the fat pony off in the opposite direction, without even a backward glance at the school house and the crowd.

§ 3

She took the low road, and drove down a steep lane, between deep tangled banks and black arches of May. The darkness was heavy and sweet with the soft penetrating scents of a night in spring.

Suddenly, at a turn of the road she became aware of

234

another scent, faint, acrid and harshly disquieting. The hedge sloped down from the bank; the level lane twisted towards the Fell. The pony dropped into a sputtering walk.

She heard voices. From above her on the hill-side came shouts and muffled sounds as of axes against timber. Bearing to the south and climbing rapidly, the pony turned again and rounded the first ridge of the hill. And now she saw.

About a mile to the north, a few feet below her, along the side of the Fell rose the Finnish Camp. It had blossomed into flame; it waved scarlet banners of fire. Above it into the dark tranquillity of the sky rolled clouds of smoke lit by warm red and amber lights. She could not see the men who sought to extinguish this blossoming beauty, to cut down the trees, to batter down the huts, to check the marching onroad of the fire. She only saw the strange, exciting place flowering at last into its true perfection. Dangerous, forbidden magic streamed on the wind, like the fiery sparks and flaming streamers. The fairy enchantment which had opened upon the hill-side returned at last to its own element.

She stood up in the cart with the wind on her cheeks, and watched it burn.

Then she spoke to the pony, gathered up her reins, and drove home to Scatterthwaite.

§ 4

Downstairs at Scatterthwaite, Bidgood drowsed over the kitchen fire. Upstairs, Teddy lit his candle for the sixth time to look at his watch. His head ached so badly that he preferred to lie in the darkness, but he had no notion of sleep.

It was nearly half-past twelve. He could see the dance-room decorated with bright May flowers and Chinese paper lanterns, and among the dancers Szermai and Joanna, clasping each other closely, swaying to the music, before they slipped out quietly into the starlit field beyond the school house. Moonlight lay on the May blossom like summer snow, and the sweet cool wind of the spring night intoxicated them. And there they could clasp and kiss and part again. Had he not dressed Joanna for this triumph of her proud youth and her splendid, unweary body?

" I myself have done it. I myself." He drew a torturing triumph from this immolation of his pride. He had dressed his sacrifice for the altar. In spite of weakness and frustration he had made one bold and splendid gesture.

In the darkness he was smiling strangely. When the lighted match flickered, it showed his face illuminated by a wild and airy triumph. Sometimes he muttered to himself, " The zeal of the Lord of Hosts shall perform it."

At the sound of wheels in the yard below, he started. A light wavered up and down outside the window. They had returned then. It was very early. He had not expected them until two at least. Was that a laugh when the door rattled? There were no voices. Perhaps they had no need of words. Perhaps their hands clasped in the dark kitchen. Perhaps they lingered on the moonlit threshold. Love has no need of words. " Ah, Love, that I may touch thee, touch thee, dear hands, dear lips."

Somebody was cautiously climbing the stair. The door opened.

Only a faint vapour of starlight gleamed in the window square.

The door closed again.

He spoke. " Joanna, is that you? "

" Yes. Yes, darling. All right. Go to sleep again."

" Come here."

She came to the bed.

" Strike a light, will you? "

A match scratched on the box. Joanna's dress glittered as she bent over the candle. Tall and shining as an angel she stood by the bed in her silver gown.

" Where is Szermai? "

" He went straight back to the camp." Her voice was trembling. " Have you been all right, dear? I've sent Bidgood to bed. He was asleep in the kitchen."

" Give me a drink of water."

" Sure you wouldn't like anything else? "

" Can I have a little whiskey with it? I have indigestion."

She gave him what he wanted. He lay watching her.

" Is that all? "

" Yes. Yes. Go to bed now."

She gave him a brief, wondering look, then meekly went.

The door closed softly, and he lay in candle-light, staring at it and shivering violently.

She moved across the passage to her own little room.

The stars gleamed wanly along her bare floor and through her uncurtained window. Without lighting her candle, she pulled out the pins from her shoulder and unfastened her dress. It slid, glittering, to her knees. She loosened the straps of her petticoat, and like the petals of a flower her garments slipped whispering to the floor. She stood gazing vaguely into the clear starlight, entranced by misery and fatigue.

A light flickered behind her.

She turned with a soft cry and saw Teddy standing in her doorway, a candle shaking in his hand and dropping hot grease on to her floor.

" Oh! What is it? "

" It is your husband. Perhaps you had forgotten? "

He staggered forward like a drunken man, his dressing-gown falling aside from his lean sickly limbs.

" I am your husband. Do we need introducing? " He laughed stupidly.

" Teddy. You must go back to bed at once."

She caught up her dressing-gown and took the candle from him.

" Oh, yes. I am going back to bed. And so are you, my wife. It's my turn now, you know. I let the other fellow have his turn. You can't say I wasn't generous. There's nothing mean about me. But now it's my turn, d'you hear? Lie down, Joanna."

He came quite close to her as she shrank back against the chest of drawers. His body smelt of sickness. His breath nauseated her. He laid wet, fumbling hands on her shoulders.

" Oh, no, Teddy, no."

Panic lit up her eyes, for she dared not struggle. She, who could have carried his wasted body, dared not resist him, because of his treacherous heart. She whose strength of nerve and will might have controlled him, became helpless through her own exhaustion. Her strength was at the mercy of his weakness. She shrank from him with futile protest.

" No, no, Teddy. Not here. Not now. Not like this."

" Yes, now, now! " he shouted triumphantly. " The zeal of the Lord of Hosts shall perform this."

The candle, pushed by his sudden movement from the chest of drawers, fell to the ground and went out.

CHAPTER TWELVE

THE UNQUIET PALMER

§ 1

THE cocks had begun to crow. Their hollow, melancholy music, echoing from the valley, roused their friends in Scatterthwaite.

" Cockadoodledooooo! "

" Cuckacuckakoo! "

Joanna, lying face downwards on the rough matting of the entrance floor heard them but did not stir. She had lain like that, her arms outstretched, since, two hours earlier, she had rushed downstairs and flung herself prostrate in the dark hall.

" Face the facts now," she told herself, but lay, shivering and sobbing, without coherent thought.

" I must know where I am," she cried, and opened her eyes as though she could look into the heart of truth. Yet opening them behind the screen of her hands, she could see nothing but blackness revolving behind blackness, the dance of fiery sparks and a shifting negation of light. For beyond her physical confusion, her shame, her disgust, and her terror, a strong compulsion urged her to the satisfaction of a more vital need.

She had thought her mind free to create its own enchanting world. She had refused the evidence of her eyes and ears and of her anxious heart. She had defied the knowledge of her life's disastrous circumstance, believing reality to be more than the farm at Scatterthwaite, the disheartening burden of poverty, the gloom of her husband's illness, the fear for her children's future. From these she had escaped into a lovely land of her deliverance, wandering at will along its pleasant pathways. She had climbed the sunburned hills, explored the islands, or rocked in her boat in the small, hill-girt harbours. The tall cities befriended her; she knew where the blue violets spread their carpets before a Chinese temple and where the yellow tulips blew on a Persian plain. She knew how the albatross caught piercing sunlight on the sweeping angle of his wing, and how the arum lilies flowered on the green slopes of a southern mountain.

And all the time reality had imprisoned her. She had been bound captive to her body, with its capacity for arousing desire and pain. She was bound captive by her heart, and by her instinct and her conscience. If she fled to the ends of the earth, she could not escape her husband's need of her. If she entered an enchanted city, and its gates closed fast behind her, she could not shut her children out of her mind.

Fool, fool, to feed upon fantasy till the life of the flesh betrayed you. Fool, to think in your vanity that you could conquer disease and poverty by a dream. Fool, thrice fool, to measure the frail integrity of imagination against the stumbling passion and craving needs of men. Face the facts now, Joanna. Beat your strong hands on the unresisting stone, and teach yourself the logic of physical pain. Now, where is the truth?

Yet though she sat up staring into the shadows, though she repeated to herself all that had happened within the last few hours, her name defiled, the foresters' camp ablaze, her husband out of his mind with rage and jealousy and desire, she could nct believe that this was all reality. For if life lay only in those humiliations, how was it that so often she had been happy, and that it had appeared gay and delightful to her? Or if reality lay in the mind's conception, then were not Teddy's illusions about her infidelity as true as her own certainty of good faith?

Face the facts she would if only they would keep still and let her face them. But they tossed up and down in her mind with fierce commotion, until she was dizzy and sick with effort and frustration. She saw Szermai at the dance staring into young Marrable's insolent face; she saw Teddy swaying in front of her, calling her his wife; she saw Pamela in her blood-stained coat, running to tell her that the black pig was dead. She saw Patricia, in the aunt's house at Kingsport, querulously demanding her mother who did not come. She saw Agnes, in the green field near Kingsport High School, sitting on a bank covered with daisies and singing in her clear, childish voice,

> " Oh, I forbid you, maidens a'
> Who wear gowd in your hair
> To come or go by Carterhaugh
> For young Tam Lin is there."

Surely, although her vision might betray her, though her eyes were dazzled by its enchantment so that her feet stumbled upon the common ways, though she became a fool, ignorant of all ways of living yet the truth of her protest against the tangible world remained?

" Cockadoodledooo! Cockadoodledoooo! "

The cocks crowed from the valley. A wan light spread slowly like grey water across the floor. Upstairs she heard Teddy coughing.

He had woken up then.

She ought to go to him.

She sat up, very still, on the floor, her hands clasped round her knees.

After about five minutes she rose stifly, walking with numb, chilled limbs into the kitchen. There she lit the spirit stove and heated milk in a saucepan. This she poured out and carried upstairs, her other hand on the banister, dragging her reluctant body as she walked.

Teddy lay on her tumbled bed, coughing hopelessly.

She lifted him from the pillows, fetched his medicine, and when he was quieter, gave him the milk. His hand shook so violently that he spilled some of it on to the sheet and she had to help him.

Then she went to his own room and made the bed for him.

" Wouldn't you like to go back now? " she asked.

He did not answer, but when she put her arm round him, he obeyed her like a child. She half carried him across the passage, and laid him on his bed. He turned his face away from her to the wall, still never speaking. She stood looking down at him, then quietly left the room and closed the door.

§ 2

At half-past nine she stood in the kitchen mixing sodden crusts and potato parings into a mash for the chickens. Teddy was still asleep, lying with a heavy immobility which alarmed her, and she kept pausing in her work to listen, lest he should wake up and ring his bell. A sudden knocking on the door made her start violently. She put down her bowl and went, the big wooden spoon still in her hand, and her apron messed with chicken food.

The girl from the post office stood outside by her bicycle. She looked at Joanna with loutish curiosity.

" There's a telegram for you, Mrs. Leigh. I'm sorry we couldn't get it through before. It came last night, but with that business up at Camp we couldn't fairly do anything. I've never known such a night. We had a special wire through to fire-station an' police an' all."

Joanna was tugging at the orange envelope, which would not open in her trembling fingers. At last she unfolded the paper and read in the postmaster's pencilled scrawl. " Patricia very poorly anxious can you come auntie."

"Patricia very poorly anxious can you come auntie."

"Patricia very poorly anxious can you come auntie."

She read and re-read it before the words conveyed any meaning to her shocked mind.

The girl from the post office meanwhile was enjoying a long stare. So this was Mrs. Leigh who had been carrying on with the Hungarian while her husband was ill. This was the woman who had blackened the

good name of the dale, insisted, so rumour said, upon
the retention of the foreigners, and driven to desperate
violence the village lads whose sisters and sweethearts
were not safe from the marauding lusts of alien men.
This, in other words, was the woman who was hot stuff.

The post-office girl, whose name was Maudie, had
been to the Council School. She had heard of a certain
Helen and of Troy burning, and she looked at the tall
woman beside her, in shabby shoes and a coarse, dirty
apron, holding a wooden spoon as she stared at the telegram. Maudie wondered.

Then she gazed with eyes rounded to astonishment,
for Mrs. Leigh had begun to laugh. She laughed with a
hard, painful laughter, which made her look very
strange indeed. Maudie said, " I say, Mrs. Leigh." Then
she said " Oh my! " Then she remembered that she had
been a Girl Guide in Miss Marshall's own patrol and
that hysterical persons must be severely scolded.

" Now then, Mrs. Leigh. Pull yourself together and
stop that," she said. " Sit down here." She pulled forward a wooden kitchen chair, her self-confidence growing stronger with each demonstration of her authority.
" Think shame, and your little girl ill, to laugh like that.
Stop it now. Where's your brandy? Got any sal
volatile? "

" Y-yes. N-no. It's in there," sobbed Joanna meekly.

" Sit right down. Bend your head down. I'm going to
get some water. Keep still."

The post-office girl felt really serious and important.
Mrs. Leigh had, she considered, shown every sign of a
guilty conscience. Other wives received the news of

their children's illness without flying off into hysterics. Besides, what were her children doing away from home anyway? She had got rid of them to carry on all the better, and now one of them was going to die. Perhaps there might be an inquest and it would all come out. It all served her right. It was a Judgment of Providence. Why, it might even be in the *News of the World* next Sunday.

" Now. Drink this water."

" Thank you," said Joanna, her teeth chattering against the glass, in her mind a mild wonder that she could have behaved so oddly. She was a satisfactory patient, however, for she responded immediately to treatment and convinced the post-office girl more than ever of her own efficacy as a nurse.

" That's right. Feeling better? You know, shock's an awful thing, but there's nothing to be frightened of with luck an' a good conscience. That's what my mother used to say."

Joanna wiped her eyes, sipped the water and re-read her telegram. Then she set down the tumbler and looked at the post-office girl.

" I want you to help me," she said. " I'm in a great difficulty."

" I know. I'm sorry," the girl muttered, less sure of herself now that the situation was passing beyond the range of the Girl Guide's Book of First-Aid.

" I want to go to Kingsport at once. There's a train at half-past eleven from Clarington. There isn't another one till late to-night. If I go down straight away, I could catch this one, but the cart's gone off with the milk." She rose and began to move about the kitchen, thinking aloud. " I can't leave Teddy — Captain Leigh — alone here. You know he's an invalid, don't you? Oh, I must go. I must go. They wouldn't send unless she was really ill. They know how difficult it is for me to get away. What time did you say this came? Perhaps there's another one come already." She did not speak her fear aloud, but to her heart came the chill horror of shock as she thought, " Suppose she may be dead already? Pat, Pat. I must go." " Listen," she continued aloud. " This is fearfully urgent. You've got to do something for me. You've got to stay here with my husband. If he wants anything, he'll ring on the bell, and you must go upstairs. I'll go down now and explain to Dr. Hutton. He must send somebody up until we can get a nurse. Will you wait here till somebody comes? Please, please. You must. There's no other way."

" Oh, I couldn't I'm sure, Mrs. Leigh. We're that busy."

" I can't help it how busy you are. You've got to do it. You can't let me down."

" Oh, I'm sure I don't know anything about nursing. What if he got ill? I'm sure I couldn't."

" I'm going to borrow your bicycle. You'll have to send to Clarington station for it. No. Bidgood can fetch it. I'm sorry. This is really important. You're going to do as I say. You're going to."

" Oh, I couldn't stay up here alone. I'm sure I couldn't. I'll go down to the village and send somebody."

" There's no time. I might miss my train. And I need

your bicycle. Look here, you've got to help me. There's probably never anyone you've ever met needed your help so badly. I'm not asking much of you. You're going to stay, do you hear?" In her urgency she crossed the room and stood over the diminished Maudie. "Do you hear?" she repeated, and when Maudie shrank back snivelling, she took her by the shoulders and shook her soundly. "You're going to stay. You are going to make him a cup of tea and take him some bread and butter at half-past ten. And if he coughs, you're to get him some of this medicine here. A tablespoonful in water. Here's the glass. Do you understand?"

She began to pull off her apron and to roll down her sleeves. She gave a sharp look at the frightened girl and ran from the room. Her husband lay with his face to the wall.

"Teddy," she said. "Teddy."

He did not stir.

"Teddy, I'm sorry to wake you, but I've got to tell you something. Listen." He did not stir and she went up and laid her hand on his shoulder. "Listen. Do you hear?" She saw his face move slightly and knew that he was awake. "Listen, darling. I've just had a wire from the aunts to say that Pat isn't well. It mayn't be anything much, but I think that I ought to go and see. I'm going down now to the village and I'm leaving the post-office girl — her name's Maudie — to look after you until Dr. Hutton sends someone up from the village. Darling, are you listening?" It was dreadful that he should not speak, dreadful that he should lie like that,

with the set sullen twist to his mouth and the dull un-
comprehending stare of his eyes. " Teddy, I hate leaving you. You understand that, don't you? But I'll try to
get back to-night. I'll wire. I'll let you know. Darling,
don't look like that. It's Pat, you know. I must go."
Still the same bitter line of the lips, and the brooding
stillness of the flushed face terrified her. " I'll come
back to you. Oh, I'll come back soon. Teddy, it's not
because of last night." She knelt down by the bed and
turned him over till his face looked into hers. " Darling.
Darling. You do understand. Oh, you do. It's Pat.
I must go."

With tears on her face, and with a sickness of foreboding in her heart as though she had left a task unfin-
ished, she turned from the room, and went downstairs
with her coat over her arm.

But the post-office girl had gone.

When Joanna rushed to the door and out to the
farm gate, she saw the last of her bump, bumping on
her bicycle over the rim of the hill, then disappearing
down the low road to the village.

The clear blue cup of the sky fitted tight down upon
the circle of hills. She was entrapped. There was no
one to help her. She cried softly to the serene, cloudless
sky, " Oh God! God! " She looked round at the huddled
buildings, at the calm line of the hills and the winding
road in front of her.

Her eyes half blinded with tears, her breath coming
in little choking sobs, she began to run away from
Scatterthwaite.

§ 3

Szermai, climbing the Fell slowly, told himself that it was for the last time. Well, he had, of course, been a fool. But so had Mrs. Leigh. She was, after all, to blame for placing herself in that position. Thank God he was cured of the madness which had beset him. This vulgar scandal, this bucolic encounter with the conventions and stupidities of an English village. Good heavens, was this what he had come to?

He was tired and stiff. He had burned his left hand, and after an over-strenuous night, his eyes felt sore and ached until they wept. But he felt sane again. The despair and the obsesssion had left him. During the hours of contest with the fire, with the angry temper and uncontrolled excitement of the men, and the shock of his own indignation, he had shaken off the spell under which he had lain ever since he had left Hungary.

He knew now what he would do. He would say goodbye to Mrs. Leigh. He would see his heterogeneous pack of foresters safely landed again in Finland, and he would return to his own country. He would find out his uncle. He would put an end to the futile wandering and discomfort of his exile.

As the road dipped down to the Scatterthwaite yard, he could not imagine why his heart had ever beaten faster to open the clumsy gate in the stone wall, or why the grey house had ever filled him with frenzy. Under the calm sky the buildings lay as solid and commonplace as the white-walled cottages near his home.

The yard, except for the pigs rooting in the straw

and two hens picking delicately near the manure-heap, was deserted! Nobody answered his knock, and in accordance with his custom he entered the kitchen through the half-open door. A bowl of chicken food stood on the table, with a half-empty tumbler of water. A wooden spoon lay on the floor and a discarded apron. On the dresser Captain Leigh's ubiquitous medicine bottles and two glasses had been set out as though for some special purpose.

Szermai raised his eyebrows. He was accustomed to the disorder of Scatterthwaite, but there was a sinister intention about this disorder and a strange unfamiliarity about the silence of the house. Perhaps an unexpected caller had come, he thought, and went through the hall to the dining-room. But this also lay empty, with no signs of a breakfast, and with the sewing materials used the night before still on the table.

At the foot of the stairs he bent down to pick up a crumpled piece of paper. As though it might provide a clue for something which quite irrationally appeared to him as a mystery, he smoothed out its folds and moved to the coloured glass of the rarely opened front door to read it. "Patricia very poorly anxious can you come auntie," he read and re-read with wrinkled brows. Patricia. That was the little girl. The elder. She was delicate. Mrs. Leigh had spoken the night before of her illness. But the date was the date of the previous night, and the paper had been flung down carelessly on the stair, and the house was apparently deserted.

With a sudden curious expression on his face, Szermai put the paper into his pocket and went upstairs.

251

Captain Leigh's door was wide open. The coverlet of his bed was neatly turned. His body lay, as he had moved immediately Joanna left him, with its face to the wall. Only his harsh breathing told Szermai that he was still alive.

The Hungarian returned to the kitchen and looked round the room. Joanna's old felt hat, which usually hung on the peg by the door, was missing. So was the black leather bag which he knew well, from which she took money for tradesmen who called at rare intervals, and which accompanied her to the village. Had she gone? And left her husband all alone? Surely not. That seemed most unlike her.

He shrugged his shoulders. Perhaps it was as well. Fate, after all, might have ordained that they should not meet again. He would write to her. He took up his hat which he had set down on the chair and was about to depart when from the room upstairs, faint yet unmistakable, came the sound of Teddy's bell.

He paused, and stood wondering. Again it rang, its angry familiar tinkle scattering the oppressive silence of the farm.

Szermai did not want to encounter Teddy. He did not, indeed, wish to remain at Scatterthwaite a moment longer than was absolutely necessary. Every minute he was growing more and more certain that he had been upon the verge of a fatal blunder there. Yet the man was ill and alone.

With a sigh he set down his hat again and climbed the stair.

" Hullo, Leigh. Has your wife deserted you, yes? I come to tell you that your beautiful and handsome suit shall be returned after I have contrived to have it cleaned. One should not put out fires in boiled shirts. Why . . ."

His voice died away. He was looking into the face of a man undoubtedly mad. For Leigh had risen from his bed at the first sound of the Hungarian's familiar voice, and stood in his pyjamas in the middle of the room, staring at the intruder.

" Why, had you not better return to bed? " asked Szermai.

But Leigh continued to stare, whispering hoarsely, " Oh, it's you, is it? She has gone and you have come, have you? To have the last laugh, eh? The last laugh. Come here. You think you've been very clever, don't you? But I'll tell you something. She's my wife, d'you hear? And she knows it now." He began to cough, fighting gallantly for self-control. " And I'll tell you this. If you think that you can trick me from my heritage." The coughing caught his voice and checked it. He began to pluck at the already opened neck of his coat. " I tell you," he put out one hand as though to stop the speech of the Hungarian. Having something to say he could not bear to be robbed of articulation through the tyranny of his sickness. " I tell you, she's mine, see? She's mine, not yours, not yours." He clutched at his thin ribs with sudden pain. His voice died to a whisper so low and harsh that the Hungarian could not catch his words as he cried, " I've won, d'you understand? Get out, get out of my house! "

He swayed forward, coughing. He struck out at the Hungarian's face with blind, futile hands.

Then he bowed his head and fell forward into his enemy's arms as the blood flowed, suddenly and inevitably from his mouth, down Szermai's coat, and on to the floor.

CHAPTER THIRTEEN

THE LAND OF GREEN GINGER

§ 1

"BUT what were you doing last night?" asked Aunt Emily.

Joanna turned her head from side to side as though searching for the memory of something obscured to her by a lifetime of anxiety and dread. Then she remembered. "I was at a dance," she said.

"A dance?" cried Pamela, jumping up and down. "Oh, Mummy, how lovely! You never told us that there was a dance."

"A dance?" echoed Aunt Emily. "My dear, what sort of dance?"

They stared at her as though she were an adventurer from an unknown world. Had she said that she had swum the Nile or flown across Mount Everest, or dined at Monte Carlo, they could not have been much more astonished. They only knew that she had arrived from the five-thirty train, in her old tweed coat and gardening hat, without even two shillings to pay the cabman. She had borrowed that from Aunt Kate on the doorstep. She explained that she had only just had time to catch the train from Clarington because she had had to find Doctor Hutton and persuade him to go up to Teddy at Scatterthwaite. Teddy, they understood, was not so well, and in her disordered appearance, her untidy clothes and haggard face, her aunts had read the story of her hard, difficult life. And now she said that not twenty-four hours ago, she had been dancing. It seemed incredible.

Patricia was very ill. She had pleurisy again, and the doctor was coming at eight o'clock with an anæsthetist to perform the operation which should remove the fluid from pressure on the lung. Joanna, already in a clean apron borrowed from Aunt Emily, and with her sleeves rolled up, was helping to prepare the spare bedroom. They had been moving the light, pushing furniture against the wall, and airing sheets. Every few minutes, Joanna ran back to her little daughter, who lay flushed and crying, saying, "I'm so frightened, Mummy. There's a pain like a knife. I'm so frightened. Don't go away again. Don't ever go."

"No, darling, no, I won't. Not unless Daddy needs me frightfully."

"Don't go. Tell me about the dance."

"Oh, no. Not now. I will to-morrow."

"Tell me now. When you talk it does not hurt so much. Tell me what you wore."

"I wore a dress of blue and silver, made from Aunt Helen's cloak . . ."

"How?"

"Oh, Daddy helped me. It was cut with a sort of scarf across the shoulders, falling down one side. And we drove to the dance in the float. It was quite fine, almost light, and so funny to be in evening dress with the sunlight still on the fields. I even put the chickens to bed, with my dress tucked under the old tweed coat. . . ."

" About the dance. I know about the chickens."

" Very well. Beatrice Marshall was there. The tall, dark, eldest one, you know. She was in white, I think. She stood at the entrance to the dance room, and behind her hung festoons of red and yellow bunting, and branches of young green stuff cut from the trees. And the tables were piled with pink jellies and creams for supper, and there was a band from Clarington, playing rag-times. They do a new dance called the Charleston."

" Show me."

" No, sweetieheart. Not now. When you're quite well, I'll teach it to you. Mr. Szermai taught me. He dances beautifully."

" He shall teach me. I like to dance with grown-up men."

" Perhaps. But he's going away soon."

" Show me, Mummy. Dance for me."

" There's no music. I have no partner."

" Show, show," Patricia wailed, and Joanna stood up in the little room, with bright, dry eyes and fiercely tender lips, saying, " Look then, darling. Weight on the left foot, up on the toe, right foot out . . ."

" Sing. Sing. Oh, it hurts, Mummy."

> " When the Sahara sleeps
> To your side I'll creep . . ."

hummed Joanna, but her breath would not come, and her eyes were upon the sick child who cried, " Dance, Mummy," yet did not look at her, as she swayed, and sang, moving slowly about the bed in her lonely dance. She did not hear the front-door bell ring, nor know how Aunt Emily ran to open it and saw the telegraph boy on the step. Nor could she see her aunt opening in surprise the yellow envelope, addressed to " Entwhistle, 36 Park Street, Kingsport."

Aunt Emily read, " Please tell Mrs. Leigh her husband died of hæmorrhage at noon to-day. Can she return to-morrow. Please wire instructions. Hutton."

" Oh dear," cried Aunt Emily. " Oh dear, oh dear. What shall I do now? "

She was still staring and wondering when the doctors arrived to operate upon Patricia.

§ 2

The front bedroom looked chill and white and unfamiliar. The electric light had been pulled down low over the kitchen table, which, covered by a blanket, stood in the centre of the carpetless floor. The bed had been moved away and in its place stood tables with white cloths and enamel trays and bowls and kettles with boiled water. When Patricia saw the strange appearance of the room she cried again:

" Oh, Mummy, what is it? What are they going to do to me? "

Joanna laid her daughter on the hard table under the unshaded light.

" It's all right, darling. They are going to make you quite well. Nobody's going to hurt you. I shall stand here all the time."

" Promise."

" I promise. And you'll only smell a nice smell and wake up ever so much better."

" You're cheating me, I expect. I shall die and wake up in heaven. I hate heaven. I don't want to die."

" Now then," said the doctor.

Joanna's mouth set in a sullen line. Harsh anger burned in her eyes. She was caught in a cold unreasoning fury. She watched with bitter composure every movement of the surgeon and the anæsthetist. She heard the clinking of steel instruments on the enamel bowls. She saw their absorbed, almost inhuman, faces. When they asked her to do anything, she obeyed them with mechanical efficiency. They thought her wonderful in her sensible placidity, as with steady hands she watched and waited upon them, handing swabs and bowls, making no false move and misunderstanding no direction. They did not know that she was hating them. There was no mercy in her angry heart for them or for herself.

They were hurting her little girl. They had terrified Patricia. Patricia might die. Let them do their worst. She would never forgive them. She could watch them with satisfaction being tortured under her eyes. She would never forgive Teddy for making it necessary to send the children away. She would never forgive herself for her impotence in failing to keep this suffering from her child.

Who spoke of motherhood as joyous? Who talked about proud mothers? This was her little girl. This, the child that she had brought into the world, the child who without her would never have known her days of distress, her wearing vanity, her exasperation and fear. She had given life to Patricia, and now she could only stand by and watch her suffer.

"Swabs, please, Mrs. Leigh. We're doing grandly."

It came upon her then that if she found that she were going to bear another child as the result of last night's wild encounter, she would almost rather kill herself and it.

It was after ten o'clock when she came downstairs at last. The operation had been successful; the doctors had gone. Aunt Kate was sitting upstairs with Patricia. Pamela was in bed.

Aunt Emily carried a tray into the dining-room and set it down on the brown plush table-cloth which Joanna knew so well.

"You must eat something, dear," she said.

Joanna ate ham sandwiches and drank tea, not speaking.

"Darling little Jo," said Aunt Emily, "you've got to be very brave."

"Yes, I know," replied Joanna. "I am."

"You — why, do you know then, dear? Oh, Joanna, don't look at me like that, dear. Can't you cry, darling? I'd rather you cried. It's God's will, after all. He was taken mercifully. All suffering over, darling."

"Who was taken mercifully?" asked Joanna, a ham sandwich half-way to her mouth. "I wish you'd make some black coffee, Auntie."

"Why — then you don't know. Oh, Jo, darling. Be very brave. We didn't tell you before. It came this evening. It's all for the best, darling. It is indeed." And she showed her niece the telegram from Doctor Hutton.

Joanna read it with stern attention.

" When did this come? " she asked finally.

" Just before the doctors arrived this evening."

" Well, what does he expect me to do? I can't leave Patricia. We'd better make arrangements with an undertaker. How are these things done? I suppose that he can be buried here at Kingsport."

" Jo, Jo, darling, don't take it like that. Don't look like that."

" I'm going upstairs now to Patricia. You had better get some hot tea for Aunt Kate."

Folding the telegram carefully she left the room and went upstairs to her daughter.

§ 3

" I shan't be away long, dear, and Pam's going to stay with you, and Nurse Whately says that she'll read to you," said Joanna, and bent over Patricia to kiss her. She smiled reassuringly at Pamela, the sturdy little creature mounting guard beside her sister. It was impossible not to feel confidence in Pamela, who was so round and placid and comfortable.

Then she went downstairs, drawing on her new black gloves.

At the turn of the steps she stood, watching the undertaker's men emerging from the drawing-room with the polished coffin. Without its canopy of flowers it looked raw and shining and businesslike. She stared at it, telling herself incredulously that within this box lay Teddy.

She watched the men shuffle carefully past the hat-rack. The marble-topped table had been removed to facilitate their progress. The front door was wide open, and as the first couple stepped cautiously down, growling muffled directions, the sunlight flashed on the brass plate and handles of the coffin.

Joanna moved slowly downstairs and followed them to the door. After a night of rain a bright breeze blew through the gardens, shaking wet laburnum and lilac blossom on to the black shoulders of the men and the path and the coffin. A blackbird jubilated in the lilac bushes, scattering notes golden as the laburnum flowers, and in the sky blew clouds as soft as feathers over the house. A large bee blundered heavily down the path, hung over the green grass, and tumbled into a scarlet tulip. Joanna noticed all these things.

"Oh, my dear. I did not know that you had come downstairs," Aunt Kate said, sniffing a little. "Poor Teddy. But the coffin looks much nicer when all the flowers are there. Really, they've done it very nicely, dear."

"Yes," said Joanna.

The wreaths and crosses lay on sheets in the drawing-room where the coffin had stood, or were propped against the trestles.

"We'd better carry some out. It will save time," suggested Joanna. "I want to get there and back again." She picked up a wreath in each hand, and, holding them by the moss-covered wire behind the

262

flowers, carried them out at arm's length to the hearse.

Aunt Kate looked timidly at her, and then at the cross marked by an ink-smudged card, " To Daddy. From Patricia and Pamela." She thought that Pamela should have been allowed to attend her father's funeral, but Joanna had been so firm about it. She had, indeed, been firm about everything, quite unnaturally so. But very wonderful. Aunt Kate picked up the children's flowers and hurried out after her niece.

Aunt Emily looked round the transfigured drawing-room. A white narcissus flower had fallen beyond the sheets and been partially trodden into the pink carpet. Dear, dear. They stained so. And carpets nowadays were carpets. Aunt Emily carefully picked it off the floor, threw it into the waste-paper basket, and wiped the place with a corner of the sheet. Then she, too, lifted the final wreaths and carried them from the house.

In the one mourning coach Joanna sat very still on the seat with her back to the horses, as she had always sat when, as a child, she had driven on rare occasions with her aunts to concerts or to parties. Her aunts looked at each other in perplexity, certain that the widow, who was an important person, should not take the humblest seat in the carriage, but intimidated by her unapproachable determination.

Presently Joanna remarked, " I suppose that no one will want to come back after the funeral to eat and what not. With Patricia ill we really can't do with them."

" No, dear. Of course they will understand," said Aunt Kate, with subdued optimism. She was glad to find one consoling thought in the day's sad business.

The sleek black horses trotted cloppetty clop, cloppetty clop, down the sunlit road. So modest a procession aroused few glances from the scattered pedestrians, although in Park Street from behind discreet lace curtains, many eyes watched the single carriage accompanying the body of Miss Entwhistle's nephew-by-marriage to the grave.

They turned past the shops and past St. Michael and All Angels, into the more crowded thoroughfares of the city. Joanna sat smoothing her black suède gloves upon unaccustomed fingers. As the houses grew higher, the carriage darkened. Passers-by raised their hats to the flower-covered coffin, and Joanna, who had refused to close the carriage window, saw them staring furtively at the mourners.

"I didn't realize that we should pass up Friarsgate," she observed conversationally.

"Yes, dear. It's the quickest way. We cut through into Bridkirk Alley."

A man wheeled a barrow of flowering plants and ferns along the road. They were destined to decorate the Town Hall for a municipal festival that evening. Two girls in bright cotton dresses, the first that Joanna had seen that year, came out of a shop and stood giggling on the pavement. A shaft of sunlight slanting between two towering warehouses made sudden summer in the street.

The hearse had turned. Its fine black horses with their gleaming coats paused for an instant, pawing at the hollow-sounding wood-blocks of the road. A group of young men in new straw hats, coming out of a bank at the corner, saw the funeral procession and turned with casual reverence to do homage to the waiting coffin. It was the bank where Martin Leigh had served the last of his self-condemned sentence of hard labour.

Joanna looked out of the window to see the cause of their delay, and as a motor lorry which had been obstructing them rattled out of a side street, she saw the hearse, flashing in sunlight, move round from Friarsgate and turn before her into the dark by-road called The Land of Green Ginger.

CHAPTER FOURTEEN

THE HOSTILE VALLEY

§ 1

JOANNA was unpacking in the bedroom which had been Teddy's, and which was now to be hers. Dresses, shoes and bundles of sewing, all a little shabby and desolate, lay on the chairs and floor and bed.

Downstairs Bidgood and his sister, a woman of overpowering respectability imported from Harrogate, ate their belated supper with the aggrieved acquiescence of two companions who, although uncongenial to each other, yet resent a coming separation.

Patricia and Pamela were at last in bed, the excitement of their return quenched by fatigue.

The familiar makeshift poverty of the farm enclosed them all again. Its bleak, half-furnished rooms and creaking stairs assumed new friendliness after the neat precision of the house in Park Street and the impersonal congestion of the seaside lodgings. They were home again, back among the familiar and friendly things, and the long, spacious days and the dark solitude of the moors. Beyond their windows the light waned from the blue cup of the hills, and the road to Letherwick faded into the grass and heather.

Joanna lit her candle and bent again over the trunk, shaking out a faded skirt and an old brown jersey. It

was no use trying to wear black. People would understand that on a farm you had to let things like that surrender to the imperious necessity of the day's work.
There was a hard struggle ahead; her life lay with the
future and with the living, not with the past; and a
strange elation sometimes possessed her at the thought
of wrestling unhandicapped with the difficulties that
hitherto she had shirked. She must raise a mortgage on
the farm and settle their debts. She would sell all the
sheep and pay no grazing rent on the moor, but con-
centrate upon the cows and dairy work and pigs and
poultry which she understood. The children must go
to the Council School in Letherwick until she could
afford to send them into Clarington. Perhaps they
would win scholarships. Pat was clever.

If only Patricia would keep well. The doctor had
said " a patch on the lung." Letherwick air was good,
but when they had driven that evening down the last
dip of the road from the station into the yard, Joanna
had shuddered as though an evil omen revealed itself in
the waiting house, the grim grey buildings, and the
green hollow of the fields. What if the child began to
show more certain signs of the disease?

" I'll make money. I'll do everything for her. She
shall go to Switzerland, to California. Anywhere. I'll
give her every chance."

Aunt Helen had sent them all, after Pat's recovery,
for a holiday at Eastbourne, and lying on the sands, or
bathing in the sharp delicious water, Joanna had
planned her future life. No more dreaming over in-
accessible countries. Here was her country. She would

learn the arts which should subdue the stubborn earth. She would rear stock and sell milk and butter, and her eggs should be the talk of the countryside.

One day, perhaps, when she was a wealthy farmer, and the children had left school, they would sell the tumble-down old place and wave farewell to the dark circle of heather, and set off on their travels. Then they would visit the Canary Islands, and Barbados and Constantinople and Thibet.

A big moth fluttered in through the window and flapped into her candle-flame.

" Silly," she admonished it. " Silly."

Another followed. She rose quickly to close her window. But as she sprang to her feet, the faintness which had afflicted her earlier in the day returned again. She sat down slowly on the edge of the bed and remained there, thinking.

At the back of her mind dwelt a half certainty which she had tried, all through the past week, to ignore. It had returned again to her consciousness, and she was facing it.

" Not that. No, no. Not that," she was repeating to herself. " That couldn't happen. It couldn't. The bathing has affected me, because I'm not used to it."

But the longer she thought, the more certain she became, and with her certainty grew her dismay.

"Oh, I can't, I can't," she whispered, looking about the room as though for some means of escape. But there was no escape, and well she knew it, try as she would to deceive herself.

The practical difficulties of the situation were bad

enough, but she could face these. If she had a child in
February, it would certainly mean that she would be
disabled in one of the hardest seasons of the year. Fortunately, she thought, Bidgood was reliable. She would
need a woman too. Why not ask Hannah Bidgood to
stay? She would explain to her the situation. She had
hoped to manage without a woman on the farm, but a
baby altered the whole position. " She may not like
children." She worried. " She'll have to like this one.
I must have somebody."

" It's a good thing I'm so strong," she considered.
Her former children had been little trouble to her. Until
Christmas she would be able to go about her work unless something went unexpectedly wrong; but all her
carefully laid schemes of retrenchment and expenditure
were thrown awry. There would be doctor's bills, and
extra help in the house, and herself burdened again by
the care of something helpless when she wanted to con-
centrate upon the farm. " I'll get through somehow,"
she told herself, and began again, but more slowly, to
tidy her disordered room.

But as she moved about the place so eloquent of her
husband's presence, the severely practical considera-
tions which came first to her mind faded. Since Teddy's
death she had refused to think about him. Patricia's
need of her, the strain of the child's illness and the relax-
ation of her holiday at Eastbourne, had filled her mind
from hour to hour with small, hurried thoughts. She
had never looked back into the last twenty-four hours
before his death; she had never speculated upon his
attitude towards her when she had left him to catch the

Kingsport train. She had learned of Szermai's presence in the house before his death, and had not even wondered very much why he should have been there.

Teddy was dead. His heavy troubles were ended. Ended also was the anxiety from day to day and hour to hour which his life had laid upon Joanna. She was free. The children were safer. The problem of life was just a little easier because he had died. She had not thought herself particularly hard because in her obsession by the needs of the hour she had found no time to mourn him, but as the earth fell into his grave, a grave among so many other graves in the ugly, sunlit, commonplace cemetery, she had thought, " Perhaps now he has everything that he wants. Perhaps now he can become even a priest," and so had made an end.

But now she knew that she had made no end. It was not true that when people were dead, and the earth lay on their coffins, the account was closed, and the living could go on their way in peace, eating and drinking, loving and hating, seeing the sun rise and hearing music, enjoying the warm ardour of work and contest. The easy comfort of speculation about immortality, the life after death, and the resurrection of the body came all too readily to living minds. The dead lie in their graves, Joanna thought. They who desired life and conquest and activity have sleep at last, perhaps, and calm decay. " But these are not life. Life stirs here in my body. Life, everlasting life, even now works through me, given by Teddy to a creature which he will never see. He has not left behind his questing mind, his eager aspiring soul which sought perfection. Here is our immortality, in this fecundity of the imperfect flesh."

She saw eternity in an unending stream of birth and of begetting; she saw humanity at odds with life and captive to it, obeying its inexorable command. She saw her body as the instrument of the remorseless mandate to continue. Teddy was dead; but even in dying he had given, not the heritage of the soul which he had born with him in so much sorrow, but the heritage of his hostile and malevolent body.

And he had desired so bitterly to escape. She saw him now, a man greedy of the spirit, desiring an immaculate conception of life, hungry for a perfection which he had never found. She saw him baffled and bruised time after time by the victory of his physical limitations, hoping always that one day his personality might ride master of his imprisoning flesh. And now, with an irony so cruel that the thought became intolerable to her, the flesh had conquered. Life moved on, away from Teddy, away from the struggles which had been so real and so intense to him. Life made her, who had been his friend, his companion, his lover, inheritor of his immortality. In his passion to possess her more completely he had lost her for ever. Seeking against reason, against prudence and courtesy and love to feel his life and to enlarge his manhood, he had lost it, and given to her instead all that remained to him.

If he had wanted a child, if he had begotten it in love and tenderness and pride of their relationship, then this moment of realization would have brought healing. It would have sealed for ever the memory of their love.

If she had wanted a child, if she had conceived it as

she had conceived the others, with joy and pride and a strong sense of enrichment, then this knowledge would have come to her with the new glory of fulfilment.

But the child would be fruit of despair and bitterness, the accidental creation of a passion for life which had killed its captive. Life had been more cruel than death to Teddy. She felt that she betrayed him now by living, by living herself and creating new life, when he was dead.

" He wanted to live himself until he had won his peace of mind," she said aloud. " He's been cheated, cheated. Oh, Teddy. Darling. Darling."

She stood with her back against the door, facing the room which had been his and in which he had died, and cursed the cruelty of a relentless law, the impotence of human aspirations and the God in whom she did not quite believe.

§ 2

Joanna climbed slowly into the cart and gathered up the reins. The schoolmaster, she thought, had a curious manner. Why had he looked at her so oddly and spoken with such brusque precision? When Patricia had gone to school before she had thought him a nicish man. Of course it was a nuisance that the children's education had been so much neglected lately, but ill-health interferes with plans whether one wishes or no.

It was very hot, and although the cart had been waiting under the chestnut trees, the worn leather of the seat almost scorched her hand. She wished that her hat gave her more shade. She had put on the black straw because she thought it somehow more appropriate to wear some sign of mourning in the village. She was tired too, although she had felt so admirably well lately; but to-day she had been up very early making butter and then had driven herself into Clarington to talk to the little lawyer who had been negotiating the mortgage for her. Everything was going quite well, except for the refusal of Hannah Bidgood to stay after her month. There was no denying that Joanna enjoyed the work. She liked talking to the lawyer and the corn-and-cake merchant and the bank-manager in Clarington. She enjoyed discussing Rhode Island Reds and Buff Orpingtons with old Harding at the chicken food stores. Although she knew her tendencies to be casual and forgetful, there was a certain blithe energy in her work which, added to the experience which was increasing monthly, should bring her success. She was contemplating an adventure to the market to buy another sow. She would love to see Mr. Dukes the auctioneer, whom she had met at her lawyer's, really " in action."

The church clock surprised her by striking four, and reminded her that she was thirsty and hot, and would appreciate tea before driving home. It reminded her also that she had done nothing about the woman who must be secured to replace Hannah Bidgood.

" I'll go to Mr. Boyse," she thought suddenly. " He's been a good friend to me, and he's probably having tea now if he's at home."

She turned the pony down a rough track across the village green and stopped before a pleasant cottage, withdrawn from the road behind a garden gay with

273

sweet peas and hollyhocks and great moon-faced daisies, where the curate lodged with the two Misses Hemmingway.

The pony would stand for any length of time with the reins twisted round the rail of the cart and his nose among the clover and daisies of the green, so she left him and went up to the door and knocked.

The elder Miss Hemmingway opened the door and looked at her suspiciously, noting the blue cotton dress which contradicted her sober little hat. " Yes. He's in. But I don't know whether he's at home," she replied to Joanna's question.

Joanna repressed a smile. " Please tell him that it's Mrs. Leigh."

" I'll tell him," said the woman, and left Joanna standing till she returned with the curate behind her.

" Come in, please. Come in, Mrs. Leigh," he said with a constrained warmth which struck Joanna as somewhat curious. " What a fine day, isn't it? "

" Very hot," answered Joanna. " I hope that you're having tea because I'm atrociously thirsty."

She followed him into his little sitting-room and sat down in the arm-chair which wore a white antimacassar and blue ribbons.

" Dear me, what a maidenly chair," she remarked. " Do you mind if I take off my hat? It's too tight, and I've been in it from early morn to dewy eve." She pushed her hand through her damp hair and smiled up at the blushing curate.

Miss Hemmingway appeared at the door.

" Another cup, please," stammered Mr. Boyse. With

a backward glance at the large, sunburned woman in her arm-chair, the landlady retired to the kitchen. " And not even in black! " she told her sister.

" Well, Mr. Boyse," Joanna began. " I've been wanting to see you for ages. First of all, I wanted to thank you, more than I can say, for all you did for us when my husband died." Her voice was quite steady. The curate, gazing unhappily at the ceiling, did not notice the deep lines about her mouth and the new wrinkles below her eyes which hardened as she spoke. " Dr. Hutton told me of all your kindness. I've always been grateful to you, but now more than ever."

The return of Miss Hemmingway with a tray interrupted her, and she waited until they were alone again.

" And secondly, I don't think that it was kind of you not to call on me before," she said, and smiled at him. Then she observed his violent agitation. " Oh, of course I don't mean anything. Of course I know that you must have been busy. How have you been getting on? " What was the matter with him? she wondered. He often seemed a little shy. She began to cast back in her mind for their last encounter, to try to remember what they had said or done.

" Have some bread and butter, what? " said the curate. " You're looking better, Mrs. Leigh."

" I am. I feel very well. It was Eastbourne. Never say that it's not a blessing to have a rich aunt, Mr. Boyse. I bathed and slept all day at her expense. It was heavenly."

" I am very glad." But he looked a little shocked, as

though so newly widowed a wife, who had known such tragic experience, ought not to find bathing heavenly.

" I really came," said Joanna, her mouth half full of bread and butter, " to ask you to do something else for me."

" Anything that I can . . . "

" Hannah Bidgood's leaving. The woman I've had. Your treasured sister. She said that you couldn't call Scatterthwaite civilization when there was outside accommodation and no Early Service. You really must find me someone else. And not quite such a good churchwoman next time, please. They do complicate things. So many saints' days, you know, and two and a half miles from church."

" You — er — er — want another maid? "

" Maid or matron. I'm not particular," smiled Joanna, her mouth half full of bread and butter. " This is lovely bread. I've only just realized that I was hungry. No wonder you don't come to tea with me now if Miss Hemmingway bakes like this. It really might be better to find me a matron, after all. Someone who doesn't object to babies. I believe really that was Hannah Bidgood's objection to me, only she called it outside accommodation."

" Babies? Oh, yes, you mean the children? " asked the curate, but he had blushed deep red.

" Yes. Didn't you know? I'm going to have a baby in February."

" Oh no. No." cried the curate.

She stared at his horrified face.

" Oh, but why not? " she said stupidly.

" No. Say it isn't true! You're chaffing me. It's not true, Mrs. Leigh."

" Why, of course it's true. Why should I want to make up a silly joke like that? It's no joke at all, I can tell you."

" But to come here. To tell me. So lightly. Oh, forgive me, so, so shameless."

The poor young man was obviously shocked to the heart.

" But I don't understand you. What do you mean? "

" I told them it wasn't true. I told Mrs. Pitcock that I'd stake my honour upon yours. I said that if it was true I'd resign from Letherwick, by Jove. I said . . . I said that you might be thoughtless sometimes, and unconventional, but that you were a devoted wife, and a good woman. Take it back, Mrs. Leigh. Say it's not true."

" I wish I could take it back," said Joanna bitterly. " And I wish that I knew who you are to make so much fuss. It's my baby. Not yours. I didn't want to have it. You don't think that it's a very happy prospect for it, do you? "

" You're hard," he said. " You've been made hard and defiant. You're trying to brazen it out. But it's no use. You must face it some time . . ."

" I have faced it. I have faced it out. But it's no use whining over something that you can't help. I was angry at first when I knew that it was coming. After all that I knew of the suffering there might be waiting for it. But somehow on a farm there isn't much time to be tragic. Especially when you've got two children and one of them is delicate. I dare say that when it comes I shall be all the more fond of it because I feel that it hasn't had an awfully good start."

" But its heritage. . . . How can you talk so lightly of its heritage? "

" Oh, be quiet. Do you think I haven't thought? What do you think I'm made of? How would you like to bear the child of a consumptive man when one of your other children was already threatened with the disease and you knew just exactly what misery it can mean and how sickness takes hold even of love and changes it? Do you think that I haven't thought? "

But he had not heeded her. He was staring into her flushed and mobile face, in which so much of indignation and tenderness, or sorrow and courage and a half-ironic acceptance of life's bitterness contested. He saw her all golden and glowing, a vital, unquenchable creature, and suddenly came down on his knees before her, seizing her hands. " Joanna. Joanna. Forgive me. I had to speak. You drive me mad. You must drive all men mad. You can't help it. It was an impulse. Say it was an impulse, that you did not love him. Say that he was nothing to you but a bad dream, what? And marry me. I'll marry you. I don't care. We'll go away. We'll get right clear of here. I don't mind about the child. Let it have my name. The fellow's gone. The camp's broken. We'll never hear of any of them again. I can't bear . . . I can't bear all the things that they're saying about you in the village."

Joanna slowly withdrew her hands from his. The colour died from her face.

"Oh, that's the matter then?" she half whispered. "That's what you all think, is it? That my child isn't Teddy's. That Paul Szermai . . . As those young farmers said at the dance. Oh, yes, I see. What a fool I've been. What a fool not to have foreseen this." They were silent for a minute, then the young man, realizing even in his great perturbation that he must look rather foolish kneeling upon the mat, stood up awkwardly beside her on the hearthrug. "Yes, I see," she continued, thinking alone. "Of course. That accounts for it. Hannah going. And the schoolmaster. And . . . How long have you known? Ever since I told Hannah, I suppose. It must have gone all round the village. My fault, of course. I ought to have remembered more clearly the sort of thing which had been going on before Pat was ill. But I was so pressed," she pleaded, as though before a judge who must hear her defence. "I had so much to think about. Was it any wonder that I never realized how much the village might talk?"

"Then it's not true?" he asked.

"No. No. Of course not. Oh, what a fool!" She groaned, dropping her face into her hands. He moved forward and touched her shoulder shyly.

She started up. "Don't touch me, please. I wasn't thinking of you or of me. I was thinking of Teddy. How he would have hated this, this sort of thing. Can't you stop them, Mr. Boyse?"

Then looking at his unhappy and still incredulous face, she saw that he could not, and that even he was not yet quite convinced. And suddenly it seemed to her that here was just the one thing which she could not fight. She, who cared so little about appearances, and who had derived so little benefit from social institutions, could face almost any difficulty but this. She must leave her good name for others to clear. There was no more spirit left in her.

She rose abruptly and began to put on her hat in front of the mirror over the mantelpiece. Her hands were trembling.

"Thank you for having me to tea," she said. "And thank you — I don't think that I quite appreciated before just how nice it was of you — thank you for asking me to marry you. It was very fine of you, I expect. And now I must go home, please."

She moved towards the door.

"But Mrs. Leigh . . ."

She turned round and faced him, seeing that he was almost in tears at last. She smiled into his young, troubled, foolish, kindly, simple face.

"Poor little thing," she said softly. "I didn't mean to give you such a bad time. You were brave, weren't you?"

And putting her hands on his shoulders she suddenly kissed him and was gone before he could recover from his astonishment.

He sank down into the chair which she had left, his head in his hands.

He did not wait to see her drive away.

§ 3

Joanna had milked the cows and fed the ducks and driven the fowls in from the paddock, and sent the children to change their damp stockings. Then she set out on the kitchen table Bidgood's supper, cold potato pie and bacon cake and a saucer custard. He came in as she was filling the teapot.

" I wanted a word with you, Mrs. Leigh."

" Yes. Well? "

" I think I'll be going off to join my sister back end of next month."

" Oh, Bidgood! Does that mean that you're leaving us too? "

" Why. It's a month's notice, both ways, and fair's fair, as you might say. If there are reasons, there are reasons as you know on as well as I. Maybe my sister's found us both a place as cook and odd man at a high-class girls' school where decent church-going people are appreciated, and maybe, on the other hand, she hasn't."

" Yes. I see. It's not a question of wages, is it? "

" The wages of sin is death," he answered gloomily. " I'm not saying that I judges you. Maybe I do. Maybe I don't. But a nicer man nor Captain Leigh it would be hard to find. He was a gentleman. But he was a rare invalid, and there were only two men up here beside yourself and you're in the family way. I'm not saying that folks about here is questioning my character. They're not. But a man who puts hisself into the way of gettin' an ill name deserves all he gets. Not but what you haven't been decent enough, as you might say."

" But Bidgood, do you mean to say that you believe that silly story about my baby being Mr. Szermai's? You can't believe it. You know that it isn't true. I'm going to have a baby. I told your sister so when I asked her to stay on. But of course it is my husband's."

She blushed and bit her lip, because, in spite of her dismay, she could not help thinking it a little funny that she should be sitting at the table explaining her baby to this grim and godly man.

" What I think an' what I hear may be two different things. But where there's smoke there's fire, as the saying is. I hadn't no references to your character when I took this situation, Mrs. Leigh. You only had them to mine. An' while this sort of one-sided justice goes about, men like me have to look after theirselves. Maybe it's all a pack o' lies, an' you're a virtuous wife that's being slandered. An' maybe you'll get folks to believe that t' bairn's born in wedlock. An' maybe not. But when mud's thrown some of it sticks, an' I'm under no obligation to you. We've got to look after our own good names. A fine thing a character given by you to me would be. ' Honest, sober an' respectable,' when all over the dale they're saying you're none of these things."

" Yes. I see your point of view." They were both silent for a minute. Then she added briskly, " Of course, you must do what is best for yourself. I don't want to hold you against your will, and I'm sure that I don't want to harm your character. Now, I'm going out for a few minutes. Will you just give an eye to the children till I come back? "

Thank goodness he was thoroughly reliable; but his reliability made the thought of his departure more ominous. He was going. Mr. Boyse was alienated. The village re-echoed with scandal. Her world, which she had built so solidly about her, the concrete reality which she had chosen so hardly, was breaking before her eyes.

Driven by an impulse for solitude, she caught up her old mackintosh and went out of the back door.

A fine summer rain was falling, but the August evening was so still that no breeze lifted the hair from her hot forehead; beneath their surface the sods of close-cropped turf were dry. The light was fading from a green and tranquil twilight, and the rain brushed the hills with the caressing sweep of soft grey wings, filling the hollow of Scatterthwaite with a warm scent of flowers and earth and rain.

She left the yard and climbed slowly through the two grass fields and across the strip of the moor to Mallow Fell. The bell-heather was in blossom, and when her feet touched them, the flowers rang with a soft shrill music. She reached the edge of the moor and looked down into the winding valley. The river was hidden behind a swaying vapour, but straight below her on the plateau where the Foresters' Camp had stood, she saw the twisted limbs of charred and blackened bushes, fragments of half-burned timber, and a desolate ruin of rusting tins, sodden newspapers, burned tree-stumps, boots and tools and wire. The three pine-trees, blasted by flame, raised their mute protest against the desecration of their sanctuary. Like a dark bruise the stain of the fire spread across the side of the Fell.

All the beauty and strangeness of the alien visit had vanished, leaving the fluttering rags, the obscene fragments of trampled paper, the squalor of rusting iron and abandoned gear. Slowly Joanna made her way down the path up which her Young Tam Lin had climbed. The charred and brittle bracken broke beneath her. The sharp stones slipped beneath her careful feet.

No dark and slender stranger glowered at her now from the bushes. He had gone; as though fairyland had opened again and taken him back to herself, he had vanished. There remained behind him only hostility and evil talk and wild, incongruous memories. Where was he now, she wondered? Chasing the hidden enemies of his fierce, lovely country? Avenging the honour of his dead, lost love? Did he indeed exist at all in this world of social bonds and decent compromise?

She moved drearily about the ground where the huts had stood. There was no sound save for the rain falling now more steadily; yet she was almost certain that she heard the wraith of an echo,

"Ta-ra, Ta-ra, la-la-la, la-la-la, Ta-ra."

She stopped and stood listening, her chin lifted and the old cloak falling from her shoulders. Like the soft refrain of a lost song she heard it, clear and unmistakable, the music of the Dance of the Four.

There was one hut still standing, its tin roof propped precariously on its half-ruined walls, and whether by freak of the imagination or by true evidence of her senses, the sound seemed to come from there. Slowly she walked across the plateau and pulled at the ill-fitting door.

"Who's that?" A harsh voice, but clearly of Yorkshire, not of Finland.

284

" Good gracious! Who's in there? What is it? "

A figure rose from the darkness. " Well, I never. It's Mrs. Leigh! "

" Yes. You know me, but I'm afraid I haven't the pleasure of knowing you. I'd no intention of intruding. I thought I heard somebody."

" Oh, step right inside. This is Liberty Hall, this is. Specially for you an' me. I'm Miss Bottomley. Bessy Bottomley from the village shop. Pleased to meet you, I'm sure."

" How do you do? Do you think that the rain is likely to last long? "

" I shouldn't wonder. Not much fine weather for you an' me ahead anyway, I should say. How's your fellow, eh? Come to revive sweet memories, same as me? Soppy, I call it."

" I don't think I quite understand you." But of course, she did.

" Go on. Don't play the Lady of the Manor with me. There ain't no flies on Bessy, not round Christmas time. Talking of Christmas time, mine's January. When's yours? Rotten, I call it. It's queer street for us this time and no mistake. Just all on account of a little bit o' fun. Mother tells me I've got to clear off this time, an' Old Ma Marshall says she'll have me sent to a home for Fallen Girls. Me! Some fall it was, going with a mouldy Finn after the fine fellows I have known. Thank you for nothing, says I. I've been with the Salvation Army once. Hymns and bread an' dripping for breakfast. Bread an' dripping and hymns for tea. I'd sooner go to the Poor Law Infirmary, says I. Why aren't you taking a seat an' making yourself comfortable? "

" Thanks. I'd rather stand, I think. I believe the rain is clearing off."

" Please yourself. You'd be glad enough to sit if your back was as bad as mine. It's pouring cats an' dogs. Come to think on it, you've got a nerve, haven't you, to come back an' set up farming when you might have gone clean away an' no one know anything about it? They're so holy here they can hardly get their hats on for knocking off the haloes. My name's dirt. Always has been. But you were so grand — dinner at the Hall. Mrs. Leigh of Scatterthwaite, I don't think. And now we're here together, eh? ' I wouldn't leave my little wooden hut for you-oo.' "

Joanna wanted to say, " But my baby's born in wedlock," only this seemed to her a piece of priggish superiority which she could not tolerate. Bidgood had been right. It was not the truth but people's idea of the truth which made it possible for one to live in society. Her mind moved sadly from one thought to another, from the memory of the curate's perturbation to the prospect of her business venture, then back to the girl whom she had so unexpectedly encountered. She felt an almost unbearable pity for her, for her isolation and her anger and her defiant unhappiness.

" Why do you think it'll take a nerve to stop here? " she asked, partly for the sake of saying something, partly from a sense that the girl had some touch upon reality which in her had failed. She would be honest, whereas Joanna could only play with conjecture.

" Who's going to buy your eggs an' butter? Who'll
want dealings with you? Who'll stop in service up at
Scatterthwaite once the kid's come? It wouldn't matter
if it was a first-class place, but so shut away an' all.
Unless your fancy man sends you a nice little bit from
Finland or whatever forsaken spot he's got hisself to,
you'll be having the bailiff's in as well as the nosey
Parkers who want to make a good woman of you."

" But what if I can prove that my baby's legitimate? " asked Joanna. " It is, you know. They can't
boycott me just for a rumour."

" Well, you've got a hope, you have, if you think anyone's likely to swallow that tale. Go an' tell it to Mr.
Pitcock, an' Madame Marshall an' Mr. Hungarian
Interpreter What's-his-name. Come off it, Mrs. Leigh.
It's no good. I'll give you one tip. Get out of this hole
while the going's good. An' get as far as you jolly well
can go. An' never say I didn't do you a good turn in telling you. An' I'll tell you somethin' else too. Keep away
from foreigners. Men? Paugh! Couldn't eat a bit.
That's me. Tell 'em Bessy Bottomley told you. Oh no.
It's only a rumour! "

There seemed to Joanna to be nothing to say and
very little to do, except perhaps to go away and take
Bessy Bottomley's advice. She felt that she had strength
for combating any task but this vindication of her
character. She had never thought about her good name
or her reputation or her place in society. She had taken
her loyalty so much for granted that the implications
of Teddy's jealousy had almost amused her. This world
wherein rumours and gossip and the verdict of a small

community counted so highly was strange to her. She felt that Bessy Bottomley knew more of life than she did. She turned to her for wisdom.

" But isn't there anything I can do? "

" Yes. Get up an' go. If I had anywhere to clear to, I'd get off too."

" Well. Thank you. I'll think about it."

She opened the door again. The rain still fell lightly along the darkening Fell. "I must be getting home. Thank you for your advice. Good luck to you."

She made no promise of help, for she did not think of herself as a fit person to offer so precious a commodity.

There was no safety in this world of Letherwick. She had lost hold on its essential code of manners. She did not know how to behave. She did not feel that she was the right person to live here. She did not feel that she could bring up her children. Teddy was dead, and somewhere behind her more articulate thoughts lay the fear that she had killed him. Szermai had gone, though for all the harm which he had inadvertently done her, she felt him to have been her friend. She had known pain before, the enriching pain of love, the futile pain of anxiety, the dragging pain of impotence before the suffering of others. But this knowledge of desolation which made her feel that the ground upon which she trod was hollow, that the world which she saw was only a phantasm, that she was lost in an alien place where neither her courage nor her love could guide her, this brought the horror of defeat.

She moved wearily out of the hut and began to climb the side of the Fell. The rain dripped unheeded on her bent shoulders and her bowed head. But she felt it no more than she felt the tears upon her cheeks or the ache of her tired body.

At the top of the path, she turned again; but darkness had closed upon the hostile valley. Only down in the hollow behind her a light glimmered from a window of Scatterthwaite Farm.

CHAPTER FIFTEEN

THE ADVENTURERS' CHILD

§ 1

A CIRCLE of lamplight fell on to the tablecloth and work-basket, and Joanna's needle moving in and out of the dark threads. She sat darning stockings by the open window and it was nearly midnight.

Sometimes her head fell forward in a doze, but she jerked it up again because she dared not sleep. The rain distressed her, mingling with her consciousness, until it seemed as though the solid earth were melting away with the unseen heavens. When she slept she dreamed that she was drowning in a bottomless pool, and that every time she raised her head to the surface the rain struck and drove it down again.

She had lost contact with the firm ground; her confidence in life had gone. She felt herself astray in an alien country whose speech she did not understand. The familiar words and speech and habits of men had grown grotesque; they assumed fantastic meanings. Love, which she had thought would transfigure life, became itself transfigured, its glory quenched by disease, its sharp ecstasies ground down by the wheel of poverty. Love brought no wisdom; it offered no security. Her groping hands could touch no sheltering wall in the night's chaos; her stumbling feet trod on no certain path.

She wished to pray for understanding of reality, but knew no God to whom she could address her prayer. Beyond her window, even the stars were darkened, and the falling rain curtained a black confusion. She returned from its negation to her work, trying, as she had tried a hundred times before, to satisfy her longing for assurance by the performance of some trivial but useful task. She wondered whether most women who sought the answer to insoluble problems stifled their hunger for reality in needlework, cooking and the making of hard yellow cubes of butter. " We take to darning as men take to drink," she told herself.

How could she live in a world grown strange to her? She no longer knew how to behave. Her code of honesty and kindliness and courage did not match the complications of her daily life. She felt as though Lindersdale were bewitched! its flowers turned to serpents in her hand; its birds sang blasphemies; and all neighbourliness was swallowed up in leering curiosity.

Yet she could not escape. She felt as though there were no place in the world for her. How could she leave the farm, the house, the only home that she knew?

Was this the only world? What world? What only world? Were only worlds like only children, a little unfortunate?

Her nodding head fell forward.

" And so you see, if you watch your chameleon, you must also charm him. For chameleons are not as we thought them in our innocence. They do not emulate the colours of grass, nor transform themselves to match the brick-red earth. By no means, dear Joanna. I caught my chameleon near a bed of salvia, deep salvia flowers with flaming scarlet mouths. I set him on a square of emerald lawn. But did he turn green? Not a bit of it. He grew black with indignation. He stormed at me. He twisted his head over his shoulder and rolled his furious eyes and hissed rude things at me in a small, venomous voice. He had no sense of gratitude."

Joanna stirred a little in her sleep. The harsh lines faded from her haggard face.

"Sir Walter Raleigh stepped out of the boat and offered his hand to Agnes. She climbed on to the shallow marble steps while her chameleons, with rolling eyes and fierce protruding tongues, darted behind her, turned eight heads simultaneously, and spat at elegant Sir Walter. 'Spirited little creatures,' said Agnes indulgently. 'They are jealous of your beauty.' But Rachel, without lifting her eyes from her big book, remarked, "You spoil them. Discipline is good for the human soul. Still more so for the Protean soul of a Chameleon. You should admonish them, but not in anger." And then came Teddy, running along the garden path with sunlight on his fair, wind-blown hair, his blue eyes dancing. He held out his hand to Joanna and cried, "Dear Love, I have been given the world to wear as a golden ball." And together they raced down the goat-path to the dam, while the willows tossed their fountains into the smooth brown water, and from north to south above the western kopjes, the banners of sunset streamed across the sky.

" 'Oh, where have you been all this time, Joanna? ' he asked her.

" ' I've been trying to live at Scatterthwaite,' she said. ' But it has become a foreign country. My tongue will not speak the language of the people there. My feet stumble along their paths. I have become a stranger to myself and a dangerous, evil woman in their sight. I am neither true wife to you, my lover, nor true mother to our children. They say that I am a wicked witch-woman, and my spells have wrought havoc among the forest trees. The destruction of my magic blackens the green hill-side. And I am utterly lost.'

" Then Teddy said, ' But it was we who had lost you. Why were you not in your own country? Your marble towers lie awaiting you. Your unseen islands blossom from the sea. But where are you? Here are trees with-holding their beauty of leaves and flowers until your cry of pleasure summons them. Here are roads built for the welcome of your feet. You are lost, lost, lost, unless you seek your country."

" ' And you? ' she asked. ' And you? '

" ' I always sought for it,' he answered her. ' Was I ever at home in an alien world? It is the seeking and not the finding, the pursuit and not the capture which makes you secure. You must keep alive while you live. You must set your feet firmly on the earth . . .''

" ' But what of Scatterthwaite? ' she asked him. ' What of Tam Lin? Who is he? '

" And as she spoke she saw, bowing to kiss her hand as he had bowed once in the potato field, dark and ironical and debonair, Sir Walter Raleigh, Young Tam Lin, the Hungarian interpreter, the eldritch knight.

" ' Who are you? Who are you? ' she cried, but as she

questioned him, he vanished, and she was left alone beside the willow tree, while the prickly pears cast their fantastic shadows over the baked red earth, and the goats raised bearded provocative faces from their grim banquet of thorns.

" ' Teddy! ' " she called. " ' Teddy! ' " in sudden panic. But her voice calling aloud awakened her. She sat in the sitting-room at Scatterthwaite while the oil in the glass bowl of the lamp sank low and the clock pointed to half-past one.

She moved to the window and stepped over the low sill. The garden was musical with running water. Into the hollow of Scatterthwaite a hundred runnels and rivulets gurgled and splashed and galloped. The earth lay open to the strong male passion of the rain; locked in dark ecstasy the elements met, and when their deep embrace had ended, in due time the land would bear the fruit of this communion.

Joanna opened her arms wide in the watery darkness and raised her face to the benediction of the rain. She knew now quite clearly what she was going to do, and only wondered how she had been so blind.

As she passed again into the quiet house, removed her wet garments and dried her heavy hair, for the first time she knew that she was glad to bear her husband's child.

§ 2

A fortnight later Sir Wentworth Marshall drove through Letherwick village in his Fiat car. He was glad to be back in Yorkshire. His head bristled with schemes and his little blue-green eyes glittered with the excitement of ideas, ideas, and ever more ideas. He had just completed a journey northward from Italy, studying Fascist rural electricity, Czech farm schools, and Danish co-operative agriculture, and he had returned with the exhilarating conviction that he and he alone knew all that was wrong with British farming.

He should have learned suspicion of foreign innovation from the disastrous experiment of the Finnish Camp; he should have acquired a nice conception of the borderland between enterprise and eccentricity; but his resilient fancy after each rebuff soared to new heights of aspiration. Besides, as he observed frequently to his agent, his wife and his daughters, nobody was certain how the Camp caught fire. It might have been an accident.

His family as usual combated his new intention of introducing a co-operative colony into the dairy farms of the dales, and Lady Marshall supported her eldest daughter, who made much of her own discomfiture during the difficult period of the Finnish feud.

" It's all very well, Daddy, going off and leaving us to deal with your scrapes. You'll set up a cheese factory and we shall have the same sort of trouble, and in the middle you'll go off to Turkey or Timbuctoo, and there shall we be left with a village up in arms. You'll fill the dales with food cranks and Simple Livers until it's totally unfit for human habitation."

Beatrice belonged to the New Tories, and believed in common sense and the good old fashions and healthy conservatism, like so many young women of her generation; but Sir Wentworth only twinkled a mischievous eye at her, and speculated inwardly upon the possibility of buying Scatterthwaite if the rumour that Mrs. Leigh was leaving proved to be true.

He was thinking how opportune might be this chance of consolidating his domain from Mallow Fell to Bartledale, when, half an hour after the argument with Beatrice, he came upon Mrs. Leigh herself in the village street.

He stopped his car and hailed her. She, looking up, recognized him and came forward with smiling kindliness.

" Well, Mrs. Leigh, what's this about your leaving us? " he asked.

" It's true," she said, shaking hands over the door of the car. " Are you going to buy my farm? "

He chuckled. " I don't know. I don't know. Perhaps. It all depends how grasping you are going to be."

" Oh, I'm the world's worst business woman. But I'll trust you not to take advantage of my limitations. It's a rotten farm in many ways. Why do you want it? "

" You're the world's worst saleswoman, my dear young lady," he scolded, " if you go about scaring off prospective customers. When is it coming on to the market? "

" On the 29th my lawyer says. He's Mr. Seymour of Clarington. But if I could dispose of it by private treaty first, I certainly would. I'm awfully anxious to get away."

" What are you doing now? Have you time to climb

in and do a little private treating while I drive out to Toplady? "

"Well, I don't know. You see, I was just finishing a few errands here in the village and then I wanted to get home. My man's in Clarington with the pony, and when I've got back there's the milking and I want to get up some potatoes, and the bread to set. And I've got the children alone there."

"Well, look here; " he was growing more and more anxious for her company. "I've got to call at the blacksmith's in about twenty minutes for a jack that he's been putting right for me. Come along in, we'll drive down the road and talk, and then I'll call for the jack and run you up to Scatterthwaite. Will that do? "

"Yes, I should like it. I love motoring still. It's quite a novelty to me. Can you imagine anything more ridiculous in this year of grace? What a jolly car! "

She settled herself down beside him.

"It's Italian. Italian. Bought it in Italy. Just driven in it straight up through Europe. Did I hear 'em say that you were going abroad? Go to Italy. Italy. Most interesting state in Europe now except possibly Russia. Things moving, what? "

"I'm going to South Africa," she said serenely. "I was born there. My elder daughter, Patricia, is rather delicate, you know. And that's the best climate I believe for her. And then, I've always meant to go there. Always."

"Have you? Have you? Got friends there? "

"I think so. I'm counting on it. There was a girl I

knew at school called Rachel Harris. She's lecturing
in a university in the Transvaal. She used to write to
me complaining about the lack of accommodation in
Johannesburg for young women earning their own
living. The Y.M.C.A.'s too godly; flats are frightfully
expensive and boarding-houses are beastly. She wanted
someone to come and set up a really go-as-you-please
sort of house with comfortable rooms, and let people
live there cheap, you know. Well, a fortnight ago I
made up my mind to leave Scatterthwaite. And I sent
her a cable. I said ' Have found respectable widow start
house paying guests any objection three children.' I
thought it rather a nice cable, don't you? She cabled
back ' Depends on children,' so I sent another to say I
was the woman. It's been awfully expensive but worth
it. I had to use the egg-money for the cables. You
know," her voice took on an excited solemnity, " aren't
cables fun? I'd never thought about sending them before. If I had as much money as you, I'd live in constant temptation. I'd want to send hundreds and hundreds of cables to all sorts of people in all parts of the
world. Just imagine inquiring after the Shah of Persia's
kittens! Is there a Shah now, and has he kittens? Or
sending Valentines to Mussolini, and Christmas greet-
ings to Trotsky and to the agent of the British American Tobacco Company in Hankow? Is there one? Sir
Wentworth, have you ever had that wonderful feeling
that there are so many gloriously silly things to be
done in the world that time and space simply aren't big
enough to hold them? "

He did know the feeling. Time and space had never

been great enough for the full fruition of his teeming notions. He liked Mrs. Leigh uncommonly well.

" My wife thinks all my notions ingloriously silly," he confided. " So they are. So they are. There are too many sensible people in the world. A little silliness leavens quite a big lump of sense. But look here, I always thought women were the sensible sex, and now do you mean that you are really going off like that with your two children, or did you say three? I mean, without any sort of prospects, what? " It pleased him to think of himself giving sensible advice to this handsome, delicious woman.

" Two, and three. Two here and one coming. But not until February. Oh, and look here, Sir Wentworth," suddenly she blushed, and her red, work-worn hands tightened on the lap of her faded dress. " If you do hear people talking, you might just happen to mention that the new child is quite legitimate. I mean, not unless it's no trouble, but people have been saying such things." She tried to speak casually, but the hot colour flooded her thin cheeks.

" Tct, tct. Really, really." And suddenly the echo of a recent remark of his wife occurred to him. " Look here, Mrs. Leigh. It isn't because of all this talk that you're going, is it? You aren't letting people drive you away? "

" No. That isn't it. I know that it looks rather like it. I know that things are difficult here for me because people think I behaved so badly. But I don't believe that will last. And I don't believe that that would really make much difference to me if I wanted to stay. But you know, what I am afraid of is that it would happen again. It's not that there were any foundations for the scandal, really. I loved my husband. Mr. Szermai did kiss me, once. But he was really in love with somebody else. Only she was dead. The point is that I simply don't know how to behave here. I'd always be doing awful things because I honestly don't know how people's minds work. I don't know what things are dangerous. I'd always wanted to travel. I'm more excited by maps and things than by any photographs of people, if you know what I mean. But I thought that the right thing to do was to stay here at Scatterthwaite because it would be safer for me and the children. But have you ever known what it's like to find the safe place suddenly grown dangerous? " She turned to him, appealing for comprehension, treating him as though he were a wise and intimate friend. The little man was delighted. " You know," she continued, twisting her hands. " It's awfully dangerous to make the best of a bad bargain. That's not the way to live, is it? Life's a good bargain, isn't it? I mean, imagine what it would be like if you were dead, and you looked up and saw people just acquiescing in life, and treating it like a poor thing, and saying, ' You can't have the best of both worlds,' as a kind of reason for getting the best of none. Wouldn't you feel cheated? I should. I'd think, ' Here am I who'd give anything, anything to be alive again and there they are treating life like a bad bargain.' Why, it's the best bargain. It's the only bargain worth buying if you really live."

Her words, restrained during the difficult summer, poured out in a torrent of eagerness, leaving him silent, but he turned to look at her as he drove slowly down the arcade of massive elm trees, and saw a wire of sunlight pass across her face, leaving it again in shadow. Yet, even when the brilliant light had gone, she seemed to him transfused by a luminous and valiant flame. The warmth of her vitality made him suddenly resentful of his age, his position and the mediocre, conscientious women who surrounded him. Reacting to his regret he became uncharacteristically cautious.

" But what about the children, eh, Mrs. Leigh? "

" Well, you see. I think I can do the best for the children by doing the best for myself. Just now, of course, Pamela and Patricia and Paulina — she's the third — it may of course be Paul — they depend on me to protect them and be wise for them and all that kind of thing. But how can I be wise for them if I wasn't wise for myself? How can I help them to be more of a person than I am? You know, I'm not a good farmer. I came to it too late, and I had no training and not enough capital, and I never wanted to stay in one place. Teddy's father turned into a machine for the sake of love. I won't."

" I can't imagine you a machine."

" Can't you? I can. I've felt it coming sometimes. Well, I could run a house in South Africa. I could take my children about the world. Perhaps after South Africa it will be India or America, or anything." She began to laugh. " I really won't talk about myself any more. You know, what is so very funny is that ever since I came back to Scatterthwaite, I've always been explaining my children and myself and the new baby to people, and the comical thing is that nobody really even believes me."

But though she said that the thing was comical, the dragging lines about her mouth revealed its pain, the mocking laughter died from her voice, and when she spoke again, the youth which had delighted him had vanished.

" I've learned one thing," she said dully. " Everyone has to find his own security. The awful thing about life is that we are really alone in it. We can't live for anyone else. I wanted to. I tried to. I tried to." Her voice grew ugly with passion. " It didn't come off. I think that's the worst thing there is in the world. You can't really take someone else's pain."

He felt a paternal tenderness for her. He wanted to cover her hardened fingers by his plump white hand, to put his arm round her waist, to draw down her weary face against his rough tweed coat. But all he said was:

" Tct, tct. If there's anything I can do to help you."

" There is. Of course there is." She grew eager again. " You can make a fair bid for my farm. You can make the auction a success."

" Well, well, I'll see what I can do. As a matter of fact," the shrewd sense below his perversity quickened, " you know I imagine that your auction will be pretty well a success anyway. You've got yourself a pretty odd name about here, and people love a gossip. They'll come to buy your chairs and tables and pigs and things just to get a look at you."

This was not a thing to hurt her. She laughed. " Will they really? Oh, I say. I never thought of making hard cash out of it. Why not? I say, can't you tell a few more tales about me. So as to send up my value? "

He was a little shocked and yet somehow relieved by her levity. He turned the car and drove her back to the village, and on the way home they discussed only technical details of the sale and the ways in which he could assist her.

In the village they stopped outside the blacksmith's shop and waited for the jack. As they were waiting, Sir Wentworth suddenly remembered something.

" Oh, by the way, I'd nearly forgotten. Lorna Lavine sent a message to you."

" Lorna Lavine? Oh, the lovely sculptor woman. Of course I remember her. That was a nice party."

" We had a letter from her last week. She's in China. She went to look up a friend of yours, she said, a Miss, Miss, I've forgotten the name. She said that she wasn't there though. She went to South America to write a book. South America. Or was it South Africa? You know she writes so badly, does my friend Lorna."

" Agnes Darlington? Gone to South Africa? Oh, are you sure? Are you sure? Why she always said that she would go and visit Rachel one day. Why, don't you see, don't you see, we all may meet there, all three again? " Her eyes danced. She turned and seized his hand. " Oh, you darling. You darling, to tell me. Oh, don't you see. It's all been arranged. It must have all been arranged."

And so it happened that Mr. Boyse, coming out of a cottage where he had been visiting the sick, saw Mrs. Leigh in Sir Wentworth Marshall's car, and heard her joyous voice crying, "You darling. You darling! "

He knew now what he had been spared, yet sick at heart, angry, and disappointed, he turned without acknowledging them and walked off up the village street.

§ 3

The *Richmond Castle,* slender, steel-grey and remote, seemed to hang between the long silver river and the soft grey sky. The passengers on the crowded tender leaving Tilbury dock buttoned their coats tightly against the keen October air. Third- and first-class passengers, huddled together, regarded each other with the suspicion which precedes the separation of sheep from goats by the unequivocal barrier of a steel railing.

A young man returning to Natal with his newly-married wife, stood watching the groups uniting and disintegrating among the bundles of rugs and suitcases.

" Do you see that poor woman? " the girl asked. " Oh, my dear! She's got two children and is travelling third class from the labels on her luggage. Just think what a voyage she'll have. They'll probably be all seasick."

"She doesn't look sorry for herself." replied the husband.

" No-o."

Standing together they watched the little group with

curiosity. One fair and very beautiful little girl was sitting self-consciously swinging her legs from a pile of luggage. Now and then she would turn to smile at some passer-by who noticed her, an astonishing smile, illuminating the delicacy of her disquieting and lovely youth.

" Little minx," said the wife. " But she looks awfully delicate."

The younger child was broad and sturdy and comfortable. She kept looking at her mother with the confident grin of vast affection, or she danced up and down the deck asking questions. Her mother answered her sometimes, and sometimes she did not, but remained quietly watching the approaching ship. Her fair hair blew softly from under her little, close-fitting hat, and a long grey cloak half hid her tall figure. She did not fuss, not count her luggage, nor harass her children with injunctions according to the habit of most of the other mothers, but stood with tranquil dignity, apparently absorbed in her own thoughts. Without being beautiful, she conveyed an impression of beauty, and the young wife watching her, felt new conviction that life was a wonderful and fine adventure, and that her voyage to Africa was going to be the culminating experience of her youth. The sorrow which had marked the older woman's face held no fear for the girl, and when, as the tender drew up to the side of the ship, the young wife accidentally knocked against her and apologized, she received a smile so frank, so friendly and assured, that the nervousness and emotion of parting

from her family left her, and she climbed on to the
ship behind her husband with a sense of confidence
and freedom.

Later that evening, walking the upper deck and
watching the lights along the flat receding shores, her
thoughts turned again to the woman who had smiled
at her.

" I do wonder who she is. She doesn't look like a
third-class passenger, and they seem nice little girls.
The elder one's lovely." Her husband was looking at
a ship moving up the river, and took no notice. " You
know. I believe she's going to meet her husband. She
looks like that somehow. As though she were expecting
something splendid."

" Is that how you would look if you were going to
meet your husband? " asked he, delighted. " As though
something splendid were going to happen? "

Meanwhile Joanna and the children had unpacked
in the small three-berth cabin, explored the bathroom
and the smoking-room and the deck and lost Patricia,
to find her promising to sew on buttons for the deck-
steward. They had eaten their six-o'clock tea in a
curious room reminding Joanna of a public lavatory, a
workshop and a club-room during a Sunday-school
festival. While consuming cold ham and rock buns and
water-cress, Patricia succeeded in completely bewildering a young schoolmaster with a pimply face, who
fell victim to her ethereal charm. A comfortable
matron, on Joanna's right, laid a fat hand along her
arm.

" Ah, my dear, what was your husband thinking of to let you come out here all alone with the children, eh, and you as you are? "

" My husband is dead," said Joanna. " Won't you have some jam? It's strawberry."

" You're drinking tea, I see. You know when I was your way, and I've had six, I couldn't touch a dropper tea. Not a drop. Fairly turned my stomach even to see a word with T in it, an' my husband's name was Teddy too, that one. Well, Edward really, but we called him Ted."

" My husband's name was Teddy, too," remarked Joanna with interest.

" Well, I never. Isn't the world small? Mine drank hisself to death, poor dear. That was my first. Not but what I had much trouble with him. As good as gold, as the saying is when not too far gone. My present — he's over at M. table. I always think the gentlemen like to get together, don't you? Not so much trouble to stand on ceremony, as you might say."

" I dare say."

" Been out before, dearie? "

" I was born in the Eastern Province. But I haven't been back since I was out there as a baby."

" Oh. You're a real South African then. Think of that now."

They thought of that and of many other interesting things during a meal prolonged by garrulous acquaintance. Pamela, on the other side, was prompting Patricia with sisterly concern in a long recital of the tale of Pat's illness, of the financial embarrassments of Scatterthwaite, and of the adventure upon which now all three were bound. Before the Leighs left the table, their history, prospects and intentions were entertaining the entire company of L. table and spreading rapidly to P. and N.

Between tea and bedtime, Pamela knew the names of twenty-two children in the third class, and Patricia had borrowed a gramophone from the purser's clerk.

"You've got your work cut out for you, I can see," said the mother of six to Joanna. " I hope you won't feel the voyage too much. You look a little tired, dearie."

"Oh, I'm not tired," said Joanna, but she felt glad when the time came to escort her too exuberant family down to the cabin and to superintend their protracted toilet for the night.

"I shan't come like this every night," she warned them. "After this, you undress yourselves, young women."

"Mummy. This sheet is prickly. Is it stuffed with straw?" asked Patricia, proding her mattress.

"Don't be long upstairs," begged Pamela.

She kissed them good night and went up to the deck again. Below the lights the third-class passengers promenaded in twos and threes. When Joanna leaned over the rail she could feel their bustling, congested life behind her, but the water was quiet. It rushed along the side of the ship with silent dark intensity. The boat seemed to be perfectly still. It was the low, black coast between

Tilbury and the sea, and it was the smooth, subtle river which flew away from her.

England was flying away. Scatterthwaite and the cool, damp dairy, the churn, and its boards scoured to flaky whiteness, the bedroom where Teddy had lain watching the moors, the little pony Ezekial and his cart, the warm brown, milky-scented flanks of the cows, all these were flying away. She had left Kingsport and Lindersdale and Scatterthwaite for ever. She had left the green and white cemetery with its raw new graves, where Teddy lay below her wilting flowers. She was sailing out on a real ship across the sea. Her back ached and her body felt weary with its growing burden, but she smiled as she faced the darkness. For her child was, after all, the child of an adventure, of a passionate affirmation, a demand upon life. Though it had killed her husband, his death had not been barren, he had left her as the trustee of his immortality. And she was unafraid.

With the low flat coasts and their flickering lights, the familiar things all fell away from her and a small, round, unfamiliar moon hung in the night-dark sky to watch them go.

There was a pattering on the deck beside her, and she saw Pamela, a serge coat over her pyjamas, standing apologetically yet emphatically by her side.

"Oh, Mummy, I had to come up. Just for a little minute. Just to see. You don't mind, do you? Pat's asleep."

"Well, I don't want you to catch cold; but just a

little minute can't hurt you. Come under my cloak and keep warm, then I'll go down with you."

"It is nice, isn't it?" said Pamela after a little, with a sigh of deep satisfaction. "Do you think Paulina will be pleased we're going to South Africa?"

The children, brought up on a farm, took Paulina's presence entirely for granted.

"I'm sure she'll like it. I did. I've been so glad that I was born on a mission station."

"And shall we really see baboons and prickly pears an' rondavels? An' shall we really trek across the veld in ox-wagons, an' fry eggs and bacon by the roadside, an' eat mealies, and ford rivers?"

"I don't see why we shouldn't."

There was a pause. Mother and daughter watched the flowing water and the enchanted blue and silver of the night.

Then Pamela spoke.

"And we're going to see Teneriffe, an' Ascension Island, an' St. Helena. Real islands. Little ones. Soon, ever so soon. Not pretend islands in the cowshed, but real ones with water all round an' houses, an' lots an' lots of flowers. An' donkeys, Mummy, there will be donkeys?"

"I think so. Oh, surely."

They looked at each other with the incredulity and happiness of two who share preposterous and nonsensical ecstasies.

"Oh, I'm happy, happy, happy," whispered Pamela. "It's too lovely. Too exciting. It seems impossible."

It seemed to Joanna impossible that she could have found so perfect a companion in her pilgrimage, one who could understand her delight in the comical and strange and splendid things. And though her heart was sore with tenderness for the lover whom she had left behind, she smiled into the darkness.

"All the same, it is possible. It is true, you know. If nothing nice ever happens again, this is true."

Her hand met Pamela's under the shelter of her cloak.

THE  END

OTHER BOOKS BY WINIFRED HOLTBY

ANDERBY WOLD

Mary Robson is a young Yorkshire woman, married to her solid unromantic cousin, John. Together they battle to preserve Mary's neglected inheritance, her beloved farm, Anderby Wold. This labour of love – and the benevolent tyranny of traditional Yorkshire ways – have made Mary old before her time. Then into her purposeful life erupts David Rossitur, red-haired, charming, eloquent: how can she help but love him? But David is a young man from a different England, radical, committed to social change. As their confrontation and its consequences inevitably unfold, Mary's life and that of the calm village of Anderby are changed forever. In this, her first novel, Winifred Holtby exhilaratingly rehearses the themes which come to fruition in her last and greatest work, *South Riding*.

'It is in the vividly affectionate detail with which she describes the routine of petty squabbles, small-town pride and the rhythm of the farming year that the book finds its life' – *Event*

Already published

THE CROWDED STREET

This is the story of Muriel Hammond, at twenty living within the suffocating confines of Edwardian middle-class society in Marshington, a Yorkshire village. A career is forbidden her. Pretty, but not pretty enough, she fails to achieve the one thing required of her – to find a suitable husband. Then comes the First World War, a watershed which tragically revolutionises the lives of her generation. But for Muriel it offers work, friendship, freedom, and one last chance to find a special kind of happiness . . .

With the exception of *South Riding*, this is Winifred Holtby's most successful novel; powerfully tracing one woman's search for independence and love, it echoes in fictional form the years autobiographically recorded by her close friend Vera Brittain in *Testament of Youth*.

'Rather as if Jane Austen had thrown her cooling shadow a hundred years on – the same quiet humour and observation of the set stages in the social dance – but then there are bursts of Brontëesque passions stirring in an isolated Yorkshire farmhouse . . . it is painfully vivid' – ALEX HAMILTON, *Guardian*

Already published

MANDOA, MANDOA!

Mandoa is a small African state: at its head a Virgin Princess, conceiving (immaculately) further princesses. The old traditions remain undisturbed until Mandoa's Lord High Chamberlain, Safi Talal, visits Addis Ababa. There he discovers baths and cocktail shakers, motor cars and cutlery from Sheffield, telephones and handkerchiefs. In short, he has seen an apocalyptic vision – a new heaven and a new earth.

Meanwhile in England it is 1931. Maurice Durrant, youngest director of Prince's Tours Limited, has won North Donnington for the Conservatives. His socialist brother Bill is unemployed and their friend Jean Stanbury loses her job on *The Byeword*, a radical weekly paper. How all three, and others too, find themselves in Mandoa for the wedding of the Royal Princess to her Arch-archbishop is hilariously told in this wonderful satirical novel, first published in 1933.

Already published

Also of Interest

TESTAMENT OF FRIENDSHIP

Vera Brittain

In *Testament of Youth,* Vera Brittain passionately recorded the agonising years of the First World War, lamenting the destruction of a generation which included those she most dearly loved – her lover, her brother, her closest friends. In *Testament of Friendship* she tells the story of the woman who helped her survive – the writer Winifred Holtby. They met at Oxford immediately after the war and their friendship continued through Vera's marriage and their separate but parallel writing careers, until Winifred's untimely death at the age of 37.

Winifred Holtby was a remarkable woman. In her short life her generous, loving, talented nature shed a special light on all who knew her, on the many causes and campaigns for which she worked. When she died her fame as a writer was about to reach its peak with the publication of her greatest novel, *South Riding.*

Vera Brittain's life was marked by the tragic loss of those she loved, but in this portrait of her friend a spirit of love and confidence shines through. *Testament of Friendship* records a perfect friendship between two women of courage and determination, a friendship which transformed their own lives and illuminated the world in which they lived.

Already published